EVERY STEP OF THE WAY

EVERY STEP OF THE WAY

SOFÍA RAMÍREZ CASTILLO

Published by Castle & Wisdom Press

ISBNs:
Paperback: 979-8-9996353-0-3
Hardcover: 979-8-9996353-2-7
E-book: 979-8-9996353-1-0

Cover design by Eva Polakovicova
Interior design by Ashley Santoro

Content Warning:
This novel contains themes of grief, loss, depression, emotional abuse, and other sensitive topics. Please read with care.

Printed in the United States of America. First Edition.

dedication

To Tita Hilda and Tita Anabelle,
Growing up in your footsteps has been a blessing.
From your fierce ambition to your untamable spirit—
You taught me how to dream.
You've always been my North Star—my guide home.
I'm infinitely proud to be your granddaughter.
You'll live in my heart always.
This one's for you.

prologue

LIFE GOES BY in a flash of unexpected moments and unexpected memories. There is love and pain, curiosity and fear, and sometimes, we are uniquely and fiercely brave, only to be shut down by our own doubts and worthless thoughts. There are new beginnings and gut-wrenching goodbyes—the ones that nothing can prepare you for, leaving you empty and directionless, numb to a world of possibilities.

Life is not a single word to which we can attach a simple definition and expect it to be enough. We can't write one or two sentences to describe it and neatly put a period at the end, because life involves more than that—so much more. It has commas and hyphens, exclamation points and semicolons. Often, it is riddled with incomplete thoughts, but most of the time, it is bursting with question marks.

Oh God, there are so many questions.

And this is where my story begins.

With a single question.

PART ONE

chapter one — THEN

"WHAT'S YOUR NAME?"

I was sitting on the corner of San Francisco Avenue and Sixth Street, my usual spot when the weather was kind enough to let me busk for an hour or two outside my favorite coffee shop. Aromas of dark blends and caramel wafted through the air, coating the city in its own particular scent. Ironically, I hated the taste of coffee—finding it bitter and unpleasant—but the smell, and the way it seemed to bring people comfort and nostalgia as they waited behind the counter, grounded me in a way I couldn't explain.

We were finally transitioning to the last days of winter. The day was warm, and the sky had a distinct glow of golden orange, light purple, and pink undertones as the sun began to set. It looked peaceful and magical, as if God had been playing with colors again and decided someone else had to appreciate a masterpiece of this magnitude rather than just Him.

I would find my way here most afternoons, accompanied by my guitar. My instrument had been with me for as long as I can remember. I've come to depend on it as if it were an extension of my body. I loved spending my time sitting in my special corner, mainly because I could see everything around me. Every day was different, but in many ways, it was always the same. People walked past me, hurrying with their steaming cups of coffee while they held a breathless conversation on their phones. Dogs of all breeds and sizes ran around playing fetch with their owners, bits of grass and dirt lifting from the ground with each exhilarating step. And the road was no different. Expensive cars idled impatiently at red lights beside old, battered ones with deployed airbags taped to the wheel, worrying me for their driver's safety. The futile impatience of traffic reminded me of how stuck I felt—caught in a place in life where the world kept moving while I sat still and stagnant.

I began to lose myself in a slow, quiet spiral, picking at the ends of my cuticles while I thought of all the shitty cards I had been dealt in life, but the blaring horns as the light turned green jolted me back to the present, watching as the cars drove by in a seemingly pointless game of winning a non-existent race, always rushing somewhere. From this spot, I could see every scene unfold before me, but most importantly, I could also see past all that. I could see the mountains surrounding the lake, the start of our neighboring town, and what I hoped would be my bright future.

This little patch of sidewalk wasn't just where I played songs for strangers. It was my refuge—a million chances to begin again. A breathtaking glimpse of everything that could be. Here I could imagine the life I wished for—where my mom was alive, my dad wasn't broken, and I'd finally graduated with my music degree. After high school, I'd managed two semesters at community college, but when caring for Dad grew harder—especially around the holidays—I stepped away to waitress and help with bills. Without Mom, Christmas was just a reminder of everything we'd lost. Her absence bled into thoughts of Dad's grief, his silence, his drinking. The ache in my chest pounded alongside my unsteady heart, like a percussion duo that had lost its rhythm long ago.

I blinked hard, trying to smooth the edges of my thoughts, then took a slow breath and let my fingers hover above the strings. Music always brought me back. I was halfway through the second verse of "Holes" by Passenger when you tossed a five-dollar bill into my case. I stopped playing. You were staring intently at me in a way no one had ever looked at me before. I stared back.

"Thanks, but I don't play for money." I held out the five-dollar bill, gesturing for you to take it back. You were tall and ridiculously handsome. You seemed to be in your early twenties, only a couple of years older than me. Your dark hair and dark eyes, and the way in which you were not just looking at me but looking *into* me—eyes fixed and reflecting my own—was fascinating.

"What's your name?" you asked, genuine curiosity in your voice. You made no motion to take the money back, so I let my hand gently rest on my thigh, feeling the paper bill growing damp beneath my fingertips. I had been offered money a few times in the past, but I had been playing here for so long that by now people knew I wasn't playing for tips; I just liked to come up with my own melodies.

"Noah," I replied, looking up to meet your gaze as I shielded my own from the sun. I was suddenly aware of the small beads of sweat around my temple and the sound of my beating heart reverberating in my ears. I had to get a grip on myself.

A few seconds later, you sat down on the sidewalk next to me—not too close, but also not too far; it was the perfect distance. I was a little startled when your kneecap graced mine for a fleeting moment as you bent down and straightened your legs in front of you. You were a stranger, after all, and this was the first time I had to share my little piece of sidewalk with anyone. On one hand, there was a rational part of me that was on high-alert and praying to all the angels you weren't a harassing weirdo, but on the other, less logical part of my brain, the only thought I could focus on was the gravitational pull I felt toward you, as if my body knew we were meant to be together.

You wore an expensive-looking suit, but you didn't seem to care if it got ruined. Little bits of gravel tugged at loose strings on the cuffs of your pants, but if it bothered you, you didn't show it. I glanced at the portfolio between us. The name "Derek" embroidered in the upper right corner. *What a strong name,* I thought. I believe it translates to "people ruler." I began to wonder if you were a natural-born leader.

"Noah," you repeated my name as if it were foreign to your lips, thinking it over and getting used to it, etching each letter in your mind. "You may be the first girl with that name I have ever met. I like it. It suits you."

You extended your hand and said "I'm Derek," flashing a welcoming smile through slightly crooked teeth, your eyes sparkling like a boy meeting someone new for the first time.

I looked down at your patiently outstretched hand. A few moments later, I stretched my hand out toward yours, but instead of shaking it, I gently pressed the five-dollar bill against your palm and closed your fist around it, dropping my hand back to my thigh.

"Nice to meet you, Derek."

You smiled confidently, like you'd known me forever, and suddenly I felt like I could breathe. Something about your aura put me at ease—made me feel protected, even. You tucked the bill into your shirt pocket and spoke in the calm, captivating tone I'd later come to recognize—the one you used when you were spellbound by something, or in this case, someone.

"I now realize how creepy it must be for a random guy to offer you money and then sit beside you uninvited," you said, crimson spots spreading around your neck. I suppressed a laugh. "But I was in the coffee shop and heard you sing. I don't know why, but I had to come out and see you. I heard the barista calling for my name and next thing I knew, I was throwing money at you. I just wish I had taken a minute or two to come up with an actual plan." You winced. "Now that I think of it, this is probably a terrible first impression."

You scratched the back of your neck with your left hand and stared at the neatly folded bill that rested in your shirt pocket, but then your eyes met mine expectantly, with a subtle arch in your brow that invited me to say something, begging for some sort of olive branch that would rail this introduction back on its tracks. The way you looked at me—honest, open—was unlike anything I'd felt before, and your accurate self-assessment of your haphazard introduction gave you an innocent quality I found irresistible.

I slowly began to smile, but I didn't say a word. Somehow the silence wasn't awkward. It lingered pleasantly in the air, patiently waiting for an answer. Then you finally spoke.

"At the risk of breaking a wonderful spell of a silent staring contest, would it be okay if I asked to hear the rest of that song, Noah? And afterward, if you'd like, I would love to buy you a cup of coffee. I promise I'll say actual words and have a coherent conversation this time. No creepy money exchanges either." You flashed me a mischievous grin.

There was something about you, and I can't explain how or why, but somehow, I knew that was our beginning. "I only drink tea," I teased, and, anxious to continue our conversation, I placed my hand in A minor and kept playing.

chapter two

NOW

WHERE THE *FUCK* did it all go wrong?

chapter three

THEN

SPRING BESIDE YOU had been magical. Three months had passed since that day outside the coffee shop, and our relationship still carried the soft colors of a new beginning. Everything was exciting, and we were happy. Our dreams bloomed like flowers, and the heat of summer only made them burn brighter.

It was ninety-two degrees Saturday morning when we decided to go to the beach. There was a heatwave threatening dehydration, so we packed our bathing suits and sunblock and headed down south. As soon as we parked the car and put money in the meter, I took off my sandals. I had always loved the anticipation of pressing my bare feet against the burning sand and feeling the warmth transfer to my skin. You took notice of my little ritual, and without second-guessing yourself, you immediately followed my lead.

We found our way to a secluded spot under a palm tree and set down our belongings. After twenty minutes under the late-morning sun, we could feel trickles of sweat as they pooled in the curves of our bodies. We had been drifting in and out of sleep when the sound of your voice woke me up.

"Tell me about the scar on your abdomen," you whispered to the ocean. It was a firm but simple request, and it made me realize how attractive I found the commanding way in which you spoke. That scar had faded from years and years of healing, but if you focused on it, you could still notice the dip in the right side of my stomach where they had taken my appendix out.

"I got appendicitis when I was fifteen, almost giving my dad a heart attack in the process. Poor guy was terrified." I was told the only other time he felt that level of terror was right before Mom died, but I did not want to get into that just yet.

Your pinky brushed mine, enough encouragement to keep going.

"It happened on a Fourth of July, which coincidentally is also my grandma's birthday. I used to see her all the time when I was a kid, but as the years went by, those visits became few and far between. We mostly kept in touch by phone, but my dad and I always drove to her house on her birthday. We never failed. Even though it was her celebration, she always cooked for us. It became a tradition—we brought the groceries, and she cooked a feast that could have fed a family of eight. On the drive back, my dad usually kept to himself, as he always did after spending the day recounting stories of when I was a baby"—a motherless baby—"so I didn't mention the stomachache I'd had for the past few hours. I figured it had something to do with what I ate for lunch and hoped having dinner and some sleep would fix the issue. Walk it off—I thought. I decided on Frosted Flakes and popcorn, and I—"

"Hold on." You propped yourself on your elbow and raised your sunglasses to look at me properly. "You ate five servings of lunch and then thought milk, sugar, and butter for dinner was a smart idea?"

I looked at you with a serious expression on my face, sweat coming down my forehead. "Well, of course, Derek, I had to eat dinner. What was I supposed to do? Starve myself?"

You stared at me with what I decided to interpret as amazement on your part, and after a moment too long, you lowered your sunglasses and returned to lying on your back. I wasn't sure if this was an act of resignation or an invitation to continue my story, so I went with the latter. I suppressed a small smile—not because the story wasn't true (it was), but because, hearing it now, I could see how I had not made the best decisions. However, I promised to be fully transparent with you months ago, so I kept going.

"I was sure I would wake up perfectly fine the next morning. But I was wrong. *So very wrong.* I woke up with pain worse than the day before, but I felt it more in the lower part of my belly. I told my dad everything, and after thirty-six hours of pain relievers, intermittent episodes of aggressive vomiting, and dangerously worsening, more localized pain, we landed in the hospital."

"Did you just say thirty-six hours? That's a whole day and a half, Noah," you said incredulously. "You're terrible during emergencies!"

I ignored this observation. "Well, yeah. The last thing I remember before they put me under was seeing my grandma and my dad holding hands under the doorframe. They looked so scared and fragile... I can only imagine their fear. My dad would have been completely alone if something didn't go as planned." My voice almost cracked on the last word, but you were always in tune with my feelings. I know you noticed it but you didn't push; you knew I wasn't ready.

"To this day, my dad flinches when I bring up the story," I said. "He laughs when he remembers me trying to punch the nurse who was doing the ultrasound, but I know the fear of the memory makes him stay away from remembering it."

We remained silent for a few minutes after that. I figured you were asleep until you said, "Frosted Flakes and popcorn. What a dumb, dumb idea. What am I getting myself into?"

We both laughed at this—the kind of laughter that makes your stomach hurt. We flipped around to make sure we got an even tan. As we were lying down, we looked at each other. I was lost in your sun-kissed cheeks. Your nose glowed—shades of pink and bronze made it hard to distinguish your freckles—and after a while, the sound of the ocean swayed you to sleep.

The intensity with which the waves crashed into the shore reminded me of how I felt for you, and I hoped you felt the same. I felt the tips of my fingers graze your hand, felt the electricity between us, and with a deep breath, with a sense of belonging that was foreign to me, I closed my eyes and slept next to you—just the way I hoped to do for the rest of my life.

chapter four

THE PAST THREE and a half weeks have been difficult. I can tell something happened at your job that has made you angry, but I also know I shouldn't ask. There is a tense and worrying aura around you. I can tell you've been stressed because you subconsciously double-knot your shoes when you're anxious. You have no idea that you do this, much less that I've noticed it. This single habit of yours has allowed me to navigate your moods and has helped me keep the peace around this house for the past five years.

However, nowadays, you have a specific routine. You come into the house after work and carelessly drop your portfolio on the kitchen table—the same one you carried the first day we met, the "Derek" on the top corner faded after all these years. Then you kiss me on the cheek—you haven't kissed my lips in so long that I've since forgotten the taste of yours. You grab a cold beer out of the fridge, slip out of your double-knotted shoes, and lie on the couch with a sigh so loud and drawn out, it would induce depression in anyone who hears it.

You don't turn on the TV, you don't tell me about your day, and you definitely don't ask about mine. You just lie there on the couch, staring at the ceiling in complete and agonizing silence. After an hour or two, I make dinner. Lately, cooking has been the only activity that evokes any sort of excitement or motivation in me. You've given up on eating at the table, so I bring the food to the living room, the smell of sweet and spicy ribs filling every square inch of the room. I place your food on the small table next to the couch and sit on the armchair beside you, watching your food get cold.

We don't start up a conversation. Somehow, we've lost all communication skills we had built over time. Still, even though there's complete stillness aside from the clinking of the fork against the plate, I know that we are together, and I am convinced that brings you some comfort—or maybe that is what I tell myself to feel better. I am not sure. But I know that I am not leaving you alone, because we get through the tough times together. We always have, and I am determined to hold that belief.

You eat a little more than half your food, and then I take the plates away. I do the kitchen alone and then go to bed upstairs—alone. I leave the light at the stairs turned on, though, because I know once you think I've fallen asleep, you'll come up and lie next to me, giving me the peace of mind I long for throughout the day.

As long as you are next to me, I can protect you and make sure you are okay— within the confines of what "okay" means for now.

I just need you to know I'm here for you; we can fix this together.

Please talk to me, Derek. Let me help you. What's going on?

chapter five

THEN

I STILL RECALL the day I fell in love with you. The rain had just passed, leaving the air heavy and sweet—the kind that clung to our skin and made our hands stick together as we laced our fingers. Sunlight broke through the clouds in soft, golden shards, catching in the shallow puddles at our feet, where tiny rainbows shimmered and danced. And in that moment, with your damp palm pressed against mine, even the thick summer air felt like it belonged only to us. With matching, childlike strides, we made our way to my favorite bookstore on Prince Boulevard. It was early in our relationship. That is the thing about love, though; you never know when it will catch you, but once it does, it refuses to let go.

After going up and down the different genres, in between the G shelves, I found exactly what I was looking for. I went to pay for my copy of *100 Years of Solitude*, but before I could reach for my wallet, you handed the cashier the money and winked at me. I smiled, baffled by the thought that I was just as infatuated with you as I was with Spanish literature classics—which, at least to me, was a hard milestone to achieve. Literature had always been my weakness, but somehow, you seemed to have taken its place. Yours was a story I would never get tired of reading. I would memorize every word until I could read you front and back with a simple glance.

Hand in hand, we walked down to the local café and sat at the corner table. A dim light directly above us gave us a romantic glow.

"I'd like to learn something new about you. Tell me something I don't know," you said in that soft, commanding voice I adored as you blew on your hot cup of coffee.

"I don't like yogurt."

You stared at me, trying to hide the grin peeking from the corner of your mouth, and gave me a look—a small eye roll that told me you were unsatisfied with my answer.

"Lame."

"What?" I faked offense. "This is a fundamental fact about me."

"I was thinking more along the lines of something deeper than the fact that you hate yogurt."

"Ah! I see. Well, for starters, I hate the word *hate*. I think it's the most powerful word we have in the English language, but nothing good comes from it. It's tragic. I've never encountered someone or something I truly hate. And to be honest, I hope I never do. Once you start hating, your heart hurts and cracks a little—just enough to leave you slightly broken. Nobody wants to live like that, you know?" I chewed on my cinnamon roll.

"Wow." You stared at me, somewhat amused. "That's deep."

"Well, ask and you shall receive. Your turn!" I smiled. "Tell me something I don't know."

You took a deep breath, and I saw your shoulders sag a little. You started playing with the sugar packet on the table, rubbing it between your index finger and thumb methodically, finding the words. "Well, I haven't told anybody this before. But you know how my dad has this big-shot company? And how the plan is for me to eventually take over? Well, I'm really dreading that day. I'm okay with numbers, and I understand the basics of how to run a business. But my dad has huge clients and investments that are way too high-risk for my taste. He's edgy but also very calculating, and I don't think I can match his vision. One single mistake from me, and it's game over."

"Have you told him any of this?" I asked. I was always one for pursuing dreams and hated—look at me being a hypocrite, using that word the first chance I get—the thought of you being forced down a path you didn't choose.

You scoffed. "Yeah, right. The only son to the big businessman wants out of the family business to chase his dream? It would never work. I don't even know what else I'd do with my life or what career I could take. I don't have many hobbies. Business courses took up all my time, and now I feel like it's too late to find something I love. I approached the subject with my mom once, and her reaction was… weird. But also very definitive." You straightened your shoulders slightly, as if preparing for disappointment.

"She gave me this intense, sorrowful look, cupped my cheek, kissed my forehead, and rested her head against mine. Then she left. She didn't say a word, and we never talked about it again. That was all the confirmation I needed. I'm just hoping I don't run the business into the ground… and that I do well enough to support us."

At the mention of *us,* I looked up from my tea, and we locked eyes. I could see red spots crawl up your neck, your telltale sign that always gave you away, and you cleared your throat to distract me from the obvious plans you had of us building a future together.

"A-Anyways!" you stuttered. "I know you love playing music and writing songs—have you ever thought about going to school for it?"

I took a sip of my peppermint tea, stalling for some time to straighten my thoughts. The tea was hot and burned the tip of my tongue, but I let it rest in my mouth a little longer before swallowing it, allowing the pain to distract me from my fast-paced, beating heart. I felt a stinging sensation forming at the back of my eyes, and I was unsure if it was because of the tea or what I was about to say.

I had never mentioned this or talked about it with anybody. It wrecked my family and broke my father, but we seemed to be headed toward a grounded, steady place in our relationship, and within the five months I'd known you, you had always kept every secret I ever shared with you and welcomed them without judgment.

I still find it difficult to believe this wasn't my fault, even though I know it wasn't. It literally couldn't have been. I also know I shouldn't play the "what if" game because it always leads to shattered hopes. Still, I was determined to let you into a part of my life that had been monumentally closed off to the universe. I pushed past the urge to cry and spoke.

"I actually went to college. I was a music major, but I dropped out after a year. A few months before we met."

"Oh? How come?" You were no longer distracted by the sugar packet, which now sat damp and wrinkled next to the cinnamon powder on the table.

I swallowed another sip of scalding tea. You were asking all the tough questions.

"Because my mom died when I was born, and it changed my dad forever. He never really recovered from it. I took care of him most of my life, and I tried to balance school and everything going on at home, but it got to be too much. He did handyman work around town, and I worked as a server to help with the bills. But most of my classes were at night, and if I wasn't home to keep him company, I'd find him passed out on the couch."

I looked up and met your gaze, and when I realized you were giving me all of your attention, I carried on before you could even ask a question.

"They called it amniotic fluid embolism. I never knew who she was, what she looked like, or how we were alike. I've seen pictures, but it's not the same."

Your eyebrows told me you had never heard of the term before, so I explained it to avoid an interruption, otherwise I would never be able to finish this story.

"Amniotic fluid embolism happens when the fluid surrounding a baby gets into the mother's bloodstream. From what I understand, her heart couldn't take it. She was able to kiss my forehead once before she lost consciousness. Her name was Lane, which is my middle name. My dad says he named me after her to keep her close."

24

I felt a single tear stream down my cheek; it left a burning trail as I wiped it away. I held the necklace that had belonged to her. Rubbing the pendant of the Earth hanging from my neck always grounded me.

You shifted your weight on the chair and leaned forward, resting your chin on your propped-up elbow, but couldn't bring yourself to say anything. You were speechless because, deep down, you knew what I knew—it didn't matter what you said; it wouldn't change anything. Looking at you, I was grateful for your silence. Your kind eyes told me everything I needed to know.

"From what I hear, my dad loved my mom more than life itself, and losing her broke him completely. He obviously did his best. He poured me cereal for breakfast and made sure I made it to the school bus on time. He told me he loved me every day and tucked me in at night, but he was never truly present. Not in the emotional sense, anyway. Every day while I was in school, he visited her grave. Sometimes I'd come home to see dirt smudges on his fingers from planting flowers with his bare hands."

I twisted the edge of my sleeve, suddenly aware of how vulnerable I felt.

"I know my mom invaded each and every thought in his mind, and I respected that, but our dynamic made me pretty independent from an early age. I wanted to make it as easy as I possibly could for him. I don't think he ever blamed me for what happened, but I still carried that guilt sometimes. I never partied or caused any trouble because I didn't want him to worry about me or resent me more than he already did."

"So I take it we will not be bar-crawling on your twenty-first birthday?" you whispered as a joke. I was grateful—nothing de-escalates tension and a sob story like a bad joke for comic relief. I chuckled, but then you took both my hands in yours and gave me a serious nod.

"Sorry, I shouldn't have cut you off like that. Please, go on."

I squeezed your hands to let you know it was okay. "Right. We had some help, of course. My grandma would come and help around the house every week for the first few years. I knew, deep down, she needed this as much as we did, having lost her only daughter and feeling just as broken. She practically raised me when my dad was too far down, lost in his own thoughts of misery and denial."

I stretched my neck as if rolling out a kink, trying to find the words to finish the story.

"Some nights, I'd wake up in the middle of the night and hear him talking to my mom. He would have trivial conversations with her, almost as if he were pretending she was still with him to avoid sinking into the new reality. My grandma says I look just like her."

"Is this the grandma that cooks a full banquet on her birthday?"

"Yup, that's the one! She is the most important person in my life. I love her to pieces. Unfortunately, when my grandpa got sick, she couldn't come around as much, and I was left alone with my half-functioning dad again. I really miss my grandma, though; I always think about taking the train and visiting her, but it's been a while."

I realized then that I hadn't looked at you for a few minutes. It was already an all-too-personal moment, and I couldn't deal with the added touch of your eyes reflecting pity. I took another sip of my tea, which was significantly colder than before, took a deep breath, and met your eyes. You had so many different emotions flashing across your face. I recognized pain, empathy, admiration, and respect—but most of all, I recognized an expression reflecting off mine.

It was love.

You were falling in love with me, and I was falling in love with you. It took me a few seconds to process the situation, but after that, you spoke. Apparently, you were much better at finding the right words for difficult conversations than I was.

"So, first of all, I am so sorry that happened to you. That is more than any child should bear. That's even more than any adult should deal with. None of you deserved that. Secondly, I can't bring your mom back, and I can't tell you what she was like. But if you're wondering, I can tell you a few things about yourself.

For instance, when you're focused on something, you stick the tip of your tongue out without realizing it. I always wonder if you'll end up accidentally biting it. I can tell you that when you're nervous, you rub the center of your left palm with your right thumb, and I can also tell you that I am reasonably concerned about how dependent you are on tea, but that's an issue we'll address later."

I instinctively brought my thumb to my palm.

"But Noah, you are the most beautiful girl I've ever seen, and from what you said about your mom's resemblance, I can only assume she was beautiful too." My face was burning hot. I was rarely in a position where I had to accept such nice compliments. It felt unnatural, and they made me a little shy, but my heart melted with every word.

"It is impossible for me to take your pain away, but I can promise that I will do everything in my power to carry that weight with you. I will give you all my love to try to overpower your pain because I love you, Noah Lane."

My breath snagged in my throat, and for a moment, I couldn't speak.

I knew then that you and I felt the same way. But hearing those words out loud still took my breath away. It wasn't that I never thought I'd hear them—it was that I never expected them to feel so abundantly magical."

I took another sip of what might as well have been iced tea. I looked up and met your eyes.

"I love you, too," I squeaked, blushing.

There was a glimmer in your big brown eyes. You squeezed my hands hard.

"Also—I think you need to go see your grandma. And I'd love the chance to meet her."

"Now that you mention it, her birthday's coming up. Want to surprise her with a visit?" I said, trying to hide all the pain in my voice and the guilt I felt for not visiting her sooner.

"You give me the list of groceries, and I'll be there."

"It's a date then!"

You smiled at me. "I can't wait to see what the future holds," you said as you kissed my hands.

I winked back. "It's enough for me to know that you and I exist at this moment," I whispered coyly.

"How do you always come up with deep and insightful catchphrases?"

"I don't." I laughed, nodding my head. "I just borrow them from people who actually said them," I said, chuckling as I tapped the bag holding the copy of *100 Years of Solitude*.

"You said such nice things a moment ago I felt like I had to say something equally meaningful. I didn't have time to come up with anything original—so I borrowed it."

At this confession, you widened your eyes and let out a laugh that came from deep within. It was music to my ears. You had such a beautiful laugh.

"Well, consider me impressed! So, these words of wisdom come from Mr. García Márquez?"

"The one and only!" I replied.

"What a smart guy. What else did he say?"

"My favorite quote is: 'Cease, cows, life is short.' It really captures the simplicity of it all."

We laughed and talked for what felt like hours, and I was amazed at how you could lift me up even after I'd relived the most painful memory of my past. You had such a gift for laughter, Derek. You were such a gift yourself.

I was so lucky.

We used to be so happy.

chapter six

NOW

HAS IT BEEN three months already, or has it been four? Ever since you answered that call, I've lost count of how many days you've spent locked up in your office. Empty coffee mugs, unpaid bills, and old newspapers are piled outside your locked door. I step over them carefully, as if touching them might make your absence feel more real.

You used to spend your afternoons on the couch, at least sharing the same space as me. The cushions still hold the shape of your head from the last time you fell asleep on them. But ever since you got that one call a few months ago—the one that made you disappear into yourself—you've found solace in your office and your office alone. Sometimes I press my hand into that cushion, pretending the warmth hasn't fully left.

The magic we felt six years ago, when we were young and in love, is fading like smoke blown in the wind. I feel as alone as you do, and I've been racking my brain trying to understand what you need from me—how to help you. But the more I reach, the further you drift.

You barely eat anymore, and when you do, it's washed down with rum or vodka. There are so many bottles lying around now, I can't even remember the last one I threw away. The clink of glass has become the only sound that reminds me you're still here.

I knock on the door and call for you, but I am greeted by silence. Only the faint sound of rain echoes back, as our old wooden house groans and sighs around me—as if it, too, can feel the dread settling into our home. This gut-wrenching, suffocating, solitary silence is killing me. Everything we were has slowly faded, slipping out of my fingers despite how hard I try to grasp it.

chapter seven

WE WERE IN the train station with three grocery bags each. Our hands were red from the plastic bags cutting into our palms, but I felt happy and hopeful for the day ahead. The station lobby was decorated patriotically. Red, white, and blue garlands haphazardly decorated the desk, and there was one small American flag taped to the ticket counter. Fourth of July was celebrated in all its American glory.

"I bought this jar of lollipops for your grandma. Do you think she'd like it?" you asked nervously.

"I mean, it's a jar with one hundred and fifty lollipops for a single old lady. Frankly, I hope she doesn't like them. If you give her diabetes, I'm going to be pissed," I half-joked. Still, the fact that you worried whether she'd like it made my chest tighten in the best way. You wanted her approval almost as much as I did.

The train ride wasn't too long. I had called my grandma a couple of days after our coffee shop date to break the news, and her excitement was palpable through the phone. She let out a high-pitched squeak that was so sharp it was only audible to dogs. We agreed on spaghetti and homemade meatballs with cheesy garlic bread, but I think we may have gone a little overboard with the groceries. We also had a birthday cake, magic candles, party hats, and balloons. I didn't think so many decorations were necessary, but you wanted to make a big impression—and why not? I hadn't seen my grandma in a few months, and turning seventy was a huge deal.

I called Dad to see if he would like to come, but he said he was feeling a little under the weather. He sent his regards and said that since you were going, you could take his place. It was the twentieth anniversary of my mom's passing that year, so I understood he wanted to spend more time in the cemetery, and I gave him his space. I was a little sad that he felt the need to cover it up with a small white lie. It stung, if I'm honest. Even after all these years, he still couldn't just say he missed her. Maybe that was his way of keeping himself intact. Maybe it was mine too. He still felt the need to act strong, and I respected his wishes.

To our surprise—more yours than mine—as we were getting off the train, we heard a whistle. And I don't mean a referee, crossing guard, lifeguard kind of whistle. I mean the kind of whistle you hear on the street when getting catcalled. The kind of whistle that sets your teeth on edge.

We were going to ignore it, thinking it was a degenerate drunk. And then we heard it. Loud—very loud—and clear.

"God dangit! Are you two my birthday present? 'Cause you are fine as hell! Can I wrap you two up with a nice bow?"

Oh boy. There she was, the famous degenerate.

I didn't even need to turn around. I would recognize that voice anywhere. You looked at me, horrified.

"By the way, I forgot to tell you—my grandma has quite the sense of humor." You widened your eyes in response, an inaudible gasp forming on your lips.

I sighed in a mix of relief and resignation and turned to face Grandma Nadia, who was holding up a literal sign like she was a cab driver picking us up from the airport. *Welcome home, Noah and Derek*, it read. God, I loved that woman.

You read the sign and took in the person holding it. "This is freaking awesome!" you whispered excitedly.

I chuckled. "Happy birthday, Grandma!" I shouted back as we ran to meet her.

She hugged us both so tight that it hurt a little—in the best possible way. When she let go of the hug, I stayed there just a little longer, pressing my forehead against hers, memories of when I was a kid flashing back in my mind, feeling deeply grateful that we were here now. Her perfume still smelled like cinnamon. Suddenly I was eight again, legs dangling off the counter as she let me lick the spoon covered in chocolate cake batter.

"Man, seventy years old already? Three more decades and you'll be a whole century!"

"Hey! Respect your elders, you punk!" she joked, pointing at me. "Also, introduce me to this hot stud," she said, shifting her finger toward you.

"H-hello, Mrs. N—" was all you were able to get out before she cut you off.

"Nope. I will be having none of that." She shook her head furiously. "You are now officially my grandson, and you will be referring to me as Grandma, end of story!"

With that, she cupped your face in both her hands and planted a kiss on your forehead so aggressive it left a lipstick mark. There it was—the stamp of approval. I don't think you realized just how big of a deal that was, but to me, it felt like the universe had shifted a little in our favor. You were officially a part of the family.

"Well, thank you very much, Mrs.—ahem—Grandma." She raised her brows in warning, then gave a satisfied nod when you corrected yourself. "And happy birthday! I'm not sure if you like candy, but I bought you this in case you did." You smiled as you handed her the family-sized jar of candy.

Her eyes lit up. "Sweet! I used to love these as a kid! You're the best, sweetie, thank you so very much!" she said, cradling the jar in the crook of her left elbow and pinching your cheek with her other hand. You winced in pain but tried not to show it; I winced right along with you—her fingers hadn't lost their strength over the years. Sometimes my grandma reminded me of a fraternity bro, and others she reminded me of how a cartoon grandmother would behave.

She sidestepped to reveal the small supermarket cart she had been hiding behind her.

"Now! I figured you'd show up here with groceries unprepared, so I brought a little cart that way you'd have hands left to cook with when you get home. I know I used to do all the cooking, but as you can tell, I am decrepitly old now. I will be needing a couple of handsome sous-chefs to assist me in the kitchen."

"Sounds like a plan!" I said as we packed our bags and headed to her house. I placed my arm around her as we walked. "I love you so, so much. I'm so glad we could celebrate together like old times," I said, resting my head on her shoulder.

"Catcalling and sexual harassment aside, you two really are the best present I could have asked for!" she said, unwrapping a lime-flavored lollipop.

chapter eight

NOW

EVERY NIGHT, I lie in bed, confused, a flurry of cynical feelings residing inside my stomach. I am sad and scared, but not of you; I know you would never hurt me. I am afraid of what will become of us. Anger and loneliness pool in my chest, as present now as when I first noticed the glimmer in your eyes dim. I experience the kind of loneliness that creeps inside your bones, the one you can't get rid of. It makes me cold, a bone-deep chill no blanket or prayer can warm. The void lingers, relentless.

You haven't slept next to me for quite a few nights; I cannot remember how long exactly, but it's been enough for me to feel abandoned.

Remember five years ago when we quit smoking? The more I think of our current situation, the more I crave a cigarette. But we made a promise; I promised you I wouldn't smoke another cigarette in my life, comforted by your promise that you would be with me forever. Those were simple times. I wish we could return to that, Derek. I really do.

I know as soon as my alarm goes off that you're not next to me, but I expected that. Where did we go so wrong? I sit on the edge of the bed, feeling the cold wooden floor with my bare toes. At least I can still feel. Sometimes, I worry I might go completely numb in my mind, body, and spirit.

I go to the bathroom and hop in the shower, hoping to feel better by the end—which obviously doesn't work. The water is as hot as it allows, burning my back as it drips off me, enjoying those few seconds of scorching pain before it leads to a few more seconds of comfortable pleasure. It doesn't last long, though. After about twenty seconds, my skin gets used to it, and I return to square one, feeling hollow and dispirited.

The room is steaming by the time I'm done. The mirror is completely hazed. As I swipe a streak away with my towel, I am horrified by the image staring back at me. I see a version of myself I can barely recognize. I have lost more weight than I care to admit, my spine showcasing each vertebra like a scale model of the Himalayas in a museum display. I don't see a spark of energy, only dark circles under my eyes. I look purposeless.

The warm and characteristic spirit I was once known for left long ago. Now there was only emptiness, and I couldn't pinpoint where it all went wrong. You had left for work, so I decided to take matters into my own hands. For once, I'd make a breakfast that was worthy of being eaten. I needed the fuel anyway; it had been weeks since I had a full meal that left me satisfied.

Afterward, I scrubbed the kitchen spotless. It didn't smell dirty, but it wasn't clean either. It smelled of dust and abandonment; it reeked of a place whose owners had given up on keeping up with it the way it was meant to. The strong chemicals burned my nostrils. I felt lightheaded, but I ignored it, hoping that if I scrubbed hard enough, I could scrub away the misery that had settled into the walls. Once I finished cleaning and taking out the trash, I did the laundry and changed the sheets. I needed to feel like I lived in a place worthy of companionship again.

I had lost that sense of company in you, and now I had to find it within myself. Once I felt like my job was done, I still had a couple of hours before you came home, so I put on my sneakers and went for a run. I wasn't sure exactly what I was running from or running to, but I knew it was important because I was running fast. I was running away from the life that had become of us; I was trying to run back in time to the couple we used to be. Young and in love. Not bitter and hopeless.

After an hour and a half, I returned to our house. My breathing was shallow, my lungs burning with each gasp, breathing was physically painful, so I rested my head against the old, wooden doorframe and counted each breath, slowly and steady, feeling the oxygen replenishing my lungs. You should've been getting home by now. I was a sweaty mess, but I saw a small ray of light in my life now—the endorphins released by the run affecting my mood.

I hopped back into the shower. When I was done, I was ready to see a renewed version of myself—or I suppose, ready to see who I was only a few months ago. I wiped off a streak in the mirror again and found the exact same look reflected that I saw in the morning.

"This must be déjà vu," I thought to myself. I wiped the mirror clean, willing my reflection to look different. But there it was again—the same vacant stranger. No progress. No relief. Just proof that even my hope was delusional.

Anger flashed across my eyes. I was disappointed in myself and my inability to show even an ounce of resilience during hard times. I brushed my hair, threw some makeup on, put on a pair of clean clothes, and started running down the stairs. Your car was outside, so I knew you were home.

I was right outside your office, staring at the door. *Knock, knock, knock*—no answer. I turned the knob, but it was locked. I tried it again. *Knock, knock, knock.* I called your name. No answer. I was getting impatient, so I made it my sole and only purpose to get you to open the door.

I knocked desperately and persistently for what felt like hours, calling for you between knocks. But it was probably just about forty-five seconds or so before you despondently opened the door. You were staring in my direction, but you weren't looking at me; you were staring right past me, which hurt.

"You look nice," you noted, walking over to your chair to sit back down. It wasn't until then that I noticed you were still holding your Ron Zacapa bottle; you stood up with it, opened the door, and walked back, holding it in your left hand. Alcohol had become your security blanket.

I moved closer to you.

"Tell me what's wrong," I said dryly.

"Nothing's wrong." You couldn't even meet my gaze.

"Tell me what's wrong, Derek. And don't you dare lie to me, I'm not an idiot. I want to help you. I need to; I feel like I'm living alone in this house. I am your wife, which means I'm entitled to know what is breaking us apart."

The silence was deafening, but I wasn't giving up so easily.

"A few months ago, I heard you screaming and slamming your hands on this desk, talking to someone on the phone around midnight. Tell me about that call." I was surprised by how steady my voice was, how firm, knowing full well that my heart was threatening to explode in my ribcage.

At the mention of the call, your head snapped up to meet my eyes. I took a step back.

"Please drop it. Please don't ask me any more questions." Your tone was calm, almost pleading. You sounded exhausted, and I was getting a little fed up as well. I snapped the hair tie around my wrist three times to keep myself from screaming. The stinging red mark that pulsated with each snap helped me focus on my breathing and dulled the headache that threatened to become a migraine. "Just know that I am doing everything I can to get us back to where we were. I just need a little time and a lot of trust." The words should have comforted me, but instead they sliced me open. How could you beg for trust while barricading yourself behind that locked door? "I know I have been awful lately, and I'm sorry, but I'm begging you, Noah, just give me some space to sort things out. Please," you begged.

I can hear the sob wanting to cry out from your throat, but you keep yourself together—for your sake or mine, I am not even sure.

"Give you space?" I scoff. "What do you think I've been doing all this time? This is the first time I've seen you in days, Derek. How am I supposed to feel when we promised to fight for each other? Through thick and thin? When lately, I have been fighting not for you or me but for your attention. Jesus Christ, you're supposed to at least *try* Derek."

It isn't until I hear the words coming out of my mouth that I start feeling the stinging sensation behind my eyes after months of pretending they did not bother me. This time, I make no effort to keep them inside. I'm tired of trying.

I stand there, looking at you, as tears pool in the corners of my eyes and leave my face a hot, salty mess. For the first time in months, I see you looking at me—really looking at me—and I see understanding flash across your eyes.

"Do you trust me?" you ask. I can barely hear your soft voice over the pounding in my ears.

I have to think long and hard about this question. I used to trust you. I used to think we would die for each other. Together forever. Forever and always. But even though we live under the same roof, we have been strangers for far too long.

After seeing the scene unfold before you and fear creeping into your bones, I see the compassion in your eyes that I thought was long gone. You were afraid, and the muscles in your jaw that are tense with worry tell me you are anxious—if not desperate—for my answer.

I realize you had no ill intent; you had just approached the situation horribly wrong. But in your eyes, I see a glimmer of the man I used to love.

"Noah. Do you trust me?" I rearrange and examine your words in my brain until I am sure of the answer. I give you the most elusive of nods.

I can physically see the relief coursing through your body. You let out a breath as you walked over to me and kissed me. I ignored the taste of bitter alcohol, and you ignored my salty breath, tears still pooled in the corner of my lips, and after waiting so long to feel the soft touch of your familiar lips, I kissed you back.

Your mouth found mine with a kind of desperation that matched the ache clawing behind my sternum. I clung to you, not because I was ready to forgive, but because I couldn't bear the distance another second. Your hands framed my face, pulling me closer, as if you too were afraid of vanishing. Every brush of skin against mine felt like a promise we were too fragile to make out loud. We sank into each other, not to forget the cracks between us, but to hide inside them for as long as we could.

We made our way to the couch, unable to let go of one another, and after months of misery, at least for a couple of hours, we went back to being what we were, experiencing all of those forgotten feelings at once. Your breath tangled with mine, and for the first time in weeks, the world felt steady. We unraveled each other with hands that trembled, not from hesitation but from need. Every kiss was a plea, every touch a vow we were too broken to speak aloud. Your body pressed against mine, warm and desperate, and I let myself drown in you—your scent, your weight, the sheer relief of belonging. The night blurred around us, but it wasn't about passion or forgiveness. It was about holding onto each other like the world might end if we let go.

Later that night, I laid next to you, on the crook of your shoulder, just like we used to. At least for a little while, we had our normal life back. I finally felt like I could breathe again, ignoring the quiet voice inside my head that tried to remind me of how you'd been treating me these past few months. I urged the voice to stop.

I sat up, relieved to know that the love we felt for one another never wavered. It had always been there; it was just masked under all the issues that arose with whatever that call was about. Finally lying beside you, finally sleeping next to you, was an idea that brought peace to my heart.

I looked at you, and with a smile, I said, "You're coming upstairs, right?"

You looked at me, pity taking residence in your eyes.

After a second too long, you whispered: "Sure, let's go."

I knew you didn't want to come upstairs with me; you were fighting against your instincts to stay put. I knew your safe haven was your office, but I also knew that you could tell how much I needed you. How much I needed to feel protected by your body lying beside mine. And for that, I loved you. I knew deep down you felt the same way.

We came upstairs, and we fell asleep intertwined with one another. I knew in my gut that this was a charade, that you weren't in a state of mind where you could slip back into old patterns and sleep soundlessly. But you did it—or at least tried to—and it was all for me. I slept throughout the whole night. It was the best night's sleep I'd had in months.

When I woke up at 7:00 a.m. the following day, I didn't have to turn around to know you weren't next to me. The mattress felt cold, and I couldn't feel the weight of your body pulling me toward you. I knew you'd be in your office trying to right your wrongs, whatever those were.

But I felt at ease. At least now I knew for a fact that the old you was somewhere in there. That underneath this stress and havoc, the Derek I knew and loved was still there, fighting for me; fighting for us. All I have to do is have a little bit of trust…

chapter nine

THEN

WE HAD ALWAYS been simple-minded people, or so we thought until we played "Would You Rather" under the stars one cool summer night. God, I loved our special talks. They felt like our own private story, our little secret. Those conversations where we shared ideas and opinions without any sense of judgment. We just wanted to get to know each other better.

We had taken one of our nightly strolls down in the forest and looked for a spot to lay our flannel blanket to look at the stars. We settled under the Three Kings. I told you how that was my absolute favorite constellation because it didn't matter how old I had been, where I was, or at what hour of the night—I had always been able to find it. It felt like the Three Kings were always watching over me, protecting me. Whenever I felt lonely, I would look up, and without fail, I would see them there, and suddenly, I would not feel alone anymore. I felt like I was a part of them: King Alnitak, King Alnilam, King Mintaka, and Queen Noah.

After listening to my fantasy of being the fourth star, you shared the most fascinating fact. I had told you that I could never find any other constellation, but you said that every time I saw the Three Kings, I was looking at part of the constellation Orion, because those three stars made up Orion's Belt.

My jaw dropped. I was speechless. You couldn't help but laugh when you saw the expression on my face. According to you, it looked like a child's face when they saw cartoons for the first time—completely in awe. Things like that were the ones that had me going crazy about you. You seemed to know a little bit of everything, a whole galaxy of information in your brain. You were mesmerizing.

Once we got past my astonishment about the Orion's Belt enigma, I asked you a question. And thus, the game began.

"Would you rather know the history behind every object you ever touch or be able to talk to animals?"

You answered in less than two seconds. "Talk to animals. I don't care much for history; it's in the past. People dwell on it. But what's done is done—and should stay that way. People tend to overanalyze and try to understand what happened years—even ages—ago, with the promise that understanding it can prevent us from making the same mistakes. But the problem is, we're so focused on the past that we ignore the present. So many issues need our attention now, and they go unnoticed." You shrugged, kicking the grass with your foot. "Modern times require modern solutions."

I arched my eyebrows in appreciation as I twirled a small flower between my fingers. Turns out I was dating a philosophical genius.

"Animals, though? I could talk with them for hours. I'd ask dogs how they remain so loyal to humans. I'd ask horses if they hate being ridden." You pointed at a bird's nest perched on the branch of an old oak tree. "I'd ask birds how far across the ocean they've flown and how many sunsets they've seen." You paused for a moment and looked at me. "Have you heard Michael's story?"

"Myers?" I joked.

"No." You snickered. "Not that one. Michael was a gorilla who was taught Sign Language, and when they asked him about his parents, he started crying. He told his caretakers a man had shot his mom right in front of him." The muscles in your jaw were twitching again. I could feel the tension coming from your body. "The capacity of animals for understanding is astounding. And the vile, heartless actions some people take against animals for profit? Despicable. I have no interest in human history. I don't really care for humans. I care for animals—for their innocence and ability to love and experience pain, just like we do." My heart ached for Michael, and I wondered if I was projecting some of my own tragedy. We stayed silent for a minute or two, paying our respects for the suffering we, as humans, have caused him—and every other innocent creature whose life we have chosen to destroy—while realizing that the more we hear stories like these, the more faith in humanity we begin to lose.

The night air pressed heavier around us, as if it, too, felt trapped by the injustice and the pain. I sympathized. You noticed how bothered I was and held my hand. You squeezed it tight—not once, but twice—and I responded accordingly.

Tiny blades of grass cut into my thighs, and I allowed myself a moment to be distracted by the needle pricks. I touched the tip of my four fingers with my thumb to ground myself, and tried to find different shapes in the leaves of the trees around us that were illuminated by the soft glow of a few dragonflies.

"Did I ruin the mood?" you asked.

I shook my head.

"Do you want to keep playing?"

I nodded.

"Okay." You took a deep breath. "Would you rather lose the ability to read or lose the ability to speak?"

I exhaled, taking advantage of that moment to choose my words carefully. We were back in the game. "Option B. But I think this applies not only to me—but to many others."

"How so?"

"Because people waste their words on stupid thoughts. I've heard some outrageous things come out of people's mouths. They choose to be ignorant and irrationally close-minded. Then they ramble about topics they don't understand." I held my hands in front of me with my palms up, as if pleading for everyone to change their ways. "It's terrifying. Imagine if we couldn't read as a society. A huge source of knowledge would be inaccessible. Now imagine people receiving random, inaccurate information from the same idiots who choose ignorance as a lifestyle? God, no. I vote for no talking. That way, we might actually have a chance to listen."

I heard you clap in slow motion—four times—just like they do in *Friends*.

"I would like to nominate you as candidate for the presidency," you said.

"And I better have your vote."

We chuckled. It was my turn to ask a question, and I took a moment to think. I liked to pick my words carefully. I wanted to say things that mattered—thoughts I would admire others for expressing.

"Would you rather be in jail for a year or lose a year of your life?"

Your eyebrows furrowed slightly. You still had smooth, young skin, so there were no wrinkles at the corners of your eyes—not just yet. I assumed they would show after years of countless laughs and memories. Together.

"What landed me in jail?"

"I don't think that matters."

"Um, I think that matters a lot. That might actually be the most important piece of information in that question," you said incredulously.

"Uh... You resisted arrest."

"Why?"

"Just answer the question!" I said impatiently, playfully shoving your shoulder.

"Okay, okay!" You ruffled your hair. "Jail for a year. Being enclosed in a small space surrounded by strangers can teach you a lot about yourself. It'll help you feel comfortable spending time alone. And once I'm out, maybe I'll have a bigger appreciation for the little things."

"Like for me?" I said coyly.

"I would never take you for granted," you said, and I could tell you genuinely believed that. I loved when you reassured me. "But also, I would work out for the whole sentence and come back jacked. Like a beast!"

"Boys…" I rolled my eyes and shook my head slightly.

"Would you rather live a life where you feel somewhat numb and emotionless? Or would you rather feel everything with every fiber of your being? Both the soul-crushing moments where you feel lost and the moments where you feel on top of the world?" you asked.

"I want to feel everything. I want to cry until my soul aches and laugh until my stomach hurts. I want to be terrified—and still choose to be brave. I want to know what it's like to fight for a dream, and to fail so hard it shakes me. I want to feel the weight of disappointment, and the fire of hope that refuses to go out. I want to crave, and love, and lose, and love again. And thanks to you, I already know what real love feels like. I want it all—the ache, the joy, the everything in between."

You squeezed my hand and then put your arm around my shoulders, pulling me closer to you. I got lost in the scent of your cologne. I straightened a corner of the blanket and swept it with my hand, removing the small pebbles and leaves to give me a few extra seconds on the crook of your neck.

After a few minutes, we closed our eyes. We were done playing. We breathed the cold air of the night, smelled the grass around us, and felt the warmth of our bodies next to each other. I thought about your freckles, how they resembled the stars above us, and I imagined all the constellations I could find on the bridge of your nose. This brought me peace. You made me feel safe and loved, and I thanked the angels watching over us for allowing you to exist in my lifetime. For writing you as a main character in my story.

Your voice, your eyes, the way you used them to look at me—*into* me. The few gray hairs I could see on your head, even though you were only in your early twenties. My grandma used to say that every gray hair she got represented a lesson in life, a lesson of wisdom. I believed in that theory and wondered what your gray hairs meant. I wanted to know what stories they held. I wanted to know everything about you. I craved for you to share your knowledge with me. I wanted to be wise with you. Grow old with you. Exist with you.

As a shooting star cut through Orion, I wished for our story to last forever. Unfortunately for us, forever wasn't long enough.

chapter ten

NOW

IT'S BEEN THREE days since we spent the night together, and despite hoping for the contrary, nothing has changed. But today feels different. I don't know if it's good or bad, but too many thoughts are swimming in my head, and I'm questioning my life choices. I know sharing your life with somebody involves changes and sacrifices, but am I sacrificing too much? Am I giving myself up entirely for someone else? When I was single, I was always clear on who I was. I knew what I wanted and where I belonged.

When I found you, my life changed. Mostly for the better, but sometimes it's more complicated—way harder than what I would've put up with when I was single. I liked my freedom. I liked doing what I wanted, with no explanations necessary. I wouldn't mess with people or get into their business, and I expected the same in return, although, unfortunately, not everyone shared that philosophy.

It's like my grandmother used to say: "To each their own." Back then, I had control of my life, and I only worried about myself.

Now, I look at my life and wonder where I stand. I stopped waiting tables a couple of years ago because we—well, you—were doing so well financially that I could focus on our home and my music. Scribbling lyrics on napkins at cafés.

Dragging my guitar to open-mic nights. If I'd seen myself a few years ago, I wouldn't have recognized the person staring back at me. The change happened so gradually I didn't even notice time passing. And now, I'm scared. I need to regain control. I used to love drifting through life, meeting poets on the street who turned their words into songs. I lived in a state of joy and nostalgia. Very few musicians could capture the beauty of pain, and I admired them for it. I spent countless nights under the moon, sand beneath my toes, feeling free—not as a person, but free of expectations and commitments. Free to become exactly who I wanted.

Now I'm rotting in misery—sad, angry, and invisible. Why am I only seeing this now? I feel torn between the woman I was taught to be—strong, independent, proud—and the woman in love, who dreamed of building a life with someone, yet was held back by a broken man. But life is complicated. Was I really not aware of that?

It's not like I haven't known pain. But this—this was a different kind of pain. The pain of invisibility. Of being shut out. The sting of alcohol laced with lies. The agony of being erased from your own story.

Who am I? I needed to make this right. I had to talk to you, but I felt too emotional, too angry. My head was clouded. I wanted a cigarette. I didn't light one.

Instead, I went downstairs. To the fridge, where I've seen you go countless times a day for a drink. I followed your steps, trying to understand you—though that's all I seemed to do lately. I've been maneuvering around your moods, allowing things the old me never would have tolerated. Back then, I was selfish, unsympathetic—only-child syndrome, I suppose. I don't even know. Right now, I'm just spitting thoughts, desperate for clarity.

I grabbed a beer and sat in our backyard, staring at the stars, hoping they'd tell me something—anything. But the stars were quiet tonight. I took a sip. It tasted bitter. I spat it out and poured the rest into the bushes. Even this tasted wrong.

In the sky, I found the Three Kings. Once upon a time, they made me smile. Years ago, they crowned me; now they only judged me. I had always been independent, but suddenly, I felt tied down—and not in a romantic way. I felt stuck, as if I were taking care of a child.

I had been through this before. When my mom died, caring for my dad was up to me. And now history was repeating itself. I just want things to be okay.

Do you still love me? I believe so, and I think I love you, too. I know I do. But the road has gotten so exhausting. I had to get things back under control.

I took a deep breath, and I thought of my mom. I thought about what she would do. It was challenging, since I had never met her, but she seemed so wise from what I had been told. I had only seen a single picture of her many years ago, but the point remains—she would have made the right choice.

That's when I decided—it was up to me.

I stood up, determined, swaying a little as blood rushed to my head from standing up so fast. The stars filled the sky like ten thousand fireflies harmonizing together. I had a long day. More than that, I have had a long year, and days are beginning to blur.

I woke up this morning feeling off, like something deep down was preparing me for the chaos that tonight would become—and tonight had arrived.

With a clear purpose, I walked back to your office. My hand trembled on the knob. I didn't knock; I opened the door and let myself in.

chapter eleven

THEN

LAST WEDNESDAY AFTERNOON was so special. There was a breeze, that September afternoon when the leaves on the trees began to fall slowly, one by one, coating the street on different shades of autumn. Crimson and amber leaves crunched under the weight of our footsteps as we strolled through the park and watched the sun go down. I was learning to play the chords to Dust in the Wind with you by my side, and once I got it, I was surprised to hear you singing along with me. You were always shy about your singing, which is ironic because you had such a raw and honest voice. Hearing your voice—shy, trembling at first, then steady—sent a warm wave of goosebumps through me I hadn't expected. It was like you were letting me glimpse a secret you kept hidden from the rest of the world. Your voice could move mountains—the same mountains I liked to stare at when I needed a moment alone with my thoughts.

I recall that day with such joy. We were lying on top of a blanket I'd knitted from my old band T-shirts. *Queen, The Beatles, Bob Dylan, Eagles, Pink Floyd*— the logos were fading, but that only added to its vintage charm. It gave the blanket authenticity, personality, and a little piece of my history.

A small dog had been running around, and as we finished the last verse of the song, the dog approached you, looking at you intently. I, of course, fell head over heels for the puppy, but you were unsure about him, as if he had deceived you once before and now you were experiencing trust issues. He sniffed your shoe, gave a quick huff, then trotted off as if he had more important places to be.

We shrugged it off and set my guitar aside, taking a moment to feel the sun kiss our cheeks as we closed our eyes and listened to the melody of the trees swaying behind us. After what felt like the perfect eternity, I heard your voice, barely a whisper.

"Does your shoe feel wet?" you asked.

"Huh?" I replied, confused and still dazed from daydreaming.

"Your shoe. Is it wet? Specifically, your left one."

I began to chuckle, only now starting to connect the dots. It was unbelievable.

"No," I replied, holding in a laugh as I faked scratching my chin just to have an excuse to cover my mouth.

The next part of this memory comes in flashes; everything happened so fast. You sprang into movement so quick it belonged in an action movie, a light breeze brushing my shoulder as the guitar vanished from the blanket. And just as quickly, a small dog sprinting away from the psychotic man holding the guitar like a weapon and cursing the creature that had peed on his left shoe. For a split second, I worried more about the guitar than the dog—it was the one piece of me I never wanted to lose. But seeing the scene unfold before me, I couldn't even scold you. It was all too ridiculous.

Of course, you couldn't catch the dog—or even get within fifteen feet. By the time you stumbled back, guitar in hand, panting and flushed, I was laughing so hard my sides hurt. You looked defeated, apologetic for the attempted instrument assault as you sheepishly set down the guitar, and smelling like a sour combination of sweat and pee. God, how I loved you.

You glanced at me, trying your best to hold onto a scowl, but with the golden sunset at our backs and laughter still ringing between us, how could you feel upset?

Instead of mentioning the dog, your yellow sock, or the warm trickle going down your ankle, you simply smiled and said—more as a statement than a question:

"Move in with me."

For a heartbeat, the world went still, as if holding its breath for an answer. My chest tightened, the future rushing at me in a single, impossible moment.

There was no need for a verbal answer. I just leaned over and kissed you—long and hard. Then I laced my fingers with yours and gave your hand a gentle squeeze for good measure. Every touch, every moment of pressure meant yes. A definite yes—a thousand times over.

chapter twelve

NOW

I EXPECTED THE door to be locked, but it wasn't, which surprised me. I came in so forcefully that the momentum threw me off balance for a few seconds. The unlocked door made me wonder if you had given up trying and didn't care whether or not this ship went down in flames, or if you were so drunk out of your senses you couldn't even be bothered to turn the lock on a door. After laying eyes on you, it was clearly the latter.

The stench hit me like a wall—alcohol clinging to the desk, vomit souring the trash can beside you, and food left to rot so long the eggs had turned green. It was the kind of smell that stuck to your hair, your clothes, and your skin. It was disgusting. Part of me wanted to run. Another part—stupid, stubborn, loyal—refused to.

Clothes were strewn across the floor and slung carelessly over the furniture. The desk was sticky with spilled alcohol, its surface glittering faintly with broken glass. Drops of blood marked the trail where you must have cut yourself trying to pick up the shards. The whole scene looked like the wreckage of a storm. I knew I should have been worried, but the mess was so overpowering, it was hard to focus on anything else.

How could you let this happen, Derek?

I went over to your desk, where I found you passed out over some papers, your left hand still clutching a bottle so tight that your knuckles were white. I shook you gently and then more forcefully, but you didn't even bat an eye.

You looked sickly. You had lost significant weight and were as pale as the moon. I could see what resembled black holes under your eyes, and your teeth were turning a shade darker—probably from all the hard liquors you were drowning in. Your fingernails were yellow, like a solar eclipse in each hand—no doubt from the packets of cigarettes serving you as your meal replacements. Because judging by the trays, you hadn't consumed anything other than nicotine for the past three days.

You were broken.

I was going to shake you again when something caught my eye. Big, bold, red letters on the papers you were sleeping over. The words **FINAL NOTICE, PETITION TO FILE FOR BANKRUPTCY,** and **NOTICE TO ALL DEBTORS** flashed before my eyes. It was hard to read anything else since you had spilled drinks over the forms, and the multiple drool stains made the letters that much blurrier, the ink fading out of the words like hope was draining out of them too.

Rather than giving me the answers I was searching for, these documents only raised more questions. I decided to wait and do my research before confronting you. I grabbed all the papers from under your unconscious body; you didn't even flinch when I shifted your head to slide them out.

The smell churned my stomach inside out. I wasn't worried about waking you up; the number of empty bottles lying around was enough reassurance.

I was about to make my way out the door when broken glass caught my eye, small drops of blood littering the carpet and the documents themselves. Your scarlet fingerprint was etched perfectly into the bottom right corner of the **FINAL NOTICE** form; the curves and grooves that gave you your identity and made up who you are.

I looked back and saw the whiskey you were holding. I was mad at you, Derek. I was furious, scared, confused, and hurt. But that didn't mean I stopped caring about you. I didn't want you to shift in your sleep and break the bottle if it shattered on the floor. I didn't want you to pick up the shards of glass and cut yourself again. I just couldn't let you bleed.

And God, how I wish I had let that be the end of it. I wish I hadn't tried to take that bottle from you. I wish I had turned around and gone upstairs.

But of course I didn't.

I couldn't.

I carefully removed the bottle from your hand, slipping it out finger by finger.

First, it was your pinky.

Please don't wake up.

Then your ring finger—your wedding ring engraved with the words *you keep me wild*—covered in a sticky substance.

Please don't wake up.

Your middle finger.

Please.

Index finger.

Don't.

And finally your thumb.

As the tip of your thumb lost contact with the whiskey, your hand shot out, grabbing my wrist so tight the bottle nearly fell from my grip. Your eyes, bloodshot and unseeing, locked on mine like I was the enemy.

And so help me God, all hell broke loose.

chapter thirteen

THEN

AT FIRST, WE didn't have much, and saying that may be too generous. For the first couple of years in our relationship, you were still interning with your dad, and I was splitting my time between caring for mine, playing a few concerts for money, waiting tables, and maintaining our tiny home. We had what we needed to get by, which, in retrospect, I realize now is all we ever really needed.

Our incredibly small and humble apartment had exactly four things: a mattress that was probably ten years overdue, a mini fridge that groaned and rattled like it was begging for mercy, a gas stove that hissed every time I lit it—swearing it would explode one day—and my guitar. The faint smell of worn fabric and old wood hung in the air, mingling with the aroma of cheap store-bought candles. It was more than enough.

My favorite nights were when we would take a stroll down the woods holding hands. The cool night air brushed against our cheeks, carrying the smell of damp leaves and pine. We would always take a different pathway, in a futile attempt to cover the whole area on foot. All the trees looked the same to us, but that didn't matter; what mattered was that we had our own mission, and we were going to conquer it together.

Eventually, after a mile or two, we would find a log to sit on and play some of our favorite songs. We would lie down on the grass and stargaze, creating constellations of our own, imagining what would happen if the possibilities were endless. Sometimes I would glance at you instead of the sky, trying to memorize your face in the silver glow of moonlight. It was always you and me against the world.

At home, we would cook a modest dinner and lie on the mattress, avoiding the areas where we instinctively knew the springs threatened to poke through. The smell of leftovers, the faint hum of the mini fridge, and the soft scratch of my guitar strings became the soundtrack of our evenings. We would talk about our day and relive those intangible moments of joy, feeling that love and affection over and over. Even the silences felt full, humming with a quiet certainty I thought would last forever.

I felt so complete with you, savoring every small moment, unaware of how the seasons of our lives would shift and change us. Each laugh, each stolen glance, each quiet evening on that threadbare mattress felt infinite—but I didn't yet know how much life would bend and stretch us, how fragile our world truly was.

chapter fourteen

NOW

YOU STOOD UP, any sign of drowsiness or exhaustion completely gone, and before I could realize what was happening, you snatched the papers out of my hands. Your eyes were bloodshot, and you were heaving, your lungs taking up what felt like every bit of oxygen left in the room.

"What the fuck are you doing, Noah!?" you threw the words at me, screaming, a groan rising from the deepest part of your gut. I flinched. My shoulders snapped tight, my pulse thudding against my throat, each beat like a warning drum. I could see the veins popping from your forehead and neck as your muscles strained with the sound.

"I wanted answers," I whimpered. My voice was so low, I wondered if you heard a single word I said.

"Answers to what?" you spat. "What gives you the right to walk in here and take what isn't yours?"

You were shaking. I didn't know if your body was going to give out or if you were about to break something—or me. My palms grew slick, the bottle in my hand slippery with sweat. My stomach twisted hard, like my body was bracing for an impact I couldn't see. My pulse was screaming. I forced myself to breathe.

I could feel the all-too-familiar sting in the back of my eyes. But no tears would fall; you had scared them dry. I wanted to know everything. I wanted to know what was going on with you, with us, with your business and this house. I wanted to know every secret you had been keeping from me. I wanted to know why you were hiding like a coward instead of talking to me.

That's what I desperately wanted to say.

But I couldn't.

Why couldn't I?

I stood there, staring hazily, but the feeling of your hot, thick, drunken breath on my face brought me back to my senses. I swallowed the need to vomit.

"What's on these forms?" I asked, pointing a finger at the papers you were holding. My chest heaved, but my tone was firm. I was trying to hold myself together, clutching to the evenness in my voice like a lifeline. I couldn't let you get away with it this time.

"It doesn't matter," you growled. "It's none of your fucking business, Noah. Get out."

"No."

I wasn't budging.

"No?" you echoed. "NO?! I'm not fucking around, Noah. LEAVE."

You'd never spoken to me like this.

What is happening to you, Derek?

"Not until I get my answers."

I stood my ground, my voice as calm as the ocean when the sun begins to rise over the bay. Honestly, your tone and attitude were starting to anger me, making me brave. Still, I didn't raise my voice. I didn't want to enrage you further—though I wasn't sure if that was possible. Every fiber of my being tried to hide the terror in my soul. You clenched your fists.

"I TOLD YOU—THIS IS MY FUCKING PROBLEM, NOT YOURS! I'm trying to fix it, but I can't do that with you breathing down my neck every fucking second!" Your scream cracked the air open, splintering it around me. "You're so used to people falling over themselves for you, so used to being taken care of, but you don't know ANYTHING about the real world! This isn't about you. This is grown-man shit. Not part of your little fucking fantasy. Not your lane, Noah. SO BACK OFF."

You didn't slur a single word.

The whiskey bottle I was still holding slipped from my grip. It made a dull, sharp noise as the bottle broke into three uneven pieces. Whiskey spilled and soaked my socks, cold and sharp down my ankle.

My whole body went hot and cold at once. My hand twitched at my side, a warning tremor I should have ignored. I felt the sting in my heart, the burn in my throat, the impossible need to make you stop. Just stop. A single thought pulsed, raw and violent: enough.

Something inside me snapped—a thread pulled too tight—and before I could reel it back in, my hand moved.

The slap cracked across your face, clean and brutal, echoing off the office walls. My palm stung instantly, heat radiating up my arm, and the silence that followed was louder than the strike itself. I watched as my print bloomed red on your cheek. A drop of blood appeared on your lip.

"Fuck you," I hissed.

The iciness in my voice was so sharp it could cut through glass—meaning every word and hoping they would sting as much as my heart did.

As the drop of blood snaked its way into your lips, staining your teeth scarlet, I saw your face contort into weird angles, twisted, unrecognizable. Then you grabbed one of the empty bottles off the desk and threw it with every ounce of force toward the wall behind me.

"OUT!" you roared, eyes bulging, as the bottle flew in my direction.

I wanted to believe you weren't aiming at me. I wanted to believe you were aiming at the wall. But I still ducked, and the bottle still shattered just above my head. Even if you missed on purpose, it was close. Too close.

The wall cracked. Glass covered the floor, reflecting the yellow light overhead like thousands of tiny, broken stars.

I gasped.

The worst part was when I looked back at you—*through* you, I saw a misguided monster, yes, but underneath that, I saw the real Derek. Not the angry man in front of me, but the one behind the mask.

You looked haunted. You looked... terrified.

Not of me. Of yourself.

And in a cruel flash, I remembered the boy who once sang softly beside me in the park, afraid of anyone hearing his voice but me. The boy whose laughter lit up a cheap apartment like it was a palace. That Derek felt galaxies away from the man in front of me, a stranger with my husband's eyes.

Tears spilled down your cheeks, mirroring mine, catching in the freckles I used to trace with my fingertips. Now I couldn't even look at your face without breaking.

You were unraveling.

And yet, all I could feel was the deep hollow forming inside me.

I turned around and ran upstairs, hearing you cry as you shouted my name, apologies pouring out of your mouth like waves in a hurricane—every word soaked in wet sorrow and breathless regret.

I kept climbing.

With every step, your voice got smaller, farther away.

Until your tears and regret disappeared behind a slammed door.

I collapsed onto the mattress and cried myself to sleep.

What am I supposed to do now?

chapter fifteen

THEN

TODAY WE WENT to the fair. There was something about the fair that was magical. The smell of caramel popcorn, the distant screams of teenagers filled with adrenaline going down a rollercoaster, the thick drops of sweat leaving a faint trail of salt near your temple, and the clicking of pictures that captured hopeful memories gave this place a quality that was nostalgic and comforting—the perfect safety blanket.

I had told you about my love for carnivals in passing, in a way you'd expect the words to be forgotten, blown in the wind. But today, I got in your car, and you started to drive, the destination already in mind. I've always loved surprises (at least the good kind), because they always leave a good story in the end. As we approached the parking lot, I could hear the music in the background, see the Ferris wheel in the corner of my eye, smell the farm animals in the back corner, and feel the hum of the synchronized voices enjoying themselves and getting lost in the moment. I could feel your hand brushing against mine as we parked, the warmth of your fingers grounding me before we even stepped outside.

Despite being hyper-aware of these details, the edges of the fairgrounds were slightly blurry—because I could only focus on you. You shone brighter than any firework that night. As we held hands, fingers interlocked, I could feel a tingling sensation on the tips of my fingers—the way only you could make me feel. You were like electricity in the desert, getting all your energy from the power in the skies, strong enough to cut through the scorching heat and melt even the most elusive grain of sand. You were a force of nature.

We took a lap around the rows of game booths and food stalls to get an idea of what it had to offer, but the moment I saw the candy apples, I took off running; I didn't even have the chance to let go of your hand. I may have been running a little too fast, propelled by excitement, because the next thing I saw, was you looking a little disoriented, the heat rushing through your cheeks from the unexpected sprint, and you were rubbing your hand, sore from how hard I had yanked it. I couldn't help but grin at the way your hair had fallen across your forehead, a strand sticking to your sweaty brow.

"Jesus, you get so relentless when it comes to food," you said incredulously. The shock in your eyes made me chuckle.

"Right! Sorry! So sorry!" I said. "But I only get to have these whenever I come to the fair, which nowadays is basically never. I can see how I seem a little desperate."

"What is so great about them?" you asked.

At this question, the candy apple lady and I both stared at you. At first, we assumed you were joking, but nobody jokes about something so serious, so we settled on concern. A lot of concern. We stared at you a little longer, and you stared blankly back at us. When I caught the slightest shrug of your shoulders, I immediately processed the severity of the situation.

"Derek. We've been dating for over two years. What do you mean you've never had a candy apple before?"

You shrugged again. "My mom was particular about processed foods and sugars when I was a kid. I guess the opportunity never presented itself."

You looked down at your feet, hands tucked in your pockets, shoulders a little slouched. In that moment, I saw you as a little boy—wanting the junk food other kids took for granted, wishing you could be one of them.

I winced and turned to the lady. "We'll take one regular candy apple and one with caramel peanuts, please. ASAP."

The lady gave us the apples with an efficiency that amazed me. "These are on me. Some things in life are too good to miss," she said with a crooked, honest smile.

I nodded my thanks, which she reciprocated; we thought exactly the same thing. Watching you take the first bite of the peanut-covered caramel apple was not unlike the expression on your face when you first told me you loved me. You closed your eyes as the crunch echoed, a little caramel sticking to the corner of your mouth. I laughed, reaching up to wipe it away with my thumb, and you caught my hand midair.

"Don't," you said, muffled by the apple. "This is serious business."

The look of sheer joy spreading across your face made me burst out laughing anyway, the sound blending with the blaring music and the hum of excited voices.

"See?!" I said, nudging your shoulder. "You've been missing out your whole life. I feel like I just introduced you to a new religion."

"You might have," you admitted, your voice muffled through another bite. "I think I'm in love."

"With me or the apple?"

You tilted your head in consideration. "...Both."

I rolled my eyes, but the warmth in my body wouldn't leave. The world felt brighter just watching you delight in this small, sugary triumph.

After we finished our apples, we walked hand in hand to the small zoo they had in the corner. The lemur sanctuary waited for us, and after making our way through the sheep, lambs, horses, and camels, we spoke about how my fascination with lemurs began with Zoboomafoo, a show they aired when I was a little girl that taught me all I needed to know about wild animals, starring two brothers and a lemur. I can't remember the brothers' names—I would always call them by their shirt color: the blue guy and the green guy, and of course—the monkey. My vocabulary acquisition was very basic back then. Lucky for me, things have somewhat changed.

I caught you grinning at my childish enthusiasm, and I laced my arm through yours, letting you know I loved that you loved it too.

I noticed the way your eyes softened as you bent to watch a lemur leap gracefully from branch to branch, its tiny fingers gripping the bark like it was weightless. "Look at that one," I whispered, pointing. "It's like he's flying." You laughed quietly, your shoulders shaking, and I could feel the vibration of your joy in my palm. The air smelled faintly of hay and fresh animal fur, grounding us in this moment, alive and simple.

After arguably the best date we had ever had, sure that the night was coming to an end, we happened to run into a country music band that was playing, and without thinking twice, we went in, three minutes before the show began. That is the definition of being in the right place at the right time.

We danced and clapped as the man in worn-out jeans and a flannel sang about trucks and heartbreak. We chuckled when the guitarist went so hard in his solo that he broke a string, and by the end of the night, we knew the words to every chorus. It was our first concert together. With my head on your shoulder, I could feel your warm breath next to my ear as you sang along. I caught a faint scent of beer on your shirt, mixed with the sweetness of the fair lingering from earlier, and I kissed you. I could hear the song in the background; it felt like the lead singer was singing not for us but to us. The music, the crowd, and the late-night lights became a blur, leaving just us, the rhythm and our laughter entwined.

Around midnight, we called it a night, but as we were walking towards the exit sign, we noticed somebody offering to take pictures by a cluttered, tattered booth. I pulled you toward the man with the Polaroid and gave him the $2 he had advertised on his handmade sign. We stood next to each other and smiled. Drunk with the lyrics we had previously sung and high from the sugar in the apples, our laughter mingled with the soft click of the camera. We saw the flash right in front of our eyes, blinding us momentarily, and by the time we made it back home, the picture had revealed itself. We went to the kitchen and put it on the fridge. The Polaroid radiated love and youth. I felt your hand slip into mine as we admired it, the paper warm against our fingertips. And just like that, we now had five things in our apartment.

chapter sixteen

NOW

I WOKE UP to the blinding sunshine sneaking through the window. My head hurt, and I felt heavy, drained of all emotion, and hungover on last night's hell. I woke up alone, to no one's surprise, but when I stretched to try and revive my stiff muscles, I felt a crinkle under my elbow. It was a note. "I'm sorry," it read. I balled the note and threw it in the trash. "Sorry" wasn't going to cut it. The word rang hollow, flimsy. I felt indifferent toward you, and a simple glance out the window confirmed you weren't home. The car was gone, and I couldn't seem to care.

I decided to put my time to good use and opted to organize the attic. We didn't have a basement, so we shoved all our procrastinations and boxes filled with memories upstairs, out of sight, with the promise to get to it later. Well, "later" had arrived. I lowered the string that pulled the door, muscles tensing as I heard the screeching of unused hinges. The stairs unfolded in jerky motions, each creak echoing through the house with a groan. Dust rained down in a faint haze as I climbed slowly, remembering the first time we went up these steps together. We giggled nervously back then; the climb had felt symbolic, life-altering, as if the uncertain creaks represented the uncertainty of what the rest of our lives would bring.

Now, stepping into the attic alone, I saw the boxes covered with cobwebs and loneliness, abandoned in a pile of dust and forgotten dreams. The air was stale and dry, carrying the faint sourness of mold. I brushed my hand across one of the lids, and a cloud of dust rose into the light, scratching at my throat.

We had so much unpacking to do when we first moved in. We kept saying we'd get to it, but who ever does? Every family has boxes of secrets they tuck away, never to be seen again. I don't know what made me come up here after so much time had passed—it was like something had been calling me. These boxes held the best years of our lives, yet they sat in silence, surrounded by the scent of abandonment. This wasn't the plan. We were supposed to have adventures and scatter them around our kitchen and living room. Mementos of the places we visited and the people we met, but it didn't happen.

I walked through stacks of boxes, their edges frayed, tape yellowed and brittle under my fingertips. Some labels I couldn't even bring myself to read. *Engagement Photos. Letters. Mom.* No. Not yet. My chest ached at the thought. Some wounds need more time to heal. The void my mom left, even though I never got to hug her or tell her my wildest fantasies, still left me hollow. That's the thing about scars, though—they all tell a story. But the scar my mom left is a story I never got to read. I wasn't ready to try and piece the scattered pages together. Not just yet.

I moved on. One box said only my name—Noah. My hand lingered on it, curiosity winning over caution. When I lifted the flaps, memories rushed through me like an old-school film reel clicking to life. The first pair of fake plastic earrings my dad bought me when I was eight sat on top. I went to try them on; they were clip-ons, light to the touch. I pressed one against my ear, smiling at how absurdly delicate they were. Back then, I was too small to hold any real weight—and now, years later, it felt like the opposite. Somehow, I was expected to carry the weight of the world on my shoulders.

I kept digging and found the rusted lock from my middle school locker. It felt heavy in my hand, colder than it had any right to be. Once, it probably protected notes and secrets and gum wrappers I thought were important. Now it was just a lump of useless metal. I thought of the girl I used to be—the one with glitter pens and too-big dreams. She had no idea life would be this painful. For a moment, I almost slipped it back into the box. But instead, I dropped it into a trash bag with a hollow clang.

I kept exploring, taking my time to sort through my collection. There was a white envelope with a letter in it. Bold letters said: "DO NOT OPEN TILL I AM 30." My breath caught. The day I wrote this letter took over, pulling the memory from the back of my mind. I was eighteen—stubborn and sentimental. I'd read about a teacher who asked her students to write letters to their future selves, and I thought it was beautiful and poetic. But I wanted to take it further. So I'd written myself a letter to open at thirty, then sealed it and drank cheap wine until the details blurred, determined to forget. I traced the edge of the envelope now, tempted, curious. But I pushed it to the bottom of the box. Six more years. Something to look forward to. A gift from my younger self to an older, hopefully wiser, version of me.

I was about to close the box when I saw it. Suddenly, I understood why I had to come here. The music box you gave me on our first Valentine's Day sat waiting, small and wooden, shaped like a piano with a ballerina poised on top. A fragile pulse stole my breath. I turned the key, and the first notes of *Canon in D* whispered out. The ballerina twirled with flawless grace, her painted face serene as she spun in endless circles.

I used to close my eyes and imagine dancing beside her, lost in her world. She seemed tireless, always twirling, always smiling. But as I watched now, I wondered—did she ever get dizzy? Did she wish she could leap instead of twirl? Did she even know her own strength, the discipline it took to keep turning without falter? Was she happy?

Next to the ballerina, I found the wooden figure of the tin soldier that I gave you in return. We'd told each other our favorite stories as kids, and this one had meant something to us both. The soldier loved the ballerina so deeply he would face any sacrifice to find his way back home to her. They were both relentless, bound to their roles. She danced. He searched. They endured.

And I couldn't help but wonder if the same was true for me. I admired the ballerina's perfect spin, but I knew I wasn't her—I stumbled, I broke. I was closer to the tin soldier, steady, stubborn, willing to sacrifice for love even when it destroyed me.

But unlike fairy tales, real love isn't steadfast. It's fragile, sharp, and often broken. The tin soldier could never have survived it.

And maybe that's why I envied him. He was made of tin—unbending, unwavering. But I was not. I was flesh and blood, fragile enough to break in ways he never could.

chapter seventeen

THEN

THINGS WERE GOING great in our life together. Two autumns had passed and I was about to graduate school, deciding what my next chapter would be, what I wanted to do in my career. Going back to school wasn't just about finishing a degree—it was about proving to myself I could still dream bigger than our four walls. Each paper I turned in felt like planting a small flag in the future I wanted. I was always worried about money, but I picked up a few more shifts waiting tables and worked every weekend at the small, family-owned record store where I clerked, organizing shelves of vinyls, ringing up customers, and dusting forgotten corners. Between those shifts, playing small concerts at the local coffee shops, and budgeting tighter than I thought possible, we saved enough to cover one semester at a time. It wasn't glamorous—late nights hunched over library laptops, coffee rings on my notes, calluses on my fingers from gigs that barely paid gas money, the scent of vinyl and old paper from the store lingering on my sleeves—but it mattered. It wasn't just about a diploma. It was about proving to myself that I could still dream, that I wasn't standing still while life moved forward without me. Every time I dragged myself home after midnight, you'd be there, awake, with hot tea and a tired smile, reminding me I wasn't alone.

Your business was thriving. You had been mentored by an old friend of your dad's, and after a few challenging months, both financially and emotionally, you had gained experience with the ins and outs of consulting, and you felt confident enough to invest in your dad's company. I was so proud of you. Sometimes I thought about the difference between us—you building something solid and lasting with your business while I was trying to stitch together one semester at a time. But instead of making me feel small, you made me feel steady, like we were climbing the same mountain from different sides, both determined to meet at the top. You never let me forget that my victories, no matter how small, mattered just as much as yours.

Two months later, December wrapped the city in a quiet hush, the cold pricking my skin and making my bones shiver, while snow settled softly on the rooftops, turning the streets into a scene straight out of a snow globe. The world felt still and magical, each flake catching the pale winter light, but when I took a sip of hot chocolate, warmth spread from my stomach outward, melting the chill and making every frozen shiver feel like part of the season's charm.

I already had my graduation dress. A wine-colored piece, its fitted silhouette ending just above the knee, with delicate lace sleeves that trailed gracefully down the arms, giving it an elegant, timeless charm. I had insisted on us buying something from the thrift shop. I didn't want us spending money we didn't have, but the day I got home after that last test, you surprised me with the gorgeous dress.

"It's not much, but you deserve to walk the stage with a new dress," you had said.

My breath hitched as I felt the soft fabric under my shaky fingers.

"Oh my god. It's so beautiful." I looked at you with pleading eyes. "But it's too much, you haven't seen any money from the new investments and you have been working so hard, I, I-" I stammered, "I can't accept this."

You rolled your eyes patiently, as if you knew exactly what I was going to say. You held my face in both your hands.

"Noah, we haven't splurged on a single thing in the past two years. Our mattress has literal springs that jab into our backs every time we turn over, and every pair of socks we own has holes in it. I know we were keeping a tight budget while we paid off your tuition, but as of today, we're done with that, and we didn't even have to take out a loan. We are debt free." You shook your hands slightly, my cheeks shaking with them. "So no, you will not be graduating with a second-hand dress. Everything else we own is second-hand, but in two weeks you will be walking down the stage to get your diploma in this very nice, new outfit that the lady at the store helped me pick, and you're going to be the prettiest girl there. You deserve it. You deserve it all." You kissed my forehead. "Also, I wasn't going to mention this part, but the dress had a tiny discount, so we can't return it. So while I am not forcing you to wear it, I feel compelled to tell you that one of us has to, because we kind of have to keep it." You smiled coyly, like a small kid asking for forgiveness after doing something he was told he shouldn't.

I smiled back and made a high-pitched, squeaking noise. I wrapped myself around you and you twirled me around our small living room. We reached the kitchen four steps later.

"Do you like the surprise?"

"It's perfect. Thank you," I whispered in the crook of your neck.

"I can't wait for you to wear it!" you said as you squeezed my sides gently.

After you told me we couldn't get the money back for the dress, I fell in love with it more with each passing minute. It was hand-pressed, and I kept it hanging on a hook right next to my recently decorated graduation cap. I allowed myself to spend ten dollars at the store to make it as nice as possible, and I was proud of the results. Arts and crafts had never been my strong suit, but a couple of YouTube videos proved I didn't need to be. I was admiring my cap and gown when the ping of an email on my phone distracted me. It was an official commencement email, with the three tickets attached of the people I had included on my list. I almost didn't invite my dad. For weeks, I'd gone back and forth about it, the weight of the decision gnawing at me every night before bed. The thought of him stumbling into the auditorium smelling like whiskey made my stomach twist, but the thought of him not being there at all made my chest ache worse. In the end, I decided to take the risk—for his sake, but maybe also for mine.

Two more weeks came and went, and graduation day was finally here. I walked into the auditorium, taking in the polished wooden floors that creaked under my heels, the faint scent of perfume and cologne mixing with the warm, musty air, the rustle of programs and shuffling feet. All the music majors were sitting in the same section of parallel rows. Each major had their own section, but from where I was sitting, we were all fish in a sea of proudly decorated caps and anticipating smiles. I twisted my tassel around my fingers to keep the anxiety at bay, the frays catching on some of my chewed cuticles. I had tried to look for my family, but the crowd was overwhelming. Each face merged with the next, and the audience became a big blur. I didn't even know if my dad could make it. I had forwarded you the ticket email and trusted you to handle it.

I felt my phone vibrating in the hidden pocket of my graduation gown, and my hand instinctively moved towards it. Your name flashed above the text notification.

Fourth row to your left. In the middle.

My head snapped to my left and I immediately found you. A wide, confident grin as you waved and winked at me from the bleachers. The sight of you grounded me. It brought me to my senses and allowed me to take a deep breath for the first time today, allowing myself to appreciate what I had done and take it in for a moment. I winked back. It was only after I flashed you a small smile and waved shyly that you cocked your head to your right, arching your brow in a sign of approval as if to say "look who's here."

When I spotted him in the crowd, it nearly undid me. Dad was sitting between you and Grandma, clutching a bouquet of red roses wrapped in cellophane, his tie slightly crooked but his shirt crisp and starched. He was clean-shaven and had gotten a fresh haircut. His eyes were glassy, not from alcohol but from tears. For the first time in years, he looked like my dad again. A knot formed in my throat, and I took a shaky breath, grateful that I had invited him, but even more thankful that he showed up.

Grandma dabbed the corner of her eyes with a lace handkerchief, muttering just loud enough for you to hear, "If she trips in those ridiculous shoes, I'm suing the university for emotional damages." You smothered a laugh behind your fist.

Suddenly I saw this day with different eyes, and I took a moment to fully appreciate the magnitude of what I had accomplished. I was the first person to graduate college in my family, and in a few weeks, they would mail a shiny diploma that made my degree official.

Noah Emmett, Bachelor of Arts in Music.

I was daydreaming when our professor instructed us to stand in line towards the stage, bringing me back to the present. My palms were shiny with sweat, my heart thudding against my ribs heavy with the weight of everything that had led me here—the late nights studying, the concerts squeezed in for money, the stress I thought might break me.

Finally, I heard my name, and with shaky feet I climbed the steps towards the dean that was waiting for me with an outstretched hand. I clutched my diploma frame and forced myself to look out into the crowd. I exhaled a slow breath. Within the deafening applause of the auditorium's cheers, I was able to single out the three most important people in my life.

Dad was on his feet, clapping with the roses shaking in his hands. Every few seconds he would whistle with his fingers on the side of his mouth. Tears ran freely down his cheeks, dripping on his tie, and for once, I didn't look away.

You held up the biggest graduation teddy bear I had ever seen, a ridiculous chocolate box balanced on top of its head. The sight of you struggling to keep it upright made me laugh even through the tears welling in my own eyes. You were the loudest one in the crowd, cheering my name as veins popped in your neck. Your face was turning purple, but your bright smile and proud eyes were everything I needed.

And Grandma, my fierce, sharp-tongued anchor, was both openly crying and screaming as she held up a sign with my literal face plastered on it that read: "We are so fucking proud of you, Noah!" An image flashed through my mind of my grandma, fifty years younger, swaying a similar sign up and down at Woodstock, and the thought of it made me laugh.

For that one shining moment, it didn't matter how small our apartment was, how uncertain the future still felt, or how many fractures my family had carried. What mattered was that I had made it—messy and imperfect, but here, and most importantly, with each of you by my side.

chapter eighteen

NOW

I HAVE THOUGHT about us an awful lot lately. We are reaching that point where enough time has passed in our relationship for it to feel real—not just like a dream or an illusion anymore. Once reality sets in, it becomes a little more raw and fragile. I can see now that we were two humans engulfed in a fairy tale, and I wasn't ready for that fairy tale to end. Now, I feel discomfort; I feel like I am in a place where I don't truly belong. Maybe it started the night you began working later than usual, brushing off my worry with a quick kiss and a muttered excuse. Or maybe it was when my laughter fell flat and you didn't notice. I can't pin down the exact moment, only that the shift was slow, like a song fading off-key without anyone realizing at first.

Things have changed within us—like how sensitive you can be to certain comments I make, and how emotional I can be to your need for space. I always prided myself on being an understanding person, but now that I am put in a spot where I question our new reality, it scares me. I wonder if we can make it through. We craved the idea of growing old together so much that we forgot to grow up together. We forgot how to be young and restless.

In the beginning, we brought out the light in one another, but that light dims a little each day. I have never experienced this kind of heartbreak before. Loss and emptiness, sure—but this is different. This is different because as my heart breaks, my illusions shatter. I want to fight for you, and I want you to fight for us, but I am not even sure how to approach the subject. I wake up with dried tears on my cheeks from crying throughout the night, and you wake up with dried liquor on the corners of your mouth, a dark crust forming where your lips meet. We used to be a team, and now we were disconnected. The house feels cold and angry, as if our home resents us distancing from each other. It wasn't always like this. The house used to feel warm, alive with music and silly arguments about nothing. I think I started noticing the silence after your drinking grew from a weekend indulgence into a nightly routine. Each glass stole a little piece of you from me, until all I could hear was the echo of what we used to be. I see the wallpaper beginning to rip on the corners of a house that, through the years, had been forgotten, and I start to wonder if this house saw our ending even before we did.

I often think of the time when we were madly in love; we would laugh every other moment, and now I can't remember the last time we found anything remotely funny. I feel alone most of the day and have no direction. I struggle with whether or not you continue to love me. I wonder if I can help you in any way and help bring back those sparks in your eyes when you smile, but I am afraid I'm useless... I wish I could talk to my mom and ask for her advice. I wish I could play a song and have her sing with me. But now the strings feel different beneath my fingertips, like they've absorbed the silence that's crept into our home. The more your glass filled at night, the more my chords went out of tune, until I barely recognize the sound of my own music anymore. My fingers have somehow forgotten their placement, and whenever I try to play, what comes out is a poor excuse for a melody.

I look at the ring that you gave me when you proposed. I read the phrase over and over again, turning it in my hand—"You keep me safe"—and it feels heavy on my hand. I close my eyes as hard as I can to remember how we felt the day you gave it to me, but I can't recreate it. I can feel the memory in my brain and see it happening inside my head, but my heart can't connect with the memory itself. We are strangers bound by marriage in a life I can't recognize anymore.

I know I still love you. I know it because if I even begin to imagine my life without you, I can feel my unstable heart starting to fracture. I can physically feel a crushing weight pressing down on me, and it is too much for me to bear. Until I met you, I had always been a loner and paved my own way. Now I see how much I needed you to walk beside me. The loneliness was getting too loud, and I couldn't handle it anymore. But then you came, and you stayed, and you have printed a place in my heart forever. But now I wonder—does forever ever come to an end?

chapter nineteen

THEN

TWO SEASONS HAD gone by since I graduated. The summer sun streamed through the windows, catching on the framed diploma by the entrance like a quiet reminder of how far we'd come. To me, it felt like we were shoving the degree in people's faces, but that's precisely the reason why you wanted it there. You were so proud that I had finished school, you insisted on placing it in the one spot of the house every person had to walk by. You wanted to brag about it, about me, and tell anyone who would listen how proud you felt of that hard-earned piece of paper.

Life was beginning to steady itself. I was working full time at the record store, learning the rhythms of regular customers, organizing the vinyls by genre, the smell of old album covers and dust clinging to my clothes when I came home. I saved each paycheck carefully, tucking away small amounts for things like the new mattress I wanted to surprise you with. Meanwhile, we were finally beginning to see the first real payoff of the investments. At first, it was only small amounts—enough to cover groceries or a bill here and there—but the company was gaining traction. Your dad knew what he was doing, and you were smart enough to listen, adjust, and take risks when others might have played it safe. I guess the apple didn't fall far from the tree.

By the end of that year, your work had spilled past the edges of a normal workday. Clients trickled in, then doubled, then arrived faster than you could manage. I'd find you hunched over our small kitchen table, papers spread in every direction, your tie loosened and eyes red from staring at numbers too long. Our home was too small for your workload. I teased you about it, but inside I was quietly proud—watching your dedication turn into something tangible.

Now it was my turn to take on the supportive role. Next door to my job was a small family-owned shop that made crafted blends for teas. Every week I would stop by and make a small purchase. At night I'd get creative with the blends, steeping concoctions of leaves that promised stress relief and focus. In my head, it would help you stay sharp while easing your body. I didn't know if the effects canceled each other out, but I had good intentions and you seemed to enjoy the taste. Eventually, four cups of tea each night became less helpful and more a cause of constant bathroom breaks, so you hired a couple of employees to take some weight off your shoulders. For the first time, it felt like your dream was no longer just a fragile idea—it was becoming its own machine.

And with that machine came change. A year later, we found ourselves sitting in the offices of a real estate agent, our knees bumping under the desk as we studied glossy pamphlets. I hadn't imagined us house-hunting so soon; in my head, the apartment was still "enough." But you had a way of dreaming bigger, pulling me with you even when I resisted.

We toured house after house. Some were laughably out of reach—gleaming kitchens with marble counters, sprawling yards we had no business even looking at. Others were small, worn down, but filled with the kind of charm I secretly loved. I remember us standing in the driveway of a little yellow house with peeling shutters, you insisting we could fix it up, me insisting it would swallow every dime we had. We argued, we compromised, we laughed when the realtor tried to sell us on a place that had a leaky roof and the smell of mold clinging to the walls. Each visit felt like its own adventure, a test of how much we could picture ourselves inside the walls of someone else's story.

Eventually, after weeks of searching, we shook hands and took a celebratory picture with the world's most patient real estate agent. Standing on the porch of a modest but spacious home, the keys warm in our hands, we looked at each other with the kind of excitement that felt too big to hold.

The day we moved in, I remember standing in the empty living room, our voices echoing against bare walls, surrounded by boxes and mismatched furniture. We went from having five things in our apartment to having more than we could count. I never needed much, but you were set on giving me the life you were sure I deserved. I didn't mind the money, but I wasn't a materialistic girl at heart. I was happy with simplicity. You were always more than enough.

Later, we used the money I had saved from working at the store, every penny I had meticulously tucked away, combined with your earnings, to invest further in what would eventually become your company. Your dad was preparing to retire, and soon his shares of the business would transfer to you. It was daunting, terrifying even—but I had all the faith in your ability to be who you needed to be. After months of trial and error, late nights, and endless conversations about what-ifs, your actions and investments paid off. You became a majority owner of the company. You proved your worth to your dad, but you never needed to prove it to me.

We celebrated with a chilled bottle of champagne. A few years earlier, our income would only allow us to toast with sparkling apple juice, but now we could afford to treat ourselves to French labels with names I couldn't pronounce, bubbles tickling the roof of our mouths as we clinked glasses and toasted to our new home and your company's success.

Eventually, the business did so well that we didn't need a second income. I enjoyed my job—it was easy and monotonous, but I found comfort in the routine and chatting with customers. I got so good at reading them, it was easy to make small talk based on their taste in music.

One night, after another long day at the store, you asked me, in passing, if I would like to take a break from working and focus on writing songs again. I remember sitting at our kitchen table, receipt ink smudged on my fingers, as you leaned across with that steady, confident look.

"The company is doing really well, babe. We honestly don't need the second income right now. We'll be fine," you promised with a small smile. You let the question hang quietly in the air, giving me time and space to decide while you reorganized the papers in your briefcase. It was getting too small for your files, so I made a mental note to buy you a bigger one.

It was strange, stepping away from work that had given me independence and stability. You weren't forcing me to quit—quite the opposite. Your intention was to be supportive, as always, in pursuing the passion I had put aside when I started working. But part of me feared losing the steady ground I had grown used to. Songwriting was unpredictable, filled with rejection, and I had forgotten the rhythm of the game.

But in the end, I took the plunge. We decided together that I would leave the store, become a housewife, and work on my music.

A few days later I gave my two weeks' notice at the record store. The owner, an old man in his eighties who smelled of cigar smoke and worn flannels, his gray ponytail brushing his mid-back, gave me a sturdy pat on the back and reminded me there would always be a place for me if I wanted to return. Between snarky remarks and the bagel with cream cheese we shared during our breaks, we had become unlikely friends. On my last day, he was sad to see me leave, but as he patted my back with his strong hands that threatened to dislocate my shoulder, I caught a glimmer of pride in his eyes—the same kind of pride my grandfather used to show me. The memory made my heart skip, and before I realized it, I was placing my hands gently on his shoulders.

"I'm going to miss you, old man," I said, giving him a soft kiss on his wrinkled cheek and hugging him tightly. He didn't move, just let me rest my chin on his shoulder as I squeezed. When I let go, his eyes were watery, but he made no motion to dry them.

"Don't be a stranger, kid." He gave me a worn out and tired smile. His teeth were yellowed from years of smoking, but his breath carried that familiar blend of mint and tobacco. In a strange way, it was comforting. I waved him goodbye and took the long way home, grateful for having met such a kindred soul, silently promising I would come back every now and then to share a bagel with him.

Once I was officially unemployed—this time by choice—I fell into routines I didn't know I would love. The citrus scent of freshly mopped floors, the hum of the vacuum, and the rhythm of chopping garlic and onions for whatever recipe I decided to try gave me a stillness that clung long after the moment passed. I wanted to create a home we could be proud of.

Even cooking, with all its disasters, became part of our story. There were successes—meals you devoured until you were licking the plate—and failures that made us laugh until we cried. Pineapple salmon was quickly retired after one unforgettable night of food poisoning, but even then, you finished every bite, only to declare with a judgement-free grin, "It really could have been worse." It became our running joke, the verdict for any meal gone wrong.

What I loved most was that no matter how the food turned out, you always kissed me after, your lips brushing mine with the kind of devotion that made every mess, every mistake, worth it. At night, with music playing low and dishes drying in racks, we danced in our kitchen, sweat on our foreheads and laughter weaving its way between us. For all the change, for all the unknowns ahead, in those moments, it felt like we had carved out a little world of our own.

I loved you so much.

chapter twenty

NOW

I NEEDED TO feel like myself again. I was starting to realize that by waiting for you, I was losing myself in the process. I had put my life on pause, skipping open-mic nights, setting aside opportunities, even ignoring the parts of me that wanted to create and explore—because I was afraid of upsetting you. And somewhere in that sacrifice, resentment took root. We were supposed to be a team, but we couldn't both be stagnant forever. If you needed time to heal, you needed to take it—but I wasn't wounded. I needed to find my purpose and my strength. My instinct had always told me to explore and be free, and somewhere along the way, by victimizing myself through your misery, I lost my courage. I lost sight of who I was.

I got in the shower and washed my hair. It felt oily to the touch and had lost its texture. I couldn't even recall the last time I had washed it—days blurring together in a haze of waiting. The silky feel of it after the shower and the smell of coconut shampoo gave me a boost of confidence on its own. I put on my black jeans and my favorite crop top, grabbing my black high-heeled boots, dusty from lack of affection, and felt like a new woman. My skin seemed a little dehydrated; all my light and confidence had been withering away, slipping off me like the water dripping from the ends of my hair, shaping the flattened curves of my body. My body and mind had changed in response to your doubt and fear. Your heart had doubted itself, cracking near the edges, fracturing mine in the process. I put on vanilla-scented lotion, feeling my skin as it silently thanked me, and sprayed brown sugar perfume on my neck and wrists. I grabbed a flannel that was tucked away in the back of the closet and went down the stairs.

As I took each step, the reverberating sound of the heels of my boots against the wood made me feel alive. The sound itself was hollow, but I felt empowered and sure of where I was going—even though I didn't have any specific place in mind. I had no idea if you had heard me, knew what I was doing, if you cared at all, or if I was ever coming back. But I knew. I was obviously coming back. The heart always returns home.

I stepped out onto the street and felt the sharp, cold breeze on the exposed part of my stomach. I thought briefly about calling Grandma, but realized I had been somewhat out of reach—most of my social life had dwindled with you. It struck me then how much I had let isolation creep in. The cold air made me gasp, but then I laughed, excitement rushing through me again. A star in the sky was brighter than the rest, as if guiding me through the night, so I followed it.

I had walked over a mile when I ran into a familiar street, although I couldn't pinpoint how I knew it. I wasn't afraid of walking by myself in the dark; I felt safe somehow, and I felt brave. I had forgotten the feeling of walking in high-heeled boots; it had been so long since I had worn anything but socks. I was surprised my ankles didn't ache while walking, but I missed it. I missed how heels make you feel as if you have a presence. How good it felt to be loud, to make my mark on the world. It's the clink and the clank of awareness, pride, and self-esteem.

I kept strolling through back alleys and hidden hallways; an old, small building was on the corner, an aged sign displaying its name on the front:

Honeycomb Café

EST. 1998

I had never walked in this particular shop before. Starbucks had become our lazy habit, and local places like this had been forgotten. But if this café had been here for two decades, it had to be decent enough to withstand the test of time.

I walked in and sat at the little coffee bar. The thin lady working behind the counter took a couple of minutes to greet me. Her eyes were glimmering under the dim light of the warm bulb above her, like she was holding her tears at bay. I paid no mind to it and ordered a cup of chamomile lavender tea instead.

She brought me the cup of tea and placed it gently in front of me, the warmth of the mug gracing my fingertips. Her hands were calloused and dry as she handed me the sugar, presumably from the harsh soap she used to do the dishes all day. She asked if I would like "something sweet for the soul." There was something mysterious about her, but she also had a loving and caring quality that made her trustworthy. The crow's-feet around her eyes told me that she was tired, but the care and charm this small café still held told me how much she loved her job. She was one of those older women who make you feel like they have known you for ages—like they know your most naughty secrets but will take them to their grave.

I asked for a brownie and almost fainted when I took the first bite. It was chewy and warm, with little bits of walnuts and caramel melting in the middle. The sweetness of the caramel was toned down by the walnuts, and the chocolate was bittersweet. I closed my eyes and savored every bit of it.

As I was taking a sip of tea, the woman chuckled. I briefly looked up, made eye contact, smiled, and lowered my gaze again. She seemed strangely fascinated by me, like she'd seen me in a museum painting, making me feel somewhat uncomfortable.

Her eyes flicked to my necklace. She gasped quietly, then looked away. A few moments later, when I ordered a refill of tea, she couldn't help herself.

"That was your mama's favorite dessert, too," she whispered softly, twisting the dish rag under her fingertips.

I choked on my tea, my blood running cold. The sweetness of the brownie turned to ash in my mouth, my throat tightening as if it knew a truth my mind hadn't caught up to yet. My pulse thundered in my ears, every beat a question I couldn't voice. I could feel my skin paling by the second. *Who was this woman?* Long, strained attempts at breathing and coughing interchangeably prompted her into motion. She rushed to get me some water and patted my back softly, the caring way a mother would pat her child.

"Who are you?" I croaked.

Even though she was a complete stranger, I did not feel threatened or afraid of her; I was compelled by her soft conviction and calm tone of voice. My curiosity was overpowering me, desperate for answers.

"Your name's Noah, ain't it?"

Oh shit.

She smiled gently. "I'd recognize that necklace anywhere." She rested her gaze on the small Earth pendant on my chest.

Her voice was so serene, yet also inquisitive. She was an enigma. I could tell she couldn't wait to tell me the story behind this necklace. And to be honest, I couldn't wait either. I had been harassing my dad and grandma to tell me why there was a golden crack across the pendant, but no one seemed to know or care enough to remember. I instinctively put my hand over my neck, feeling the rough edge of the crack.

"Three letters on the back, written in Sharpie, right? O-G-R?" I nodded. She laughed, her eyes getting slightly watery. "Course. I knew Lane well enough to know she'd pass it down." I could see the memories forming in her mind. Clearly, my mom had been a massive part of her life—but if she knew her so well, why hadn't I heard of her?

Her name was Dawn. A former neighbor and childhood friend. And just like that, puzzle pieces of my mother's story began clicking into place. She didn't give me her entire history in one breath; instead, her memories slipped out between sips of tea, little glimpses of who my mother had been.

"She was stubborn. Impulsive. Fierce when she oughtta be," Dawn said, her voice steady. "But her heart? Bigger than anybody I ever known. I remember the day she got the necklace; it was the very same day we met." I was anxious to hear more, but I grabbed another piece of brownie to distract my hands.

"I was the only Black child in a town full of white folk. My mama and daddy always told me, *'Be careful. Keep to yourself. Stay quiet.'* So I tried. But even when you try your best, there's always a few kids who don't take kindly to someone different. One day, I found a little wooden airplane your mama had left by a tree. I wasn't tryin' to take it—just wanted to play a bit, then set it right back down. But sure enough, two kids came runnin' up, pointin' fingers, sayin' I stole it. Now, what I didn't know was that your mama had left that toy there on purpose—she wanted an excuse to talk to me, maybe become friends. But when she saw those kids comin', one pickin' up a rock with his hand, she didn't waste a second. That girl came flyin' out with a broom, broke it clean across that boy's back, then grabbed the girl by the hair and laid her flat.

Your mama was somethin' fierce. Savage, really. She even snatched the necklace right off that girl—the same one sittin' on your chest right now. From that day on, we became best friends."

My face was expressionless; the only thing close to indicating how I felt was the slight confusion my eyebrows gave away. Inside, though, a wave of heat crawled up my neck—half awe, half disbelief. Could that wild, fearless girl really be the same woman I've only known through secondhand stories? My fingers brushed the cracked pendant, and for a second, I swore it pulsed with a life I wasn't sure belonged to me or her.

I wanted to add, "That doesn't sound like her," but I couldn't. Because the truth was—I didn't know her well enough to say either way.

"She wore that necklace every day after," Dawn continued softly. "Told me it reminded her she could conquer the world. When the little girl fell on her back, the pendant cracked, but your mama said it was more beautiful broken. She believed in that—findin' beauty in what's broken."

Her voice grew distant, her eyes lost in the past. "Your mama taught me how to be brave. To stand tall when people wanted me small. She was a one-girl revolution."

O-G-R, I whispered, spelling the moniker in my mind. She nodded softly.

I was warm all over, as if I had been wrapped in the hug I'd always wanted.

The rest of her stories came in fragments—summer afternoons, scribbled letters, the way my mom dreamed of giving me my name. Not every detail, not a long history, but just enough to let me glimpse the outline of her, enough to feel her presence stirring inside me.

"I kept all her letters in a box, a little reminder to start livin' on my own terms. I opened this coffee shop a year after she passed, and I ain't looked back since."

"Established in 1998. That's the year she died," I pointed out.

"It's also the year you was born," she smiled. "I always wondered what became of you, but I couldn't believe my eyes when you walked in here. You look just like her. At first, I thought life was playin' a cruel joke on me—I thought I was seein' things. But the second I saw them two little eyeballs of yours, I knew. I'm so glad to see you wearin' the necklace, too."

I told her everything about myself—the good parts, the complicated ones, and the rough patches I was going through with you. I shared the fears that keep me up at night and the dreams I still hope will one day come true. Through it all, she listened. Sometimes, she would smile, almost imperceptibly, the way somebody smiles when a memory they thought they had forgotten visits their mind to say hello.

I could tell she was connecting the dots. Seeing how I was like my mom, how I was different… wondering if our stories would be the same if things had gone differently. Playing what-if scenarios in her head. It felt like she was meeting me for the second time, but as desperately as we both wanted to, we knew I was not who she hoped was sitting across from her.

Despite her look of nostalgia for who I was and where I came from, she seemed fascinated by me. In a way, the love and pride she felt for my mom had been unreciprocated and vacant for too long, and in me, she saw a mirrored image of her best friend—an extension of my mom. Suddenly, all that love and ache she had for the person she missed the most had found a new home in me.

I welcomed these feelings. Dawn was the person who seemed to have known my mom best aside from my dad, and in this coffee shop, I felt closer to her than ever. I needed Dawn as much as she needed me. Our relationship became symbiotic, aiming to keep the memory of my mom burning bright inside of us, guiding us toward each other to pick up the broken pieces she left behind.

When it came time to close the shop, Dawn kicked everybody else out and returned with a bottle of wine. She held her glass up high and said, "To your mama— may she keep on livin' inside you, shinin' bright whenever you need a little courage. Lord knows, she was always good at that."

My throat tightened, the words catching before I even spoke them. I lifted my glass with trembling fingers, the rim cool against skin still warmed by wine and memory. For a fleeting moment, it felt like I wasn't just drinking with Dawn—I was drinking with her, with Mom, and her laughter hovering in the air between us.

"To Mom," I said, raising my glass.

We cheered.

We drank two glasses each, and with every sip I craved more of my mother's courage. Dawn's presence gave me both clarity and comfort.

"Hey, baby, it's been so good havin' you here. If you ever wanna come by and help out a couple days a week, I wouldn't mind one bit. I'm gettin' old, and keepin' this place up's been takin' a toll on me. You can earn a little money and listen to this ol' lady talk your ear off some more. Think on it, all right? My door's always open for you!"

Before I left, I hugged her tight, whispering in her ear, "I'll come back next week to report for duty. Thank you for giving me clarity." If I am lucky, I can combine enough pieces together to understand who my mom was and finally get to know her.

Her reply stunned me. "Thank you baby, for givin' me closure."

On the way home, I walked slowly, feeling the cold sting my ears and fingertips. Each breath cut sharp but clean in my lungs, like the night air was carving space inside me for something new. My cheeks were still warm from the wine, and for the first time in a long time, I felt okay. The click of my heels on the pavement sounded less like noise and more like a declaration: I was still here. I was still hers.

My first instinct was to rush home and tell you everything—but the thought withered just as quickly as it appeared. Things weren't like that between us anymore. I couldn't count on your excitement to mirror mine. And so I kept the night tucked away inside me like a secret flame.

I closed my eyes with my hand on my necklace; I thought of my mom and her one-woman revolution and felt a spark in my soul that I hadn't felt in months. She was awakening a fire in me I swore was long gone, and I let it travel through my body and mind as I drifted away with her memory in my dreams.

chapter twenty-one

THEN

WE HAD A set of "rules" to keep us accountable. I've seen it a million times before, where a couple gets so comfortable in their relationship they forget things are happening outside their bubble. Staying in one night watching a movie turns into seven movies a week, and before they know it, they've forgotten about the rest of the world because they created their own within the walls of their house. That's not inherently bad; some may even call it romantic, but forgetting the last time you washed your hair or the last time you changed your PJs is a slippery slope. That's why we decided that at least once every two weeks, we would dress up nicely and go on a proper date. Outside. Surrounded by other human beings. Three and a half years later, we haven't missed a single one. And tonight would be no different.

At first, we were a little hesitant. We were warm and cozy under the blankets, and getting out of bed to shower proved more difficult by the minute. But rules are rules. So off to the shower we went. We stayed there for what felt like an hour, letting the hot water cascade down our bodies. It was comfortable and safe. It was home. Nothing would beat the feeling of you holding me tight in your arms as a curtain of hot steam encircled our bodies. Even then, I felt like the world outside could collapse and I wouldn't care, as long as I stayed in that circle of warmth with you.

After the shower, we smelled fresh and clean, like eucalyptus and strawberry.

I wore baggy leather shorts, a sparkly burgundy crop top, and high-knee black boots. The heel of the boot was worn out, and my left calf would tire quickly after walking a few minutes, but they were my favorite boots, and scratched or not, they were still beautiful—just like I hoped to be. In the end, every scratch has its own story. Sometimes I wondered if you noticed the little imperfections I tried to cover with confidence, or if love made you blind to them.

Watching you dress was the most exciting part of this rule. You would always follow the same pattern: underwear, mirror check, muscle flex, pants, shirt, mirror check, socks, shoes, shoe check, change of shoes, watch, and cologne. You were wearing your navy-blue button-down, and I loved how you quickly slid your hands twice down the front of your shirt to smooth any wrinkles. You always left your top two buttons undone, but it was the veins in your forearms when you rolled up your sleeves that I waited for the most. It was enthralling. God, you're so handsome. Sometimes I caught myself staring too long, afraid you'd see just how undone I felt in those moments. Each time you caught me staring, the corner of your mouth would go up. Once dressed, I put on the heart-shaped necklace you gave me for my birthday and sprayed my date-night perfume.

"Ready?"

It was my turn to pick a spot, and I wanted to show you my favorite street. It was one particular street—a cobblestone road that stretched for three blocks. What made it so special was that along both sides of the street were different coffee shops right next to one another. It looked like coffee-shop central. I was so excited for you to see it. It felt like sharing a secret, as if I were handing you a hidden piece of my story and hoping you'd keep it safe.

On the drive there, we listened to old songs and sang along. My left hand was on the nape of your neck, and your right hand was on my left thigh. We were always together, always connected. Every touch back then felt like a promise—that neither of us would drift too far away. We parked a block away and walked to the beginning of the street.

"What's this? It's beautiful."

We started walking down the road, holding hands as I explained. String lights zigzagged from one side of the street to the other, drenching the road in magic. Faint music played from all directions, as most of the shops had live local singer-songwriters playing that Friday night. The scene was breathtaking. Watching you take it in, I felt proud, as if the beauty of this place somehow reflected back on me.

"Aren't thirty coffee shops on the same street bad for business? Isn't that too much competition?"

I thought about it. "Well, no."

"How so?"

"Every coffee shop has something that makes them unique. They usually are known for having a specific drink that they do better than any other shop on the street. The owners are also people from different countries, so every shop has something that belongs to their culture, which adds to their uniqueness. Also, those tired of overrated and over-influenced coffee shops come to this street and support local places. They get to try coffee from all over the world and make an experience of it. If you look around, you'll see a similar number of people in line for each shop. They almost treat it like a coffee tasting. It's a genius idea, in my opinion."

"How did you find this place?"

"A couple of years ago, I was roaming around and played in a couple of these spots."

"Ahhhh! I am witnessing the street where my favorite musician had her first paid gig! We have to celebrate!"

"Well, I wasn't exactly paid, per se. You do it for the experience and exposure. Most of these places give the musicians a handshake and a $10 gift card for their shop."

You laughed. "You hate coffee."

"Ha. Well, yeah, but most of these places also have tea. And on that note, I am about to embark on a journey that will educate you on the magnificence of herbs and lessen your ignorance on the subject."

You nodded and squeezed my hand twice—"Well, that sounds like a plan. Lead the way!" I skipped twice in anticipation of the adventure.

"So!"—I pointed to the left—"the shop with purple walls has a fantastic lemon-zest tea. They put a rim of brown sugar on the cup that they glaze with honey, which is as succulent as it is classy. The shop with blue tables has an incredible caramel-apple latte—sweet, but balanced just right, with a thin slice of cinnamon apple on the rim. And the shop with the white door has a Bailey's hot chocolate that will make you rethink your life decisions."

We walked up and down the street as I pointed out the highlights of each shop. We tried about eight teas between the two of us, ordering the smallest size so our bladders wouldn't betray us. We spent the rest of the night talking, laughing, and thinking about our future. It felt like we were writing some unwritten chapter together, one that tasted faintly of sugar and cinnamon and sounded like laughter drifting under string lights.

We made it back around eleven o'clock. We locked the door, put on a fresh pair of PJs, and went to bed. We wrapped our legs around each other, and I laid my head on your sternum, listening to your breathing as it slowed to a steady pace. We whispered "I love you" to each other and kissed goodnight. It was a soft kiss, a familiar kiss. A kiss that meant I was home. Here, with you, I was home. The steady rise and fall of your chest lulled me to sleep, the sound of your breath anchoring me in a world that felt unwavering.

chapter twenty-two

NOW

ANOTHER DAY, ANOTHER night. I looked up at the sky and felt nostalgic. The gray on the horizon made me feel empty; the fog blurred my mind, and I could feel the heaviness of the clouds in the pit of my stomach. I'm running out of ideas on how to reach out. So instead, tonight, I decided to reach in. I'm reaching for the memories we once shared. Trusting you to fix our issues drove me insane; asking you directly led to a fight, and giving you time was a waste of mine. If you are still in there, this is the only way I can think of to bring you back—a last resort.

I packed a bag: a wine bottle, two glasses, a blanket, and my guitar. I could hear the water flushing and the faucet running in the bathroom. When you came out, patting your hands dry on your pants, I walked weightlessly to you, grazed the back of your neck, and kissed you.

At first, you didn't kiss me back. Your body went still, your jaw tense, like you were debating whether to let me in. My stomach clenched, preparing for rejection— but then, slowly, your lips softened against mine, hesitant but present. That small surrender unraveled something inside me.

It wasn't a deep, passionate kiss. It wasn't the kind of kiss you witness between two twenty-one-year-olds in a bar, their bodies too tired to keep dancing but their minds too restless to go home, so they drink till their sight is blurry and their balance is off, grounding themselves in someone else's lips. Our kiss was different. There was no sense in rebelling, no competition, and—most importantly—no regrets. It was a long, slow kiss. A kiss that felt like it was stepping into territory that had been long forgotten. My lips pressed softly against yours. It was a kiss worth a thousand words, a million whispers. A kiss of promise. A kiss that swore not to ask any questions—and you knew I meant it. A kiss that made you feel warm inside, a sharp contrast to your cold skin.

Today, I wasn't looking for answers; I was looking for the other part of me that had been missing for some time, and I was ready to embrace it.

"Follow me," I said softly. I grabbed your favorite sweater, the fabric thin and worn from so much use, with a few holes in the left sleeve. You seemed a little tired—but not so much physically as mentally. I could practically feel the weight of your thoughts slowing you down.

Your eyes flicked to the door, then to me. For a second, I thought you'd shake your head, retreat back into your cave of silence. But you let out a weary sigh and nodded once, as if agreeing more out of surrender than eagerness. That silence meant everything.

We got into the car, and I drove us to the woods—our woods—in silence. There was a palpable comfort in that silence, because I could tell you weren't quiet from overthinking or swimming in your thoughts, but because you were curious and expectant. Most importantly, you were at peace—no longer alone.

I pulled over at the side of the woods. We hadn't been back here since we moved from the apartment to the house. Suddenly, a bigger house meant more responsibilities and a different chapter in our lives altogether. These woods held the younger versions of ourselves, the ones that still had a whole world to discover. The versions of ourselves who weren't afraid of change. Those were the ones we needed. We needed their bravery and their courage. We needed their faith in each other. You were aware—you knew it, too. I could see you were grateful to follow the steps you once walked and do everything you could to channel the past.

I laid down the blanket, and we sat next to each other. I opened the bottle of red wine; the sound of the cork pulling free was the only noise on a rather quiet night. I poured each of us a glass and looked at you.

"Cheers," I said. "To us, and to who we used to be."

You hesitated, glass hovering halfway to your mouth, eyes locked on me like you were searching for the catch. Then, slowly, you tapped your glass to mine.

"And to the ones we will become," you said. Your voice was low, a little rough, as if testing the words on your tongue before letting them out.

You flashed an almost imperceptible smile. Not a smile of laughter, but a smile of hope.

We drank some wine in silence, and after a few minutes, I reached for my guitar. I was getting restless; I needed to do something to show you how much I cared about us—how much I loved you. I played the first song that came to mind. The first syllables of "Holes" created a melody with the stars. A tribute to our beginning, an ode to our story.

Halfway through the third verse, I felt you wrap your arms around my waist. You were trembling. At first, I thought you might be cold—but then your breath hitched, uneven, and I realized you were crying. Relief coursed through my body.

By the end of the song, you were holding me tight—almost too tight. I was sure my ribs would be bruised tomorrow, but it didn't matter. I needed to feel this—the contact of a familiar touch that had been foreign for so long it had started to become a fantasy rather than a reality. I had been waiting to feel this vulnerability again—for you and for myself.

Your strong hands were holding mine, keeping me safe, and I knew then that despite the struggle we had been through, you would hold me now—and hold me forever. Right then, as if you could read my thoughts, you realized how tightly you were squeezing me. You immediately softened your grip and apologized.

The words came out haltingly, like stones dragged over gravel. "I'm sorry." Then again, louder, more certain, until they tumbled out faster, unstoppable.

You told me how sorry you were, blushing a little across your cheeks and neck. You sobbed as you told me how much you missed me and how sorry you were for the way you had been handling everything—for the way you had been behaving lately. You owned up to the fact that you'd been hurtful these past few months and vowed to do better. You apologized again and again—and one more time, for good measure.

Each apology cracked open another part of me, making space for hope. At the same time, I caught the edge of fear in your eyes—the fear of losing me for good.

I could sense these apologies were coming from a place of guilt, born of recent developments. The drinking, the detachment, the secrecy, the pain...

A surge of hope rose through me.

I was finally reaching you.

You missed me.

You needed me.

This made me smile. It had been so long since I'd smiled that the muscles felt stiff on my cheeks, as if learning how to curve my lips for the first time. You kissed me then, sure and unwavering, pressing into me with the certainty of someone who had finally come home. My chest lifted, my hands instinctively threading into your hair, my body leaning fully into the warmth and strength of you. Every worry, every doubt, every lingering shadow of the past melted against the firmness of your lips. The forest bugs chirped, and a few fireflies began to light their way out, as if celebrating this long-awaited breakthrough, the night itself joining in on the triumph of us.

You grabbed the guitar. I had once taught you some of the chords to "Dust in the Wind." I thought it would be a good song to start with—short and simple. You played the first C chord. It sounded out of tune, so I repositioned your index finger to the correct string, and you strummed. A decent rendition of the song filled the forest.

I relaxed until I heard a sharp, uncomfortable, and yet too-familiar sound, followed by a low grunt. A string had broken—the second string, to be exact. When it snapped, it ricocheted off your left cheek, and a small, irritated bump started to form on your face. Maybe it was the wine, but we laughed.

Our musical adventures had come to an end, but the feeling lingered. Warm and cozy, the sense of the alcohol—a responsible, regulated, and conscious amount—running through our bloodstream, loosening our emotions and enabling us to be free, unafraid, and undaunted.

We lay next to each other, enjoying the wine in silence. I looked at the sky, and the midnight reflected through the wine glass looked magical. I felt like Alice. This, right now, was my Wonderland—you were my Wonderland.

A change in perspective, ever so slight, allows you to see the world in a different light. In this case, the light of the moon and the stars filtered through the reflection of the glass, mirroring a constellation that faded out at the edges—it was such a beautiful concept. The stars shone brighter through the curves of the glass than they did through my naked eye.

I twisted my glass toward you and placed it between our faces. The curve of the rim magnified your freckles. The galaxy they formed on your nose and cheekbones was only interrupted by the mark of the guitar string—a red shooting star dancing its way through space. I made a wish on your cheek. I wished for us. I wished for hope. I wished for our past and our future. I wished for our present and hoped it would shine with the love and magic we had before.

A tear slid down from the tip of my nose. You were still looking at me, those eyes shining and sparkling like the North Star itself. You knew exactly what was running through my mind. You always did.

"Me too," was all you whispered.

chapter twenty-three

THEN

I WILL NEVER forget the day we officially committed to each other. It was as spontaneous and unexpected as the day we met. The summer heat hung heavy in the air, the kind that made the pavement shimmer and the hours feel a little slower, as if the season itself wanted us to linger just a little longer. For three days straight, I'd been caught up in thoughts of backpackers—ever since I watched a documentary about their adaptable, minimalistic lives. The idea that someone could tuck all their belongings into a single bag, hop on a plane, and chase adventure wherever it called left me awestruck.

I brought it up over the past few days, but I had no ill intentions. I just thought it was a brave choice. While I was captivated by the idea, you had your own.

"Let's go to California," you mumbled. Your voice sounded small and foreign, childlike.

"Huh?"

"Let's go to California," you said again, more determined this time, more excited.

"When?"

"Right now."

"Like right this second?"

"Sure!" You nodded, raising your eyebrows effusively. "Our little jar has enough money saved for a wild weekend adventure. You haven't shut up about how much you'd like to go backpacking, and I want to make you happy, so let's do it! Pack your bag and I'll meet you in the kitchen in fifteen!"

With a quick peck, you ran to our room and threw a bag together. Before I could process what was happening, I found myself doing the same. I had my bag in my left hand and opened the drawers with my right. It was my turn to chase adventure. From all the research I'd crammed into my brain in the past few weeks, I felt more ready than ever.

I understood that human beings can be simple creatures—that we complicate our lives by cluttering our own world—and that none of the material things I owned would make me happy. Happiness was in the adventure and in being satisfied with the bare minimum. The point was to be wealthy in experiences and memories, not money.

Once I embraced this, packing was a breeze. I was wearing the only pair of jeans I needed for the weekend. I packed four shirts, some old shorts, a baggy shirt to sleep in, and a few pairs of underwear and socks. If I ran out, I'd just wash them by hand in the sink. I tossed in my toothbrush and a travel-sized deodorant.

Fifteen minutes later, I ran back downstairs to the kitchen with a flashy smile on my face. This backpacking business was a brilliant idea, and we were off to a fantastic start.

We arrived at the airport forty-five minutes later and checked the flights. The next flight to San Francisco was scheduled to depart in a little less than an hour. We bought two economy tickets, and by the time we rushed through security and made it to the gate, we had less than ten minutes to spare before the gate doors closed.

"What's the plan for when we get there?" I asked, out of breath.

"What do backpackers do when they go to a new place?"

"They usually eat, find a hostel to sleep in, and then explore."

"So that's what we'll do!"

As the plane started to take off, I kissed you. It was the sweetest kiss—partly because you were the magic in my life, and partly because I could taste the overpriced grape juice on your lips from the little store by our gate.

I looked into your eyes, and without a single word, I knew you understood. I rested my left ear on your chest. Hearing the steady beat of your heart made me feel safe and warm as the plane took off. You rested your chin on the top of my head, and we both thought about California, excited for the first trip of many we hoped would come.

Three hours later, we were walking down the streets of San Francisco, and I immediately fell in love with the city. The way people dressed and walked with purpose, the art and creativity that seemed to breathe from every wall—it was absolutely perfect.

We rented two bikes and gave ourselves a tour of the city. We saw the Painted Ladies, rode through downtown, stepped inside stores just to admire their window displays, and made our way to Castro Boulevard, where I bought a few stickers and pins.

One pin read: "LOVE IS LOVE IS LOVE IS LOVE." Each word was written in a different color of the rainbow, which made sense. The pin captured the essence of Castro Boulevard—love, freedom, acceptance, and vibrant colors. A place worthy of commemoration. I also bought a Freddie Mercury pin—one of my favorites— which, again, just made sense.

After our self-guided tour and dinner, we bunked at a hostel for the night. Exhausted from being on our feet and carrying the extra weight of our bags, we just wanted a good night's sleep to prepare for whatever the next day would bring.

The next day—the infamous day in question—was when everything changed.

We woke up that morning sore from the day before but excited to see what the new day would bring. There was a nice park where we went to buy coffee and a small sandwich for breakfast, and we fed the birds the leftover crumbs. The morning air carried exhilaration, but neither of us knew why.

We walked around San Francisco, taking in the town's architecture and overall culture, looking for our next adventure. Around noon, we stumbled upon a small pizzeria located on 16th Street. The smell of pepperoni wafted around the block, and by the time we walked in, our jaws ached from how hard our mouths were watering.

While we waited by the host stand, a very energetic twenty-something-year-old approached us with two menus. She sat us at the corner table, flashing a bright smile before returning to her post. A few minutes later, a very kind, slightly less energetic but equally happy server came over and filled our cups with water, the ice clinking as it swirled in the glass.

"We'll just share a pepperoni pizza, please," I said, trying to mask my hunger behind a sip of water.

The server wrinkled his forehead at me and pointed to a pen and paper at the table. Now, it was our turn to be confused. The three of us had an almost comical moment where we stared at one another, hoping to get an explanation or some sort of clarification, but none came.

That's when I realized how quiet this restaurant was, even though it was mostly at capacity. The next few seconds happened quickly, like a blur flashed through my eyes. I realized that the server was not speaking to us, the host had not said anything either when she greeted us at the entrance, every table had pens and papers, and the people in the kitchen were signing with each other. Suddenly, I caught on. I grabbed the pen and wrote two words on the sheet:

Deaf-owned? — I shifted the paper his way.

He nodded in affirmation, signing "yes" with a smile even bigger than before. I mirrored him in return. After understanding, we both wrote down our order and showed him the sheet of paper. He flashed us two thumbs up and left to input the order in the system. The whole environment and experience we had in that restaurant was incredible. It was eye-opening and compelling, and it was honest.

After lunch, we hopped on the trolley and rode it all the way down to Pier 39. I had heard countless stories about this place, but seeing it firsthand sent goosebumps down my spine. The pier was pure magic—string lights connected one end of the dock to the other, the smell of fresh oysters traveled all the way across the pier, and the seals in the ocean sang a captivating melody that encapsulated the beauty of the moment. I was honored to experience this by your side.

We walked along the boardwalk holding hands when something caught our attention. A lady was sitting behind a table, rings and bracelets for sale displayed in front of her. I picked up a bracelet and noticed something written across:

DON'T BE A LITTLE BITCH, it read in all upper-case letters.

"Sold!" I exclaimed.

The older hippie with a crown of flowers in her hair chuckled as she placed the bracelet in a little brown bag. "It'll be twenty," she said with a gentle smile.

I pulled out $20 without hesitation.

"This is officially my favorite piece of jewelry." You both smiled in unison.

"What led to the passive-aggressive messages?" you asked.

"You see—" the lady started on what I imagined was a daily speech. "Before I did these, I used to have bracelets with encouraging messages engraved; I wanted to spread positivity and inspiration. Unfortunately, I was barely selling enough of them to break even, and I knew I would have to get creative if I wanted to keep food on the table.

"I decided to sit back and people-watch—really look at them—to figure out what they liked. Turns out all you folks talked about was profanity and blasphemy. Ironically, I make more money selling insults than I ever did selling hope. But that's life, isn't it?"

I could tell the bracelets were starting to rub off on her. She looked distant now, as if contemplating whether she wholeheartedly agreed with the morals behind her jewelry business.

"But hey, you gotta pay the bills somehow, am I right? A girl's gotta do what a girl's gotta do! At least I'm making an honest living!" Her profound introspection quickly dissolved after reaching that conclusion.

"Amen to that!" *(Amen to that!?)* The words had left my mouth before I even knew what I was saying, and I blushed. You looked at me, suppressing a smile. I had never said that phrase before in my life. Clearly, these bracelets were powerful. I was turning into a whole new woman.

Thankfully, you deterred attention to a small machine on the side of the table.

"And what's that for?" you asked, pulling the lady's attention back to you.

"I get a lot of couples that are head over heels for one another—you two being a perfect example—and they get engraved jewelry. Some get their anniversary date, their names, you name it! I once got a young couple who engraved each other's phone numbers in case one got too drunk and got lost; they'd know who to call. Pretty smart if you ask me!"

This lady had seen it all. I loved Californians. No wonder the Beach Boys wrote a song about girls from here. They were fearless and accepting of the universe; nothing seemed to faze them.

You kept chatting with her, but I got distracted by the view of the pier, and after thanking the lady for the bracelet, I went to the edge of the pier to look at the seals while I waited for you. I took a deep breath, letting the salty breeze fill my lungs. It felt incredible. The sun was setting, and the different colors blended into a magical scene.

After a few minutes, your arms encircled my waist. I could feel your scent mingling with mine, and I melted into your chest.

"I love you so much. Thank you for making my backpacking dream come true," I whispered as I overlooked the ocean.

"Anything for you."

We stood in silence for a few minutes. The sky merged into a watercolor of different shades of purple and orange that bled into one another. After a while, you broke the silence.

"Speaking of dreams, would you like to help make one of mine come true?"

"Anything you want!"

"Marry me," you said.

I gasped—an almost imperceptible gasp. I looked at you, speechless, tears forming in my eyes.

"What did you just say?"

"Marry me. I want you to marry me." You pulled a little blue bag with a silver string out of your pocket and got down on one knee. Inside, there were two rings. I was full-on ugly crying by now.

"I love you. I want you to be my forever and always, to wake up every single day next to you and have a new adventure every day for the rest of our lives. I just bought these two rings from that passive-aggressive, kind hippie, which may or may not turn our ring fingers a little green, but I want you to wear it until I can save up enough money to buy you the big, shiny diamond you deserve. Think of it as our promise rings if you'd like. I know typically only the girl gets one, but I got these engraved for us."

Your voice was cracking by now, but your smile couldn't have been more obvious.

I got down on my knees with you, trying and failing to get a hold of myself. I grabbed the ring that I had to put on your left finger, gripping it tight because my hands were shaking too much, and noticed the phrase engraved inside:

You keep me wild, it read.

It was true. I always kept you on your toes, ready for that next adventure. It helped you break out of your routine and become more spontaneous, learning to let loose a little more each day and appreciate the little things.

Snot was pooling on my upper lip by now.

"What does mine say?" I asked—half question, half sob. You tilted it for me to see the inside:

You keep me safe, mine said.

I gave a small laugh that came out more like a wet snort. A flurry of emotions took over and I couldn't pick them apart. They were one big ball of love, exhilaration, and everything in between.

As you slipped the ring onto my finger, the little crowd that had gathered around us erupted in cheers. A group of tourists near the fountain clapped and whistled loudly. A vendor with a camera, quick to seize the moment, snapped a photo of us—me still teary-eyed, you grinning as if you'd just won the World Cup. He handed us a glossy print a few minutes later, the ink still warm, capturing the exact second my life had changed.

"Don't even think about changing these rings," I said between tears as we slipped our rings on each other's fingers. "This is perfect. This is us." I whispered, cleaning my nose against the hem of my shirt.

You looked at me with those brown eyes and that piercing gaze that melted every part of me.

"So I suppose this is a yes?"

"Yes!" I practically screamed as tears of joy streamed all the way down to my collarbone. Before you could get back on your feet, I threw myself at you and wrapped my arms around your neck. You fell with your back against the pier's wooden boards as we laughed and kissed and dreamt about our future.

As the cheers died down and the crowd dispersed, I couldn't help but think about how far we'd come. Three and a half years together, and only now were we finally in a place where travel was possible—backpacking, of all things. Before, it had been bills and long hours, scraping by and dreaming of "someday." But now, here we were, living the dream with two worn backpacks and a map folded too many times. Celebrating our engagement to the serenade of sea lions and the gentle crash of the ocean. Maybe that was what made this moment so perfect; the fact that we had waited. We hadn't rushed; we hadn't forced it. We had earned this—the laughter, the freedom, and the future you were now asking me to build with you.

When I propped myself up on my forearms, we noticed a thin string of snot connecting my nose to your cheek after I kissed you. Most people would have found that revolting, but we didn't mind.

We lay there, laughing—your back against the cool, sand-covered boardwalk and my face in the crook of your shoulder, where it always belonged—as the sun hid behind the water and the first stars shone through the sky. It was everything I ever could have asked for.

You promised me a "real wedding" once we saved enough money. You said we would have an officiant declare us "husband and wife," and you promised me a ring bearer and a lavender cake. I was happy just as we were, though. I didn't need all the extra luxuries or legalities. It was enough for me to know that we belonged to one another. Who cared what other people thought?

Lying next to you, I twisted the ring on my finger between my index and thumb. I smiled as I thought about the phrases you had engraved on them.

You keep me wild.

You keep me safe.

And you always did.

Until the day you couldn't.

chapter twenty-four

NOW

THEY SAY ONE of the best ways to shift your perspective is by shifting the space surrounding you. Just like putting clothes into a drawer—if you organize the space, you can organize your thoughts and place them where they belong, allowing you to see clearly. Clarity is the first thing you lose when stress and panic start to tickle your brain.

So that's exactly what I did. I changed into comfortable clothes I wouldn't mind sweating in and tied my hair in a bun. You had definitely made an effort since our date in the woods. You told me today you would be at the office for a few hours, but promised to bring takeout on the way back and asked me to pick a movie for us to watch. Baby steps, I reminded myself. So during the time you were gone I focused on my task at hand. I started with my closet, scared that under that big pile of clothes—the ones I had to sniff to determine their cleanliness—a creature would be plotting my demise.

I grabbed two hampers, placed them on either side of me, and began sniffing. Shirts, underwear, and even a few mismatched socks. Dirty, clean, clean, maybe worn once or twice? Eh, I'll assume it's clean enough. Dirty, clean... I fell into a rhythm and had sorted both piles before I knew it. I felt satisfied with my work despite the sweat going through my shirt. The more I cleaned, the more invigorated I felt.

I walked to my nightstand, cluttered with old receipts and water cups meant to quench a thirst that never materialized. It wasn't my throat that needed to be satiated, but my soul that needed reassurance that things would be okay. I cleaned up the mess and wiped everything down. I put some pens and notepads in the drawer in case I had a dream I thought was worth remembering, but when I went to close it, I heard a faint noise—the sound of paper wrinkling and complaining.

I opened the drawer and pulled out the piece of paper. It was a picture; the top left side was a little creased from when I tried to murder it with the drawer. I choked a little when I looked into my grandma's young and vibrant eyes. It was like looking at the Earth itself. Deep, rich blue eyes stared back into mine, with green specks like continents against the ocean in a globe. They shone like marbles when the sun reflected its light on them—fierce and confident, yet wise and loving.

I turned the picture around; it read "December 4th, 1954." I recognized her handwriting immediately. This picture was taken right before my grandparents met. I've heard that fairy-tale-like story a thousand times, but every time she told me, it was like hearing it for the first time—recreating the scenes in my mind, like pages in a book or scenes in a movie. She would always end the story the same way:

"There's magic in beginnings, Noah… You just need to know where to find it…"

Her gaze would drift away then, keeping pieces of him to herself, holding on to his memory the way she wished to. I always respected that she kept some of their stories private, and I hoped one day I would have someone worth keeping secrets for.

I started thinking about Grandma then. I remembered when I was little, she tried teaching me how to knit, and the whole point was for us to knit each other something—like a project we could work on together while enjoying each other's company. After a month and a half, I finished my poor excuse of a beanie for her. I was mortified. The beanie did an excellent job of covering only one of her ears; somewhere along the stitching pattern, I made a mistake, and now the poor woman looked like Piglet after a misadventure, her left ear poking out of the hot pink yarn.

She looked ridiculous, but I tried my best, which was enough for her. My pity party was cut short after she gave me my present. She had knitted me the most magical blanket—shades of white, blue, deep purple, and teal intertwined, creating a winter wonderland. It was ironic how colors that looked so cold could keep me so warm and cozy. I always wondered what became of it—one day I was a kid clutching my blanket, the next my life had turned, and it was gone. Wherever it is now, I hope it brings warmth to someone who needs it as much as I needed it now.

Grandma and I always had a bond that felt invincible, unbreakable, infinite. She knew all about you, and I felt comfortable telling her about us because I knew she had felt this way. She had a one-of-a-kind love, and I hoped we could have it, too.

I remembered one special moment. A phone call years ago, when I thought I had the flu. I was feverish and miserable, but Grandma insisted I wasn't sick from a virus—apparently, I was "ill from love," and my body was in withdrawal from being away from you. Her words had annoyed me at the time. It was ridiculous and wise all at once, but secretly I clung to the idea. The way she said it made me feel less broken, as though love itself was both the cause and cure. She had a way of diagnosing the heart when no doctor could.

I smiled at the memory. I could not remember the last time I had called her to see how she was doing. It must have been two months or so. I had been so caught up in my own drama that I forgot about the one person who always understood me and knew exactly what to say. I felt a sharp twinge under my ribcage, feeling guilty for neglecting her, so I picked up the phone. After two rings, I heard the voice I'd been craving for months.

"Let me guess... You wandered around your house, found something that reminded you of me, and felt morbidly guilty because you hadn't called your only grandmother to see how she was doing before she kicked the bucket?"

A faint laugh escaped before I could stop it. "Something along those lines... I won't even ask how you knew."

The conversation felt so natural and rhythmic, as if I had never stopped talking to her at all. Still, the guilt sat heavy in my stomach.

"What's up, buttercup? I have missed ya! But you sound sad. What's going on in that pretty-but-usually-matted head of yours? Everything okay?"

Silence. After a few seconds, she could hear my stifled sobs on the other line. She didn't comment with sass; she just waited.

"Remember a few years ago, when Derek and I were dating, I called and told you I felt sick, and you told me I was ill from love?"

"I remember it like it was yesterday."

"I think I may have caught it again."

She paused. "Hmm. This sounds different though. Years ago, your voice was hopeful, almost childish. Today, something feels misplaced. Tell me more."

So I did. I told her everything—the drinking, the necklace, the fights, the way sadness pinned me to the bed. I spilled it all until I had nothing left. When I finally stopped, the silence on the other end was deafening.

After a few heartbeats, I asked, "So? What's the diagnosis this time?" My voice was raw and tired from the heartbreak, from trying to swallow every feeling that threatened me with vulnerability.

"Aw, Pumpkin. I'm afraid the diagnosis isn't as romantic as before. You're not sick from love, but from loneliness, like an infection spreading through your veins and isolating every cell in your body. Derek may still live in the house, but he is not *with* you. When you called me a few years ago, you were physically far away from him but felt as close as ever. This time, even though you are under the same roof, you both act like strangers. That's such a shame, he's such a good kid."

She couldn't have been more right, and when she called you a 'good kid'—as if she saw you not in spite of your brokenness but through it—it nearly cracked my own heart wide open.

"What do I do?"

"Don't let that sparkle die alone; create a fire, rekindle your story, and reclaim your fairytale, my little punk."

If I had known then what I know now… I would've taken that sentence as a warning, and God knows I should have listened.

chapter twenty-five

THEN

YOU WERE MY *perfect fairy tale.*

chapter twenty-six

NOW

WHEN DID THE *fairy tale become such a nightmare?*

Since our marriage became rocky and inconsistent, my days have blended into each other. The progress we made that night in the woods felt significant, and even though you've improved, sometimes I get flashes of the Derek who was explosive and distant. I can see how hard you're trying to maintain the character I need, but sometimes, I can see you reverting to the version of yourself that I am afraid of.

Today, I woke up and went downstairs to cook us breakfast while you showered. Before sitting down, you kissed my forehead, which I thought was a good sign. Maybe you were in a good mood, and I was getting the happy-go-lucky, loving Derek today. Who knows at this point? But I chose to be optimistic; perhaps you were ready to talk to me about what had been going on, and I could drop a hint or two about possibly talking to someone. Perhaps therapy could help us through this.

We ate quite amicably while you asked me questions about my day. You asked what I had planned, if I was going to pick up a shift with Dawn any time this week, how I was feeling...

This was my chance. You asked about my feelings. You opened the door wide for me to step through. This was it. I mentioned how the last few months had been rough, how I was exhausted, and how going through this marriage was like walking on a tightrope. I also mentioned how happy we used to be. We had years of ups, so naturally, some downs were expected, but this felt like an infinite cliff I couldn't climb out of. You listened quietly with an empty look in your eyes. I wasn't even sure you were really hearing me, so I took a chance.

"I was thinking maybe we could try going to couples therapy."

And then it all came crashing down. That simple statement led to an argument unraveling all the words we had kept quiet, exploding out of our lungs with burning rage and old resentment. It was technically what I wanted—for everything to be out in the open—but without a third-party mediating, it escalated by the second.

"Therapy for what, Noah? We don't need someone else in our business," you growled, trying aggressively to keep calm and avoid screaming in a rageful fit.

"I think we do. We've tried to talk about our issues, but I think it would be healthy to get some professional help."

"We're not fucking crazy. What is crazy though is paying somebody $200 an hour to chat. It's a waste of money."

"Therapy isn't for crazy people. That's such an insensitive and ignorant comment. Therapy is for people who want to invest in themselves and their relationships to try to become the best versions of themselves."

"I'm not paying someone to tell me how to feel."

"They're not telling you how to feel anything, Derek; they're supposed to help you process the feelings you already have."

"No. Therapy is for losers who have no idea what to do with their lives, and so they pay someone to figure it out for them."

"That's ironic, coming from the immature alcoholic with no other coping mechanisms aside from throwing screaming fits and isolating in an office that smells like a public urinal." I didn't mean for it to go that far, and I could tell by your wince that my comment stung, but I couldn't take the words back. Even so, I didn't regret saying them.

"Drop it, Noah, please."

"But why won't you even—"

"BECAUSE I FUCKING SAID SO."

That was the last thing you said before slamming the coffee cup so forcefully on the table that it broke in half, making the silverware and plates jump.

I stayed quiet. There was no point in arguing when you got like this. The tightness coiling in my core ached in disappointment, because I had believed we were finally getting somewhere—only for it all to collapse at the mention of getting help. Hope slipped through my fingers like water. Whatever your thoughts on therapy, I would have to wait before approaching the subject again.

You gathered the broken cup and threw it in the trash. I was surprised to see that even while furious, you still placed the dishes in the dishwasher. It was almost laughable—the strange duality of you; breaking and cleaning, destroying and fixing, all in the same breath. Was this progress? Or just another cycle repeating itself?

You took a loud, deep breath. "I'm going to drive to the store to clear my head. Do we need anything?"

You avoided eye contact, but I was relieved you were at least trying to talk. I followed you to the car.

"We don't need anything from the store," I confirmed as you got inside. I didn't realize my hand was resting on the roof, my thumb catching on the edge of the door, so when you slammed it shut, all we heard was a distinctive crack and then a howl of pain.

You froze as my scream filled the air, but the sight of blood gushing from my finger forced you into action. Suddenly, our anger and hostility disappeared, washing away with every drop of blood that hit the driveway. My hand throbbed, pale with shock, my fingernail snapped clean off.

It stung and burned, but aside from that, no bones were broken. Your face turned green as you saw the shadow of where the nail was supposed to be, raw with bleeding flesh.

"Jesus Christ, Noah, I didn't—"

"Don't worry about it; hands bleed a lot. I'm okay. I know you didn't mean to," I mumbled. Instinct told me to downplay it, to smooth it over, because if I acted angry, you might spiral again. Even in pain, I was trying to protect you.

"This is NOT okay, Noah. It's far from okay."

You were sorry, I could tell. Your eyes filled with tears, your nose red. You apologized over and over, and for those few seconds, you were back.

I smiled faintly. It was flimsy, forced—one of those survival smiles, built not out of joy but necessity. But you needed it, so I gave it to you.

You took off the flannel you were wearing and wrapped it around my thumb, applying pressure. I winced. The fabric quickly turned crimson red.

"I swear if I had known your thumb was there, I would have never—" You were speaking so fast that you were not giving your mouth time to catch up with your brain, some of the words stumbling into one another.

"I know. I promise I'm fine."

Then something shifted in your eyes.

"I'm breaking us apart, aren't I?"

I nodded almost imperceptibly, but held your gaze as firmly as I could.

"I need help." It came out like an epiphany you couldn't avoid anymore.

"We both do," I agreed.

"I'm so sorry," you hissed.

I kissed your cheek and pulled you in. For once, you didn't stiffen; you surrendered. There was still hope.

"Let's go inside," I whispered. My breath warmed your ear, and you shivered. You buried your face in my neck, whispering,

"As soon as we fix your thumb, I'll start looking into couples counseling. I'm sorry I got so mad about it."

Even while pain pulsed hot through my hand, I swallowed it down. Because right now, your remorse felt fragile, and if I let my own hurt show, I was afraid it would shatter you. But carrying both our burdens was breaking me, piece by piece. I wasn't sure if I could keep this up for much longer.

We went inside, washed and bandaged my thumb, and you kissed it softly, like my grandma used to. You poured me apple juice with a straw and sat me on the counter. For once, I allowed myself to savor it—this fleeting version of the you who cared, who loved openly.

The following morning, I opened my eyes to fresh coffee on my nightstand and a smile as you peeked your head from under the covers, an innocent, almost childish quality to your eyes. This was progress—really, really good progress. I grazed your cheek as I wished you good morning. My thumb was swollen, the flesh where the nail used to be still raw and tender.

You changed my bandage gently, hand steady at my back as hydrogen peroxide bubbled down my palm. We felt like teenagers, hungry for each other, and for a moment it felt like we would make it.

Or at least I thought so, until 4:30 in the afternoon when your parents decided to show up unannounced. I had no issue with this. I had a great relationship with my in-laws, so I didn't mind them dropping by, but when I opened the door, I could see your reflection in the mirror. You looked like you had seen a ghost. Your body stiffened in defense, and even though I clearly wasn't aware of what was going on, I could already tell it would not end well for anyone. I could see the tension emanating from your muscles. My intuition tried to say something again, but before I could listen to it, your parents gently pushed the door open and invited themselves in, apologizing for not calling ahead.

"Nonsense!" I said, recovering as quickly and nonchalantly as possible. "It's so great to see you! Please come in; I can order some pizzas if that's okay with you guys?"

"That would be wonderful! We came straight from the airport; we are starving!" your mom said. She was swaying gently from side to side, exaggerating her mannerisms and clasping her hands anxiously as if trying to regain her composure, but I could see right through it. Your mom is very well-mannered and intentional.

This was strangely out of character for her, which only added to my already anxious attempt to test the waters and figure out their motive for the surprise visit.

"Three pies coming up!" I replied as chipperly as possible. It probably sounded a little fake, but I was overcompensating for your total lack of emotion toward your parents, which confused me. I went to the kitchen to order the pizza and left you and your parents to catch up. We had only seen them during the holidays since they moved to Florida, so I assumed they had stories to share. To my surprise, you followed me into the kitchen to grab four wine glasses.

"Did you know they were coming?" I asked.

"Nope."

"Why didn't they call to let us know they were flying in?"

"Whatever it is, it can't be good." You went back to the kitchen, back stiffened and jaw tense. My instincts were practically screaming into my eardrums by now.

When I returned, your mom was in the middle of a story that didn't involve anyone we knew. Your dad was silent, looking at me intently. It was almost like she was buying time by rambling about her Floridian acquaintances to avoid the unavoidable. We politely pretended to laugh as I handed you the wine, looking forward to having something to keep my hands occupied. As I brought the glass to my lips, your mom gasped as she saw the bandaged thumb. It had already stopped bleeding, but there were some dried blood stains visible through the bandage.

"What happened to your thumb!?" she asked, sounding a little exasperated. I did not like her dramatizing it so much. I blamed it on a cooking mishap. She looked unconvinced, but thankfully, and to my surprise, she let it go. Your dad asked about my family and we exchanged a pleasant, though clearly forced, conversation. He was stone-faced throughout most of it, but I tried to smile and act invested for the both of us. A futile attempt, but I had to do something.

Dinner was awkward; there was a tension I had never felt before when they were around. The pizza boxes sat open in the middle of the table, steam long gone, the smell of grease clinging heavier than the conversation. After we were done eating, your mom said something that had been nagging at me for a while, but I had not been able to place it.

"We are so glad we got to see you both," she said. "If we're being honest, retirement was refreshing at first, but it has been a little boring lately." She played with her napkin, eyes locked on her plate. Your dad drank his wine silently, now staring at you, as if trying to pry information out of you through telepathic wavelengths, but you were avoiding him.

That is when it hit me. They were *retired*. That meant you were now entirely in charge of your dad's company. I hadn't heard any new developments about the company for a few months, and you stayed home with me all day without giving any notice or taking any calls. All those months locked in the office, claiming you were working—what were you doing? Were you ignoring the business completely? Had the weight of running everything alone been too much? My mind was starting to spin. I felt the room tilt, like the chair beneath me wasn't steady anymore.

As if on cue, your dad asked how the business was doing, and that is when I knew we were in deep trouble. You couldn't take your eyes off your plate and refused to answer. After moments of awkward silence, you could only say two words.

"It's fine."

You answered bluntly, cutting through the tension in the room with a knife. Your dad looked at you; I could tell he knew something I didn't, but you did not beat around the bush.

"Why are you here?"

Your dad tried to keep his tone even and businesslike, speaking calmly as he said, "I got a call from Damian a couple of days ago."

Damian had been the business's accountant for as long as I had known you, always a loyal business partner and friend.

"He shared some concerns he has about the company—and about you. He says you have been dodging his calls and mentioned the company is going through some financial issues, and he really needs to touch base with you." Your dad's voice was flat, but it reverberated around the room, almost like a fifth presence.

You were at a loss for words. I couldn't read the expression on your face, but suddenly, it all made sense: the sudden free time, the papers I saw on your desk, the drinking, the anger, the shame. The truth hit me like a blow. The business wasn't being run. It was unraveling, and you were drowning under the weight of it. We were up to our necks in rough waters with no life jacket in sight.

"May I speak with you in the office?" your dad added.

The chair screeched against the floor under your weight as you pushed your feet away from the table. Out of the corner of my eye, I could see your closed fists trembling, and the fear and nausea came rushing back to me. I took a sip of water to stabilize myself. Your mom and I stayed at the table, the silence growing louder by the second. She stared at me intently. She wasn't fidgeting anymore. She was back to her normal self; calm, cool, and collected. I could see where you got your piercing gaze from. I felt so uncomfortable that I drank some more wine just to distract myself and have an excuse to look away.

"You didn't cut your thumb cooking, did you?"

I knew she already knew the answer, but my palpable silence and diverting look gave her all the confirmation she needed.

"I should start cleaning up," I coughed as I excused myself from the table.

I allowed myself to meet her gaze again before leaving the room. In her eyes, I saw pity, but I also caught a glimpse of understanding. Had she seen this happen before? Was she as scared as I was? Did she know how to handle this better than me? Was this a cycle repeating itself—a wound she had once lived through and never healed from?

I loaded everything in the dishwasher, and by the time I came back, your dad was leaving the office, disappointment written all over him. You followed behind, and when our eyes met, I saw helplessness etched across your face. Your mouth was a thin line, and you looked drained. As your dad walked past me, he gently placed his hand on my arm and gave me a compassionate nod before he walked out the door.

Your mom spoke softly as she thanked me for dinner and followed your dad. As she walked to the door, I thought I heard her whisper, "It's not your fault," but I was unsure if I had imagined it. When she got to the doorway, she stopped and turned her head back to me.

"Put Neosporin on your thumb. It will prevent an infection. Your nail will grow back, but it'll take time," she said as she closed the door.

Confused, tears started streaming down my cheeks. I was too weak and tired to try to make sense of anything. I walked to the office and tried to turn the knob.

Locked.

"Derek?"

Silence.

I heard the swish of alcohol being poured in a glass and the thump as the hollowed bottle hit the desk. I let out a deep breath and made my way upstairs.

All that progress, only to go back to square one.

I will be sleeping alone.

Again.

chapter twenty-seven

THEN

I'D HOPED WE'D last forever.

chapter twenty-eight

NOW

I WENT UPSTAIRS and laid on my bed. I was shaking, and I felt like I could not contain the anger that was coursing through every inch of my body. My hands trembled so violently I had to clench them into fists, but even that didn't stop the tremors. Heat flushed through me, feverish and stifling, and when I finally glanced down, I saw the skin of my thumb breaking open again, tiny trickles of blood seeping out as if my fury had split me from the inside. Eight minutes had passed since your parents left, and all our progress had crashed and burned in front of my eyes. I don't know if the wine encouraged me, but I had had enough.

I kicked off the covers, stomped to the kitchen, opened the drawer, and grabbed a knife. For a split second, my breath caught—was I really doing this? The thought flickered like a match and burned out just as quickly, drowned by rage. We were going to settle this once and for all.

I stood outside your office, jammed the knife into the doorknob, and forcefully pried the lock open. For half a heartbeat I braced myself, expecting a storm, a confrontation, or maybe even nothing at all. I slammed the door with my weight, and it was the clatter of the knife dropping against the floor that snapped you out of the trance-like state you were in.

chapter twenty-nine

NOW

I BURST INTO the office, guns blazing. My chest was already tight, my pulse rattling in my ears like a war drum.

"What the fuck is going on, Derek?"

"Don't worry about it." Your words were sharp and dry.

"Don't wo—are you fucking kidding me? After everything that just happened, do you still think you can keep your secrets?"

"It's none of your business, Noah. Cut it out."

A bitter laugh slipped out, sharp and ugly. My hands were trembling so hard I could feel the vibration in my ribs.

"Except it *is* my business. You may be too much of a drunk and an addict to realize it, but I am so fucking done with your bullshit act, Derek." Your gaze pierced through me. You looked maniacal. "Are we broke? Bankrupt? Poor?"

"WE'RE FINE!"

"We are *not* fine! We are far from fine; you are just too much of a coward to accept that—"

"To accept what!?" Your eyes bulged, blood vessels clouding your sight like red cobwebs.

"To accept that because of your stupid secrets and your stupid decisions, you shut me out and ruined our lives! To own up to your mistakes like a real man would, and to understand that I'm sick and tired of you!" I was gasping; the agitation of the argument had me feeling like I was running the back end of a marathon. My vision blurred, hot tears pricking but refusing to fall. I hated how my body betrayed me in the middle of this fight.

"You want me to accept that!? How about you take some accountability and accept that you have been on my ass, whining about how much I drink, or about how you're so fucking emotional and lonely all the time? If you had made the minimal effort to stop being so antisocial and made at least one friend, you'd have someone else to depend on—someone else to cry your ridiculous, nonexistent problems to—other than me!"

You were blinded by rage at this point, every vein in your neck threatening to burst, completely indifferent and unaware of the words spilling from your mouth. You swept a vodka bottle off the edge of the desk, sending it crashing to the floor. Glass shattered, scattering sharp fragments across the hardwood.

"Oh, fuck off! Being married to you these past few months has been exhausting—it feels like a chore. You and your victimizing, isolating personality are pathetic. You've been treating me like shit these past few months! Don't you think it's embarrassing for me to have to beg for your attention? But it's even worse walking into this office and looking at the excuse of a man you've become, covered in vomit and reeking of cheap liquor. If you took a second to look at yourself in the damn mirror, maybe you'd stop acting like such a fucking asshole!" My throat was raw from screaming.

"Have you stopped for a second to consider how *I* feel? Are you aware that there are other people in the world aside from you? Do you know how emasculating it is not to be able to provide for your family and give you the life I promised you? Maybe if you stopped being so useless and selfish, you could be a little more helpful—instead of acting like such a fucking bitch, Noah!"

"Fuck you, Derek! *Fuck. You.*" I dragged my words, hoping each letter would cut like glass shards down your throat. "If I am such a fucking inconvenience to you, then why don't you just fucking leave—and don't fucking come back!" I screamed as I slammed the door. The slam rattled the room, tipping another bottle over. It shattered loudly, the sound echoing like a warning as the liquid and shards spilled across the floor. My throat burned, my whole body shaking with the force of the words. I barely recognized my own voice anymore.

Those last words reverberated off the walls, echoing inside our brains. Those were the last words I ever said to you, and they will haunt me till my dying breath.

With just one sentence, I sentenced myself to a life of heartbreak. A prison of loss. The regret and the guilt make me want to carve my heart out and step on it until it bleeds dry, because that is what I deserve. It's all my fault. I feel empty and hollow. A shell of the human I once was. Condemned till my last breath with the knowledge that I destroyed the only thing that ever mattered.

I want to make one thing perfectly clear: I loved you, Derek, and I still do. Past and present. I always will. I do not blame you for any of the things you said that night. I am forever thankful to you for showing me what pure love feels like, and I know that nobody will ever love me as desperately and genuinely as you did. I will miss you every single day for the rest of my life, and in my heart, you will always be my forever.

Till death did us part.

chapter thirty

NOW

AFTER YOU WALKED out and drove off, I fell asleep on the couch, the last conversation with you replaying in an everlasting nightmare. At 9:02 PM, I jolted awake, the sour taste of a bad feeling rising in my gut. Something wasn't right. My face was wet; the tears had left a salty taste on the back of my tongue, and my stomach was churning. Something was definitely wrong. I immediately called you—I needed to hear your voice in a futile attempt to quiet my fears.

Beep, beep, beep.

Voicemail.

Beep, beep, beep.

Voicemail.

Beep, beep, beep.

Voicemail.

Fuck.

It was 9:39 PM when I hung up for the eighteenth time. The weight of this feeling was killing me. My head hurt, my soul ached, and the memory of how we met kept reminding me of how much I truly loved you and how much I needed you to be okay. I was drowning in anxiety; the cuticles on my nails were actively bleeding dry from where I pulled them every time I got sent to voicemail. I grabbed one of the cigarette packs I knew you kept hidden in the bottom drawer of your desk. I needed to do something. I hadn't smoked in years, and the smell made me lightheaded, but at least it would give me something else to be preoccupied with. The thought of shortening my lifespan seemed appealing.

You're useless, Noah.

Fucking.

Useless.

That word kept circling my brain as I sat on the couch and tried to steady my hand enough to strike the lighter. It took me several attempts; my hands shook so badly that they avoided contact like uncoordinated dance partners whenever I got the lighter close enough to the cigarette. I couldn't even do that. *Useless.*

I sat on the couch and waited, a cloud of smoke impregnating itself into my hair and clothes. I felt like my lungs were physically becoming smaller with each breath. I couldn't breathe. Was I having an anxiety attack? I lit another cigarette and called again.

Voicemail.

Fuck.

I tried to take a deep breath and steady myself, my thoughts flooding my brain with the worst-case scenario. I waited. I waited for the call that I knew would inevitably come. It was already 10:57 PM, and I only had one cigarette left. I lit it, praying for that phone to ring so I could hear your voice.

Finally, putting my torture to an end, at 11:04 PM, it rang. My heart sank, relief flooding through me once I heard that ringtone, but it was short-lived once I glanced at my phone.

Private Number, it read on my screen.

It wasn't you.

I felt sick. I immediately got to my knees and puked in the decorative bowl that served as a centerpiece for the coffee table in the living room. My heart was pounding in my head, and I was exhausted from crying. I answered the phone, but the blood rushing through my veins was so loud that it was hard to hear the officer's voice on the line. My mind was racing; I couldn't seem to understand what he was saying. His words seemed slurred and muffled, but I knew it wasn't his fault, the phone reception, or anything other than my brain trying to process and comprehend what, deep down, I already knew. I could only make out specific words; everything else was washed away in a panic, along with any hope left in me.

"There's been an accident.

Driving in the rain.

Lost control.

Fatal crash.

I'm sorry.

I'm so sorry."

At that last sentence, everything went dark; my knees gave in, and I collapsed on the couch.

I can't account for the time I was unconscious. I don't know how much time had passed. I was in a state of nothingness; my will to live seemed to have vanished with that phone call. I was ready to give up, to stay in this broken-hearted, coma-like trance, because nothing mattered—nothing at all. A life without you wasn't a life I wanted to live. I was ready to be swept away by the all-consuming, burning darkness.

But you seemed to disagree.

"NOAH!"

The sound of your voice jolted me awake. It was not a dream. You were here— your spirit, your presence—it was you. That cry for help, those four letters that made up my name, was your last goodbye. There was desperation in your voice, your final effort to keep me safe, because that's what you always did.

I gasped, my eyes shot open, and they immediately started to burn. I could feel the thick smoke irritating my pupils. I was straining my eyes to see anything, make anything out, but as tears tried to relieve the sting from the smoke and blurred my vision, it seemed impossible. I was completely disoriented and confused. The smoke in the house was so dense and heavy that breathing was nearly unbearable. I felt lost and terrified; my skin was so hot I could feel the welts forming on my forearms and neck.

I tried to sense my surroundings. Rather than seeing it, I felt the familiarity around me—the worn edges of the couch beneath my fingers, the way the fabric had softened in the spots we always sat.

I was in our house.

"DEREK!?" I yelled, trying to find you. I didn't know if you were here with me or had left the house, but I wasn't going to leave you.

It wasn't until I threw myself from the couch to the hardwood floor and knocked the wind out of me that it all came back with an overwhelming, soul-shattering clarity.

The fight.

The call.

The cigarette.

The fainting.

The lit cigarette.

It must have fallen out of my hand when I passed out and caught something on fire. Then I remembered your voice calling me awake, and it all made sense. You needed me to get out—fast.

By now, the heat was penetrating my lungs, consuming all the oxygen within me. The air felt thick and heavy. I was starting to cough up blood. With a struggle, I grabbed my shirt and covered my nose and mouth. I was coughing every few seconds now, gasping for air, as thick tears streamed down my cheeks, my eyes trying to defend themselves from the smoke, leaving clear streaks on my soot-covered face.

I shrieked as something sharp cut my left knee.

There were broken liquor bottles on the floor from our fight earlier. It's no surprise the house was going up in flames. It was a flammable pile of wood and alcohol.

I was crawling my way to the door; luckily, the fire hadn't spread to the rest of the house yet—it was mainly focused on the living room and office—but the smoke it created was as harmful as the fire itself. My mouth tasted like ash, metallic and bitter, coating my tongue until I thought I'd choke on it. The fire roared so loudly it filled my ears with a constant, punishing ring, like the house itself was screaming in pain. Every sense was under siege—sight, sound, taste, touch—and I felt myself unraveling under the strain.

I was a few steps away from the door, about to escape, about to leave everything I knew behind—my life and your memory—as they went up in flames. I was abandoning everything I was, everything I am.

A paper house for a paper girl, both burnt down to ashes.

I was three steps away from the door when I caught an all-too-familiar shape calling out to me. I paused—maybe from exhaustion, maybe instinct. My guitar was propped up in the corner of the living room closest to the entrance. I could see the flames of the fire reflected off its body, but it was completely unharmed, as if protected by a spell. It was the only thing I had left, and I'd be damned if I didn't fight for it.

It felt like the last lifeline in a world collapsing around me, something solid to cling to when everything else was consumed. My fingers itched to touch it, to feel something that belonged to us, that had survived the fire like a guardian for the both of us. I'd lost everything else and needed something to hang on to. I was able to get my feet under me as I limped from my bleeding knee, struggling like a baby deer learning to walk, and I lunged toward it. My fingers wrapped around its neck.

I howled in agony.

The metal strings were scorching from the fire around it, and as I held on to it, I could feel the six strings searing into my palm. I was hyperventilating, suffocating now.

The five steps between myself and the door seemed never-ending. The smoke and the heat crippled my every move.

The noises the fire made as it tore through the house were heartbreaking. I could hear all the cracks and snaps of the wooden beams, and I knew with complete certainty that the house was grieving, its core shattering as ruthlessly as mine.

This was no way to say goodbye, but we didn't seem to have a choice. These four walls had seen the best and the worst of me. Of us. It kept all our secrets; in return, we promised to care for it and make it a home. Now, I had no choice but to abandon it; the only comfort was knowing it didn't die alone. It died with you and with a piece of my soul, and the three of us will be bonded together for eternity.

I turned the knob as I whispered a silent thank you to our home, my fingertips sizzling with the heat as my skin began to melt against the metal. I couldn't even tell if the pain was real anymore.

I stumbled onto the front porch, gasping for breath as the cold air of the night cooled my burning body. I ran toward the grass and fell to my knees as I cried and screamed and begged for God to bring you back. It wasn't your time yet; I still needed you, and I couldn't understand how He could be so selfish.

What's a few more decades in the grand scheme of things?

I sat on the lawn, tiny beads of blood forming on my skin as the grass pricked my legs, cold sweat dripping down my back. You hadn't mowed the lawn in months, so I leaned my full weight on the grass a little harder this time; the pain of the new tiny blades cutting into my skin reminded me of you, and I smiled at the memory. Each sharp sting was a reminder that pain could still coexist with love, that even in destruction, traces of you lingered in the smallest of sensations. It hurt to feel, and yet it grounded me, tethering me to the reality of what we had shared.

I didn't want to correlate pain with the thought of you, but right now, at this moment, watching our life go up in flames, it was all I had, and I wasn't ready to let go.

I tried to be brave and look up at the house as I watched everything we owned burn to the ground. All of the memories and stories we created were fading, and even though the heat from the fire was still scorching my face, I stayed put, because the house deserved for me to grieve it and pay my respects to the life we had.

I sat there for a few minutes, and a few more minutes passed before I saw the familiar red and blue lights in the distance. I couldn't hear the sirens just yet; the flames were so deafening that I didn't hear them until they were parked in front of the house—or what was left of it.

Paramedics and firefighters came rushing toward me, bombarding me with questions.

"Are you badly hurt?"

"Is there anybody else inside?"

"Do you know what happened?"

"What's your name?"

"Where does it hurt the most?"

"What happened?"

"What happened?"

"What happened…"

So many questions…

I didn't feel like answering any of them. I just sat there, silent tears soaking my face and neck, watching the firefighters as they did an immaculate job of putting out the destruction. Thousands of gallons of water flooded what was left of our home, and by the time they were done, the house looked like it was crying too.

I felt someone's hand on my shoulder; it was rough and calloused, but his touch was tender and cautious.

"Give us a minute," he told the paramedic who was unsuccessfully trying to gauge and cleanse my wounds.

I was being extremely uncooperative; it was like trying to bandage a dead woman. I figured it was appropriate since I was already dead inside.

I recognized the man's voice, kind and raspy, although it felt like I had heard it a lifetime ago.

It was the officer who called to tell me you had—

I couldn't bear to think about it. Not just yet.

I looked at him slowly, my spine cracking as I turned my head, hollow-eyed and empty inside. He stared straight into me; I could see how sorry he felt for me, desperate to comfort the stranger whose world he had shattered just a few hours before. He was an older man, probably in his mid-sixties, with a receding hairline and kind eyes. His mustache covered part of his upper lip, and the wrinkles on his forehead told me he had lived a thousand lifetimes in the span of his career.

We didn't speak for a few moments, looking at each other silently, a quiet agreement of understanding and heartbreak. There was a heaviness in his eyes, the kind you only see in someone who has carried too many ghosts already. He looked at me not like a name in his report, but like another weight he would have to shoulder, another memory that would haunt him long after his shift ended. Tears were pooling in the corners of my eyes, and it was at that moment, without any warning or obligation, that he pulled me into a gentle hug. Instead of pulling away, I let him hold me.

"I'm so sorry, kiddo," he said as he patted my back.

By now, snot was coming out of my nose as I heaved and sobbed into his chest. At that moment, I felt cared for, I felt safe. It also felt strangely familiar, and it wasn't until I could compose myself for long enough to take a deep breath that I noticed it. He was wearing the same cologne my grandpa used to wear when I was a kid. The scented memory comforted me, making me feel like he was here with me, holding onto me through the arms of this kind stranger.

I pulled away slowly, a slight, almost minuscule smile of gratitude tracing my lips. I looked at him gratefully, wiping the tears, snot, soot, and sweat from my face.

"I thought officers were supposed to deliver bad news in person," I said inquisitively.

"Yeah." He paused, looking down shyly. "Well, when we collected his phone, I saw about thirty missed calls. I know it's not the call you wanted, but I didn't want to keep you waiting. I'm sorry if I made the wrong choice, but I would've liked to know, you know?"

I nodded. It was a lose-lose situation, but the uncertainty and agony were killing me, so I understood where he was coming from.

I looked terrible. Blood and welts covered my entire body. I let the paramedics bandage me up properly, stitch my knee, and clean the wounds to the best of their ability in the limited space the ambulance provided. They insisted I go to the hospital, but I refused. The officer asked me to recount what happened, and with a knot in my stomach and a stifled scream in my throat, I summarized the story as quickly as I could. I couldn't fully recount it yet, and he knew I wasn't ready. But I told him enough to satisfy him.

When the paramedics left us to finish the procedures, I looked at the officer and whispered:

"Could I borrow $10? I promise I'll pay you back," I said, my voice raspy from the soot residing in the back of my throat.

"Where's your wallet?" he asked me. A gentle but mischievous arch in his eyebrows told me he was half-heartedly joking. We both knew the answer, but his off-beat sense of humor managed to cheer me up a little. We chuckled. Despite the tragedy, I was thankful for this man. He destroyed my world, condemning me to what felt like everlasting darkness, but at the same time, he showed me a small ray of light. I immediately associated him with the theater masks. The dichotomy of Melpomene and Thalia reminded me that you can feel pain and happiness simultaneously, and that was my new reality.

"Where do you think you're headed? We need to take you to the hospital to monitor your vitals, and I need to finish my report with you in a few days," he said, with the fake authoritative voice a parent uses on a small child.

"I'm exhausted," I begged. "I can't do this tonight, and I can't stay at the hospital. Can I give you the address and phone number of where I'll be? You can call or stop by anytime. I just need all this to stop for a little bit. I can't take it anymore," I said sincerely.

He looked at me reluctantly. Legally, there were other procedures he needed to follow, but for some reason, he had developed a soft spot for me, and I could only imagine how pitiful and broken I looked. I'm sure it wasn't the first time in his career he bent some rules. He huffed as he gave me a notepad to write down the details of where I'd be. He then pulled out two twenty-dollar bills and one ten, placing them in my hand.

I gave him back $40. "This is all I need to cover the train ticket."

"We can give you a ride to the station," he said.

"I'd rather walk. I need to clear my head a little, plus the night air feels nice."

"Aren't you in pain? How can you even walk?" Concern clouded his eyes as he looked at the stitches on my knee.

"I feel pretty numb at this point," I said reassuringly. More like dead, at least on the inside.

He nodded and pushed the money back toward me. "Get yourself some food and something to drink too. Dinner's on me; it's the least I can do." He handed me back the forty dollars with an air of finality that told me there was no changing his mind.

Another round of tears threatened to fall down my face.

"Thank you... for everything," I whispered as I gave him a small kiss on the cheek. I started walking away with nothing but my clothes and the guitar across my back.

"Wait!" he shouted as he caught up to me. "Take my card, please; don't hesitate to ask if you need anything. We have many resources that can help guide you if you need them at any point. And normally, I don't do this, but I would really appreciate it if you could give me a ring once you get to where you're going, just to know you're safe. My daughter says I tend to worry too much, but you can never be too careful, I don't think."

I nodded.

"You remind me of her—my daughter," he confessed as he showed me the small picture in his wallet of a girl, around my age, with a bright smile and curious gaze. We had the same eyes.

"She must be lucky to call you Dad," I said as I thought about all the ways in which my dad couldn't be there for me. I smiled as I gave him my word to call and placed his card in my back pocket. I turned around and walked away. It was about a twenty minute walk to the train station, but between the limp on my knee and the exhaustion, it took me closer to forty to finally make it. I was dehydrated, in pain, and scared. I smelled disgusting and was filthy from all the smoke and sweat. I was pathetic, and I was broken, but at least I had a place to go.

Nobody was concerned about my state when I arrived at the train station. The 2:32 AM train didn't provide services to influential businessmen or high-end lawyers. It housed homeless people, hookers, and crack addicts that probably smelled better than I did, but everyone minded their own business. We were all lost, so we walked numbly and alert, hoping to stumble into something worth chasing. Despite being broken, there was an air of togetherness and empathy that felt welcoming. I was thankful for it. There were only eight people on the train, so I had a wide variety of seats to pick from. Once I found one in the back corner, away from the doors and as isolated as possible, I sat down. As I heard the hiss of the doors closing, I cried once more. I cried for you; I cried for me, for what we had, and for what will never be. I cried out of anger and frustration, but also out of happiness and gratitude because I was lucky enough to have known love and been loved, and not many people experienced that.

I held my guitar like you would hold a baby, resting my head on its neck as I closed my eyes. But even as I clutched it, I couldn't shake the truth; you had been slipping away from me long before tonight. The laughter, the patience, the softness I loved most in you had been dimming piece by piece, leaving me to grieve fragments of you long before your body was gone. Still, knowing you were truly lost—that there was no chance left—felt like a wound that would never stop bleeding. I tried to fall asleep, hoping that all of the ache and draining misery I was feeling would soon disappear, hoping against hope that if I fell asleep on this midnight train, God and all the heavens would be kind enough to let me die, because living did not seem worth it without you next to me.

It sounded tragic and cliché, but it would be different if you were still here. A burnt home wouldn't hurt as much if you were still here with me. I would've slept anywhere with you; under a bridge or in a mansion, it would have made no difference. If I had caught you cheating, or if I had slipped up somehow—if we had gotten divorced after a plate-throwing, punching-holes-in-the-wall, neighbors-calling-the-cops kind of fight and kicked you out—it would be different. Because those words would carry no meaning. I would still know you and I existed together in this intricate world and under the same galaxy. I would know that you are okay. But now you are gone, and I will have to wait until I die for us to see each other again and have our adventures in eternity.

But that's just it; the words we exchanged last night did carry meaning. They carried a fatal meaning that had the indecency to dictate the rest of our lives—and the end of yours. They killed you and left me wishing I was dead. These thoughts consumed every part of my brain. I didn't know how to even begin processing what happened tonight, but the train's metric movement and rhythmic sound against the tracks had me in a trance. My eyelids grew heavy, and I was finally able to sleep. Thankfully, I didn't replay our last conversation like I feared I would. I wasn't forced to relive the trauma. Instead, I dreamt of you. I dreamt you were finally happy and free—free of problems and all worries—and at that moment, I felt at peace, too. It was a peace that felt both foreign and familiar—I had already been grieving you in small, quiet ways, long before this night. Your absence had carved a hollowness in my heart, and though you were gone in life, I had been saying goodbye piece by piece, preparing for this moment without even realizing it.

I guess dying of love is the most romantic of deaths, but for some reason, I'm still standing. I don't know what it is, but something is keeping me here, and I need to find out what. Many people have come and gone, but there is only one person who has suffered through worse fates than mine, and she will be the only one who can help me, if there is even a remote possibility of getting through this.

Grandma always knows what to say.

She always has.

PART TWO

month one

THE DAY AFTER

I'M NOT SURE if I fell asleep in the end. I'm unsure how much time had passed since the end of my life as I knew it, and a chapter I did not know was written. The first rays of dawn grazed my eyelashes, and as I opened them, I realized enough time had passed for my tears to dry and create long, crusty streams down my cheeks. The screeching sound of the slowing wheels against the tracks shot sharp bursts of pain up my spine. My breath was bitter; I felt drenched in silent thoughts and heartbreak, and my head was pounding—no doubt a mix of dehydration from my tears, the soreness in my body, the smoke I inhaled, and the empty space in my heart, so hollow that it felt as if a black hole was sucking my soul from inside my body.

I was confused for a moment. Why was I on a train? And most importantly, where was I headed? I blinked three times, and then I felt the dread all over again. I remembered the fight, the screaming, the call, the cigarette, and the fire. I could see it flashing through my mind like a film reel burning in reverse, jagged and sharp, the faint scent of smoke clinging to my throat and the crackle of wood snapping in my ears. I had to use all the effort I had left to get up from my seat and make my way out into the train station. My body was tired and sore, but my heart knew where to take me. The route to Grandma's house was very simple; it was only a fifteen-minute walk from here—four minutes if you took a cab—but I would rather save the money the officer lent me, and quite frankly, I didn't want to be surrounded by anyone else. I slowly walked off the train and started toward the lobby, following the people, dreading having to explain everything to my grandma, terrified that recounting the events would make them real.

A few steps from the lobby, I walked past an old man sitting spread-legged on a lawn chair, using a coat as a blanket, and he had a nearly empty lollipop jar next to him. The hood on his jacket covered most of his face, but I could hear faint, peaceful noises every time he snored. The sight of him warmed my heart. I reached into my back pocket to find two dollars and fifty cents. I put the money in his jar and gave a silent prayer, wishing he would be okay. I heard the clink of the quarters as they reached the bottom of the jar, and I stopped dead in my tracks with my hand on the lobby's doorknob as I heard an impatient, yet all-too-familiar voice snarl at me—

"I'm not a fucking hobo!"

I gasped.

Surely, I must have been imagining things. It wasn't until the woman—not a man—looked up in my direction that I saw her reflection in the glass panels of the double doors. I turned around slowly, too stunned to speak. She had bent down and was struggling to pick up the two quarters from the jar that danced around her fingertips, but there was no mistaking her posture and body movement—it was her. Grandma.

It wasn't until she managed to pick up both quarters that she straightened up and met my eyes. Immediately, I saw her expression soften; I saw the love and compassion in her eyes I had been craving. The tension she held in her shoulders had been replaced by a sigh of relief and a crooked smile.

"You made it!" she spoke softly as she slowly got up from her chair with the help of her cane. The kinks in her spine from sleeping on the lawn chair reminded her that time is unforgiving and aging is inevitable.

"How did you know I'd be here?" I was so glad to see her, I struggled to process any words. I couldn't move.

147

"I came to get you, Pumpkin," she said, her voice soft. "I saw it on the news—the whole thing. Scared the living shit out of me. I tried calling, but it went straight to voicemail, and that's when I knew I had to come here and wait for you. You think I'd let my baby girl face all this alone?" I blinked back twice. "But, Jesus, what happened to you today was *fucked up*. No one should ever have to go through that." She opened her arms towards me and gave me a small, inviting smile.

I was momentarily taken aback, if a little amused, by her choice of words. Still, I felt a rush of love and affection for the woman who had clearly spent a significant portion of the night waiting for me, sitting on an uncomfortable chair in a cold, outdated lobby that had had the same snacks in the vending machine for the past two decades. I looked into her eyes and saw that familiar wittiness, edginess, and, most of all, tenderness that I have kept so close to my heart all these years—but there was something else as well, something that wasn't there before. A flicker of heaviness. Grief? Fear? I wasn't sure, but it unsettled me. I didn't dwell on that thought for too long, though, because the image of my grandma sleeping on a lawn chair in the cold to wait for me broke what was left of my heart.

I ran to her with so much force that I was afraid I'd push her too hard and make her fall. She was shorter than me by a few inches, but just like when I was a little kid, I could still fit my chin in the nape of her neck when I hugged her. The winds from the west blew her scent in my direction, and the mix of cinnamon and sweet perfume brought happy memories of when my life was simple and safe. I wanted to stay in this moment forever. It was her newfound tact that brought me back to the present.

She breathed—and aggressively exhaled—into the back of my head.

"Shit. You fucking stink, baby! Come here, let me look at you." She wrinkled her nose, but her hands fussed at my shoulders, like she was making sure I was real.

She said it so casually and innocently that I found myself laughing within seconds, my shoulders shaking as I laughed and sobbed all at once. I wasn't an expert on aging, but I could see how time had shaped my grandma—etching wrinkles into her skin, softening her frame, and loosening the filter she once carried so tightly. The swearing felt less like rebellion and more like honesty finally freed, and somehow, it only made her sweetness shine brighter.

I caught a glimpse of the TV inside the lobby and felt a pang in my stomach when I recognized what used to be our home on the news. I saw what used to be my safety embraced by flames in every corner. The house seemed smaller now, consumed by smoke and the ashes of who we were. Five hours ago, it was a regular home, full of love and problems, like any other house. But now it looked helplessly vulnerable. Devoured in flames that screamed freedom and authority. I understood then. My life had become local news. I realized that everyone at the train station was staring at me. I was not used to being such a poetic disaster.

People were drawn to tragedy, and right now, I was tragedy personified.

I pulled back from the hug, and that was when I really took the time to look at her. She was wearing light purple leggings, a baggy flowery nightgown, and a pair of Converse—one white and one gray. She wore glasses that made her eyeballs look enormous, another pair hanging from her shirt, and a long necklace with the biggest Tree of Life I'd ever seen. She took off her jacket to reveal the pink beanie I had knitted all those years ago—the one with a hole in the left ear—and she was sucking on a red lollipop that was dyeing her tongue scarlet. It was like a color-blind clown had dressed her.

When did my grandma become such a hippie?

"It's going to be okay, sweetie," she said as she squeezed my hands. "I changed the sheets before coming here to make sure you slept in a clean bed and cleared out the closet for you to have your own space, which, now that I think about it, is kind of fucked up since you literally have no clothes, but we'll go shopping tomorrow," she said reassuringly.

I nodded absentmindedly.

What was up with all the cursing?

The last time I saw her, she was as good as a nun, and now it was like she'd been raised by pirates.

She grinned and offered me a purple lollipop from her nightgown pocket.

"How many of those have you had?" I asked.

"I suspect about fourteen, but don't worry, I've got a bunch more at home. You can have the whole jar if it makes you smile. I bought a family-size one, just like the one Derek bought me the first time we met," she said, her eyes turning somber with grief and ache.

At the sound of your name, my stomach lurched. For a split second, I'd forgotten—forgotten you were gone. But then it hit me all over again, the way it always did, a hollow weight dropping straight through me.

She missed you too—I could tell. She held my hand and squeezed it twice, telling me the three words I needed to hear the most.

"Let's go home."

I wondered if Dad knew—if he'd be sober enough to care—but the truth was, I couldn't lean on him now. Grandma was the one I needed to be with.

I sighed and hoped the small smile I showed her told her everything I couldn't. It broke me, realizing the place I once called home had ceased to be, but I felt safe knowing I was returning to a place that had never left me. I zipped up her jacket to protect her from the cold and pinched the lawn chair between my armpit and elbow. With the lollipop between my teeth, I squeezed her hand and followed her lead. I made a mental note to ask her about her fashion choice and compulsive cursing later, but I needed to stay present for now.

I remembered a phrase she always said to me growing up: "Every day is a chance to begin again." The only difference was that tomorrow would mark the beginning of the rest of my life—a life without you in it. For a moment, I wavered, unsure if I could step into a life where you weren't waiting for me.

Then I let my fingers tighten around hers, drawing strength from her presence. If I was going to move forward, it would be by leaning on her, like I had always done.

I took a deep breath. Fingers interlaced, we were coming home.

As soon as I walked inside her house, I was greeted by a home that had not changed in fifty years. Porcelain dolls and houseplants that were older than me decorated the living room. Flowered tapestry and hand-knitted blankets were placed strategically on the couch, and one of the Lay-Z Boys recliners sat directly in front of the box TV, two antennas protruding from behind it, and one wooden foldable table where she had dinner every night, watching *Wheel of Fortune* or *Family Feud*. All I wanted was to go upstairs and sleep, but I had to do something first.

"Can I borrow your phone, Grandma?"

She raised her eyebrows in confusion as she nodded and pointed me toward the kitchen, where I knew I would find the house phone.

I pulled the wrinkled card from my back pocket and waited for the phone to ring. It was late, but he said to call as soon as I got home.

"Officer Jones," I heard on the other end of the line. His raspy voice had traces of sleep, making it sound like I had awoken someone from the dead, but as soon as he heard my voice, he cleared his throat and had the same kind quality he did when I last spoke to him—a lifetime ago, though it couldn't have been more than three or four hours.

"Hey Officer, it's Noah. I'm sorry to wake you. I just wanted to let you know I'm already home with my grandma. And to thank you again for everything," I whispered.

"Noah. I'm glad you made it all right," he whispered. "I will be keeping in touch these next few days, okay? For now, get some rest. You've had a long night. Let me know if you need anything."

"Okay, you too. Thank you."

I was about to hang up when I heard him call my name.

"And Noah, thank you for calling. I really appreciate you letting me know you got there safe."

"Have a good night, Officer Jones," I said as I hung up softly.

I turned to my grandma, who was standing behind me, pretending to put away dishes.

"That was the officer who was called to Derek's crash, and he was also the one who came to my rescue when our house burned down. He told me to let him know when I was with you. He was like an angel in disguise."

"I see," my grandma said as she came over and wiped my face with a damp towel. I was filthy and covered in soot. "How about you go take a nice shower and get in bed? We can talk tomorrow. There are clean towels, a toothbrush, and one of my pajamas for you to sleep in on top of the bed. Oh, and I left some Neosporin for your hands and arms. You don't want those to get infected," she said, gently squeezing my cheek.

I smiled at her, infinitely grateful for her support and for welcoming me back into her life with open arms. I hugged her.

"Thank you. I love you so much." I planted a kiss on her forehead, and we both went upstairs.

Feeling sore and exhausted the following day, I was awoken by a loud clang against the wooden boards beneath me. I jolted awake and saw my grandma sitting in the recliner beside my bed, a tray in hand and an innocent smile that was borderline mischievous.

"What the hell was that?" I croaked, suddenly aware of every jolt and twitch in my body as I tried to sit up. My arms trembled under me, muscles spent from crawling out of the fire, every vertebra screaming in protest. My skin was streaked with welts and scrapes, bruised and raw, as if a train had run me over—not once, but three times.

"Sorry, sweetcakes, I accidentally dropped a fork; I didn't mean to wake you. Also, we don't say 'hell' in this house," she said as she traced a cross with her thumb and forefinger on her forehead, middle of her chest, and both shoulders. "That's fucked up and could upset the man upstairs. I brought you breakfast, though! Your favorite: grilled cheese sandwich and honey lavender tea."

I looked at the fork on the floor suspiciously. She may be old, but she's as clever as always, and her tricks never changed.

"You don't need a fork to eat grilled cheese," I commented accusingly.

She stared through me; a now fully mischievous grin that silently screamed "busted" traced its way onto her lips as she deviated from the subject.

"Well... you're awake anyway, so why don't we start from the beginning?"

I took a deep breath and groaned.

"Ugh, do I have to?"

"You absolutely do! But first, eat this; the cheese is melty, and you look like you haven't been fed in months," she said, no trace of judgment in her words.

"And you want all the details, I assume?" I scratched my head in a failed attempt to organize my ideas.

"Consider it your final step in the roommate interview process."

"I thought you said we were already roommates."

"That depends entirely on your storytelling techniques and whether or not you eat that sandwich," she said, glaring playfully.

I rolled my eyes and rubbed my head, hoping it would make the headache disappear like magic.

"If I tell you, will you explain why you are cursing like a pirate and dressing like you don't own a mirror?"

"Cross my heart," she said as she winked at me and traced a cross with her small, frail finger on her chest.

And so I folded in on myself, knees tucked under my chin, regretting every single movement and wincing my way through the pain, beginning the tale of tragedy I called my life. I told her everything: how it started, how it ended, the good times, the bad ones, what I said and what you said, how I felt, and why I felt it. Through it all, she didn't interrupt me once; it was a no-questions-asked, unwritten rule. She just listened. It had been so long since I'd been heard...

Once I finished, I immediately felt lighter. All the pressure, dread, and guilt I had been feeling was somehow lifted away from me, and I could finally breathe.

My grandma didn't say anything. She just sat next to me in my bed and handed me a green lollipop. I looked at her...

"Fucked up, huh?"

"Very..." she answered introspectively, and we both nodded, acknowledging the misfortune.

"By the way," she added, putting Neosporin on my stitched-up knee, "Derek's parents left a message this morning. They said they spoke with Officer Jones but really need to talk to you. They're still in town, in a hotel. Give them a call when you're ready."

I felt my stomach sink again. I had been so wrapped up in my own grief that I hadn't thought about calling them yet. I pressed my lips together, feeling a tight knot in my throat, closing my eyes as hard as I could.

I'm sorry, Derek.

"Hey, look at me," Grandma said, lifting my chin gently with her hand.

I met her eyes and felt the weight of her gaze—steady, warm, and unwavering. In that moment, I realized she had lost a child too, and somehow, she still knew how to guide me through this. I nodded slowly, deciding to trust her in how to handle this conversation, knowing she would help me tell your parents what they needed to hear.

"Eat your sandwich first. We'll worry about that after your stomach's settled," she commanded.

I nodded and ripped little pieces of sandwich with my fingers. Butter seeped into my skin, coating them with a shiny layer of grease. It was the first solid food I had had in almost a full day, and I savored it slowly, hoping the longer I chewed, the more I could postpone the call.

"Okay. I did my part," I said. "Now it's your turn. What's up with all the cursing and candy?"

She sighed, green-stained teeth showing.

"So... about a year and a half ago, I had a little mishap, an accident of sorts."

"A car accident!?" I half-screamed, half-interrupted.

"No. You could call it a walking accident."

I thought she was being sarcastic, but while I looked at her incredulously, her mouth didn't move a single muscle, so I kept quiet and let her continue.

"You know the sliding glass door with butterfly stickers I have downstairs?" she asked.

"Uh-huh."

"Well, before the stickers, I'd spent one morning cleaning the windows and really outdid myself. They were literally spotless. Later that afternoon, I went to check the lights outside and... smack!" She tapped her forehead gently. "Hit that big ol' glass door head-on. Left me with stitches, a bruised ego, and a little note from the universe reminding me that I don't bounce like I used to."

I blinked. "That's why there's a huge crack in the door?"

"Bingo. And after that, things started... changing a bit. Sometimes I forget stuff, sometimes I drop fuck bombs like candy at Halloween," she said, shrugging with mock innocence.

"F-bombs, you mean?"

"No, *fuck* bombs, honey. I say *fuck*, I don't go around saying 'F' all over the place; that makes no sense... People would think I lost my marbles.

She leaned closer, lowering her voice. "Anyway, the neighbor heard the windows shatter and called an ambulance. That's when they told me I've got early-stage dementia. Been creeping along ever since, nothing I can hide from you anymore."

I frowned. "But... Why didn't you tell me before? Derek and I came to see you over a year ago."

"Ah, Pumpkin, I didn't want to worry you. Birthday, lollipops, happy to see you… I felt mostly fine then. And when you called a few months ago, I felt you needed me more than I needed to unload on you. Some things a grandma keeps tucked away, you understand?"

I nodded slowly. Her eyes glistened with a mix of pride and worry.

It bothered me that she felt like she couldn't call me. I didn't resent her, but I wished I could worry about her as much as she worried about me. It explained everything. That's what I recognized in her eyes back at the train station. It was fear—not of me, but of forgetting.

My heart sank. I had been so wrapped up in my own life that I forgot to call her every week and ask how she was really doing. I teared up, about to apologize, when she put her finger on my mouth rather sternly.

"Shhhhh." She pressed a finger to my lips. "No time for guilt trips. We'll save that for when I'm dead. Right now, you need your strength, kiddo."

She started getting out of bed and motioned for me to do the same. She may have been old, but she had more energy than I ever did.

"Do you plan on dying anytime soon?" I asked her, hoping the sarcasm was bleeding out of my pores.

"Not just yet! First, I gotta make sure you get back on your feet and that I leave my affairs in order. Now chop-chop! But brush your teeth first, your breath smells. Meet you downstairs in five!"

And with that, she left. I couldn't believe she was playing the *soon-to-be-dead* card on me. That's such a grandma move—guilting you into productivity. Also, I felt like it was a little too soon to be pulling that card, but the worst part was that it always worked…

I eased out of bed slowly, every movement calculated, every shift threatening to make me scream. My muscles burned, protesting even the smallest effort, and the hardwood floor felt sharp beneath my feet. I used the wall for support, but before heading to the bathroom, I popped my head out the door.

"I love you!" I yelled, my voice raw and rasping, my throat scorched from the ashes. The metallic tang on my tongue made every word feel like it was ripping through my lungs.

"Love you lots-a-tots, kid!" she answered back.

Later that afternoon, we sat down at the dinner table and had a steaming cup of tea. The flower-laced white cloth over the glass table reminded me of old times, and the taste of the butter cookies that crumbled inside my mouth comforted me, bringing memories of when I was a young child and hadn't truly understood what loss felt like. The yellow rotary dial phone sat heavy between us, in the middle of the circular dining table, challenging me to make the phone call.

"It's been almost a full day. What should I say?" I asked, terrified of not knowing how to handle this.

"Just tell them the truth. Let them take the lead."

Her voice was soft but steady, like the hum of an old lullaby. She reached across the table and brushed her thumb over my knuckles, warm and certain.

I took a deep breath and dialed each digit, one by one, waiting for the circle to do a full rotation each time I spun it.

Fifteen seconds passed before I heard a voice on the other end of the line. I know because I counted each weak pulse of my beating heart, begging me to hang up the phone to avoid hearing your parent's broken hearts.

Your dad picked up, clearing his throat before he spoke. His voice sounded heavy, wet, and tired. But his tone was even and composed, just like it had always been. I was amazed at his strength and wished to have even an ounce of it.

"Hello?" he said.

I waited three beats before answering. My throat was dry; it felt like sandpaper, and I couldn't find the words to begin.

I looked at my grandma, and she gave me a small smile as she placed her fragile hand gently on my back, steady as a stone, giving me the courage I was looking for.

I cleared my throat as well. The familiar sting in the back of my eyes prickled my eyelids and made me salivate, soothing my throat for a moment before I felt a ball of fire nudge my windpipe.

"Um—hello, Mr. Burke. I—It's Noah." My name came out more of a sob rather than an actual syllable.

There was silence on the other line. A hollow static hum. For a moment, I thought he had hung up, but before I could ask, I heard him sigh onto the phone.

"Noah." A pause. A breath. "Hi. I... We've been meaning to call, but—" His voice caught. He cleared his throat sharply, like he could erase the crack. "Officer Jones told us what happened. We saw the news. We're... we're so sorry. We wanted to give you some space before we called."

I gripped the cord so tight it bit into my skin.

"No, please, I'm sorry. I am so, so sorry. For everything. I should've called sooner. I just didn't know what to say. I was so embarrassed, and I thought you would hate me and blame me and I—I am so sorry."

My voice caught on repeat like a scratched record. My grandma slid a box of tissues across the table.

Your dad spoke like each word was a stone he had to push uphill.

"Is it okay if I... if I tell my wife you're on the line? She's been... she's been desperate to hear your voice." His tone cracked open, heavy with swallowed tears. "She's been devastated—we both have been—but she's... she's barely gotten out of bed today. She drifts off, and when she wakes up... God, it's like reliving it all over again. I'm worried about her; I don't know how to help."

Silent sobs choked my lungs. I closed my eyes to steady myself and tried to take a deep breath, resting my forehead on my closed fist.

"Can I speak to you both? You can put me on speaker if that's okay."

"Of course. I was at the front desk getting water. Give me one minute."

I heard silence for a few seconds and then a soft knock on their bedroom door. I heard the key card beep, then the heavy thud of the door closing. From what I gathered, your mom was drifting in and out of sleep, but when your dad told her I called, she scrambled to her feet and cried my name over and over—hopeless, broken, wild. She sobbed so hard I could hear her palms slap the dresser for balance. Between raw screams and grieving, awful sobs, she fumbled with her hands to grab the phone so desperately that it fell on the floor.

I pressed my forehead to the table, squeezing my skull like maybe if I held it tight enough it would stop splitting in two.

"Noah—Noah—Noah," she gasped through the phone.

"Mrs. Burke…" I whispered between raspy heaves. "I am so sorry…"

We couldn't form real sentences. Just three people crying into the void.

My grandma silently wiped her cheeks beside me and set a warm palm over my fidgeting hand, grounding me like an anchor. I slid her a tissue with shaking hands.

"Noah," your mom finally said, voice small and hoarse, "We… We saw it on the news. I am so glad you made it out. Are you hurt?"

I couldn't believe it—their hearts were still big enough to worry about me while theirs had been shattered.

"I'm okay. Just a few cuts and burns, nothing major. I'm so sorry I couldn't call before. Derek and I had gotten into a huge fight, and I told him to leave, and he was drunk and I—" My voice crumpled. "I am so, so sorry, so sorry, I am so…" I stammered. I couldn't finish the sentence. Begging for their forgiveness was all I could do.

"Aww, sweetie… it wasn't your fault," your mom sobbed, but it sounded like she was trying to convince herself more than me.

"He hated being told what to do," your dad said flatly. I had the impression that he couldn't bring himself to say your name. His voice was so calm it was jarring, like a man standing in a house on fire. "I… I pushed him anyway. I pushed too hard. I left him upset and then left your house without much of an explanation. I was so proud and stubborn. He never even wanted to take over the company. I could tell, and I forced him regardless, and now he—"

"Please stop," I begged. "We had been in a bad spot for months. He shut me out too. It wasn't just you. I just wish I hadn't started that argument yesterday. Maybe then—"

"No," your dad cut in, firm and quiet. "No maybes. Don't do that."

There was a long silence, like he'd run out of words. Like we all had.

"Sweetie," your mom said, her voice trembling like glass about to crack, "we don't blame you. I only wish he had come to us—or to you—and that we could've fixed it together. But what happened… wasn't your fault. It was an accident. And we… we still love you."

I nodded even though they couldn't see me. Tears slid down my neck.

In my mind, I heard your voice—warm, and teasing.

That's how they say 'I love you,' you know. All clipped like that. Drives me nuts.

"I just feel like a part of me died in that car too. I really thought he would come home," I whispered.

"And he would've," your dad said, though his voice broke on the word. "But Officer Jones found skid marks. Said maybe an animal jumped out. He swerved. Lost control."

I heard your mom crying into her hands, her sobs muffled by wet heaves, her throat raw.

My heart felt like it was going to explode. My eyes were swollen, and my face was hot—it was so difficult to think.

I was drenched in sweat; my grandma brushed the hair that was sticking to my forehead.

Your dad drew in a sharp breath, like he was steeling himself, and then his voice shifted—quieter, flatter, like he'd put on a mask.

"The funeral will be Friday," he said. His voice caught on the word and he cleared his throat roughly. "They… they'll release the body that morning. I—" A choked sob cut through, and then another, as if he was trying to smother the grief with his own hand. He forced his tone steady again. His words were precise, surgical, like if he spoke too softly, they'd dissolve. "I'll handle the arrangements. I just need your signature on a few things."

I was grateful for your dad, because I couldn't even begin to fathom the logistics of losing you, let alone planning a funeral. The thought of it felt unbearable—like the world expected me to stand beside your coffin when all I wanted was to be buried inside it with you.

Together forever. Forever and always.

He paused, breathing ragged, each word shattering on the way out.

"Is this your grandma's phone number?" he asked. "Can we reach you here?"

"Yes," I said quickly, almost tripping over the word. "Anything you need. Please. Anything at all."

"Good." He exhaled, short and clipped, like he was trying to finish before his voice gave out. "We'll see you Friday."

"Wait," I blurted. "Doesn't someone have to… to identify—"

There was a long pause. I heard muffled static, a shaky inhale.

Your mom spoke then, soft and trembling like a sheet in the wind.

"We… Oh God… We already did, sweetie," she whispered, and then stopped. I heard her trying to breathe through a sob. "The officer called us last night. We… went to the morgue this morning." Her voice wavered like she was about to splinter into pieces.

The word *morgue* landed like a stone in my chest.

Cold. Sterile. The opposite of you.

An irrational thought burst through the fog; I wanted to go there. To see you. To wrap you in a blanket so you wouldn't be cold, to smooth back your hair, to tell you that you could come home now. The thought gutted me, sharp and senseless, but it rooted itself deep in my core anyway.

"I… I didn't want to," she stammered. "But my husband… he couldn't… he was our baby boy… he just stood there, and I—" Her voice cracked and disappeared. I heard a chair scrape and something crash. She sobbed like she was trying to tear the grief out of her body. "I kept thinking if I didn't look, it wouldn't be real…"

I pressed my hand hard over my mouth. My vision tunneled. For half a second, my mind pictured what she had seen—your face still, pale—and I nearly threw up.

"Was he—um—" I choked out, unable to finish.

She knew what I was asking. "He looked… like himself," she whispered at last. "Like he was sleeping."

Then silence. Heavy, suffocating, endless.

"I love you both, all of you," I finally said, my voice a rasp. "And I am so sorry."

There was a faint chorus of broken voices.

"So are we," they said, almost together, barely above a whisper.

And we hung up the phone.

I stayed frozen, the phone still pressed to my ear long after the dial tone buzzed. My breath came shallow and fast. My hands shook until I had to set the receiver down or risk dropping it.

My grandma wrapped her arm around my shoulders, pulling me into her side like she used to after nightmares. She didn't say anything—just held on, fierce and warm. I stared at her wrinkled knuckles until they blurred.

In my head, I heard your voice again.

You did good, babe.

The sound of it broke something in my chest, and I let myself fall apart.

month one

DAY TWO

THE CALL WITH your parents left me exhausted, and the following morning I woke up with a knot in my stomach. I had a dream about us, and during the early hours of the night, I got to relive a moment we shared when we first moved in together. We were sitting on the couch, cuddling under a blanket we had knitted together from watching a video on YouTube, and I can't remember exactly where it was, but I distinctly remember watching a scene on a show or a movie where a couple was reminiscing about the idea of Death. Heartbroken about the thought of living without one another, the passing of time, and the importance of goodbyes, they decided to write a letter to each other in life, bidding their goodbyes for when the dreadful time came. It was simple and intimate. It gave them peace, knowing their last words wouldn't go unspoken, regardless of how or when they died.

We were entranced by the gut-wrenching and romantic idea, and that same night, we wrote our vows of Death to one another, unaware that one day, it would become the most important piece of paper I'd ever own. We dropped off both letters at the bank, put them in our deposit safe, and hoped we would never have to read them. Now, years later, that single sheet of paper was all I had left of you—your final goodbye.

I got out of bed at the crack of dawn and showered under cold water, hoping the drastic temperature change would help me feel alive—but the icy sting only made my skin crawl, reminding me of the cold, still weight of a dead body. I shut my eyes to drive the image away, but it only made it more vivid. I was pressing the heels of my hands against my eyelids so hard, black and purple spots danced in the air. My lungs felt hollow, like they couldn't remember how to breathe without you. I took a deep breath and steadied myself against the wall.

I took the earliest train to the city. Only a few people were on board, and the deserted scene reminded me of that awful night. Every sound was too loud in the silence—the squeal of the tracks, the rattle of the windows—as if the world was trying to jolt me awake from a nightmare that wouldn't end. Flashbacks of flames turning to ash—the memory physically hurt my body. I could feel the blisters boiling on my fingers again. I clenched my fist just to keep my hand from melting.

After three stops down memory lane, the train pulled into the downtown station. The bank was only a twelve minute walk, but I was still sore and limping from the cut in my knee, so I walked slowly, each step an act of penance, as if pain might somehow balance the scales.

I sat on the curb outside the bank, waiting for the teller to open the doors so I could retrieve your last words. I saw the first rays of sun peeking through the clouds, but not even the cold breeze against my face kept my clammy hands from sweating. My heart thudded dully in my ears, like it was trying to warn me away from what waited inside.

At nine in the morning, the bank teller unlocked the doors, and I was able to enter. I found myself standing inside an empty lobby. The only two people there were the teller and me.

"Can I help you with something?" she asked inquisitively.

"Um, yeah, I need access to my safe deposit box, please."

"Of course. If you wouldn't mind stepping right over here, I can go ahead and verify your account with us. It won't take more than two minutes."

She kept staring at me as if she were trying to place my face. There was a familiarity she couldn't pinpoint, and I wasn't really up for chitchatting.

"Of course," I said compliantly.

"May I please have your name?"

"Noah," I said. "Noah Emmet."

"Yup! I found your account. Co-owned with Mr. Burke."

I looked at the ground, hoping the sight of my feet would ground me. The sound of your name was a punch to the ribs. I felt dizzy, and I wanted to do this as quickly and painlessly as possible.

"Okay, I will need your key and your ID, please."

Suddenly, I realized I didn't have any kind of identification. Much less a key—it had all burned down in the house.

"Uhh... I don't have either of those things," I confessed.

"Oh, okay. Well, would you be able to go get them and come back? We are open till 5 p.m. today."

I stared at her vacantly while I tried to gather my thoughts. I hadn't even started to think about the process of replacing all the ID cards and documents I'd lost in the fire.

"Um, I don't have them at home either. My house caught on fire two nights ago. I lost everything. I have no wallet, no phone... nothing."

She looked taken aback for a second, and then I saw her connect the dots.

"Noah..." she looked at her computer to verify the name. "And Derek... your husband was driving—" she covered her mouth with her hand. "Oh my God," she mumbled under her breath. "It's you. Oh my God, I am so sorry."

I could barely meet her gaze. So much for being quick and painless, after all.

"Yeah," I nodded. "It's me. I came because Derek left me a letter in the safety box, and a little money we had saved for emergencies. Please, is there anything else we can verify the account with? Our social security numbers? Security questions? Thumbprint or something like that?"

Most of my fingertips were charred from the fire, raw with melted scar tissue and flesh—grabbing the guitar and turning the doorknob had come at a cost. I still couldn't make a fist without wincing, but I hoped she would let me into the box out of pure pity, which is pretty much what ended up happening.

She sighed and looked around her keyboard. I'm not sure what she was looking for—I think she was just trying to find a way to help me.

"Okay, there is a way we may be able to do this. Since one of the co-owners of the deposit box is deceased, if you wouldn't mind giving me both of your social security numbers and a signature so I can compare it, I can make an exception. But I'm so sorry—I have to be legally present at the time of retrieving the artifacts for policy reasons. I don't want you to feel like I'm intruding on your privacy, but I do apologize—it's the only way I could justify this exception."

I nodded in understanding. What's one more pair of eyes, after the whole town saw us on the news? Our lives gutted and displayed like a cautionary tale.

"Sure. I really appreciate it."

She typed some keys into her computer, and after a few minutes of me signing documents and reciting numbers, she let me into the vault. She opened the safety deposit box and then stood in the farthest corner of the vault, giving me as much privacy and space as she could in the confines of such a small room.

The air inside the vault was dry and cold, carrying a faint trace of metal and dust—like time itself had stopped breathing. The tang of it caught in my throat, sharp and bitter, and I gagged quietly before forcing a slow, steady breath. Now I stood in front of the safe, petrified, unable to move and wishing time could stand still just for a minute, leaving me suspended in my grief. If I didn't read your final goodbye, well then maybe it wasn't goodbye after all.

My hands shook as I picked up both pieces of paper. I recognized your handwriting and traced my name with my index finger, remembering how you looked when you wrote a single phrase in the center of the envelope:

"To Noah. Do not open till I'm gone."

Your eyebrows were furrowed, focused on making sure each letter was even, the movements of your wrist slow and methodical.

I clenched the letter to my chest to steady my heartbeat and prepared myself for your farewell.

I lowered myself to the cold vault floor. My knees wobbled as if my bones were hollow. My fingers trembled as I broke the seal and unfolded the page. The words inside were yours—raw, unfiltered, and final. My vision blurred with tears as I read the first line:

"*Dear Noah,*

I suck at writing."

A strangled sound escaped my throat. The words swam, then disappeared altogether, swallowed by the agony residing inside me. I folded the page shut, pressing it to my heart like it was the only thing tethering me to this Earth.

I couldn't do it. Not now. Not yet. I couldn't survive losing you twice in one day.

My hands shook so badly that I had to place the letter against the floor to keep it from wrinkling. The thought of knowing your last words—of closing the book on us—was unbearable.

Please come home… I thought as I sobbed.

I sat on the vestibule floor of the bank for an hour. Defeated, alone, and empty, I slid the letter back into the envelope with shaking hands and tucked it gently into my purse. It felt heavier than stone, like carrying your coffin on my shoulder.

The ride back to the house felt eternal—almost like floating in a black void, chained to the weight of your memory. Once I got home, halfway up the stairs, my knees buckled and the hallway spun. I gripped the banister until it steadied. Maybe it was the grief—or maybe my body was starting to give out on me too. I stumbled my way to my room and got under the covers, clutching the sealed envelope to my heart and squeezing my wedding ring so tight that it cut off my circulation and turned my finger purple.

I set your letter down on my nightstand, carefully, reverently—the way someone might lay down a loaded weapon. It could wait for me. Until I was strong enough.

A few minutes later, sadness sent me into a deep sleep, as if trying to shield me from the misery of losing you.

Luckily… when I felt that moment of absolute peace right before surrendering to exhaustion, I saw you.

I saw you in my dreams, and I saw you in my heart. You reached out, and I saw you. No… I *felt* you.

"*Come home…*" were the last two words I mumbled before we disappeared into nothingness.

As the days went by, so did the legal proceedings. Death certificates, wills, testimonies, funeral arrangements—legal stuff that happens when someone dies… I had no idea how to do this, but luckily, my grandma and your parents were there to help me. I knew it was painful for Grandma too, reliving everything she went through when Grandpa died, but she was my rock, and right now, I couldn't afford to stand on my own.

The funeral was a few days away, and even though all the arrangements were in place, I was dreading seeing you lowered in a casket while I was left on the surface—alone. It was unbearable. The funeral home asked your parents if they would rather have you incinerated or buried, but I couldn't stand the thought of you burning away in a fire. I had already lost our home to those flames. I couldn't lose you that way too. So we agreed a burial would be better. A place where we could come visit you, to remind you that you're still in our hearts.

Two days before the funeral, on a cloudy morning, I heard a soft knock at my door. I slowly opened my eyes to find my grandma's head poking through—almost comically—with the cordless landline in her hand. She was one of the few citizens of the United States who still owned a landline. That thing was older than me, but from the looks of it, it still carried out its job perfectly, which was more than I could say for myself. This, however, wasn't the usual morning ritual, so I already knew something was amiss.

"What's up?" I said, my voice hoarse with the effort of pronouncing the day's first syllables.

"It's for you. Someone named Damian. He says he was a friend of Derek's," my grandma's floating head whispered—rather loudly.

My stomach lurched, and I felt the faint tang of metal in my mouth. Damian was your accountant. If anyone knew the company's hardships and whatever secrets you harbored around work, it was him. I remembered your dad mentioning that Damian called to say you were ignoring him. How did I not think of calling him? How stupid could I be? He had the one thing I needed. He had answers.

I jolted awake. "Give it to me!" I whispered just as loudly, flailing and waving my arms in a ridiculous attempt to emphasize the urgency of the matter and get my grandma to move quicker.

The rest of her body materialized to accompany her head, and she mimicked my gestures with an irritated and exaggerated expression as she walked toward me. She handed me the phone and sat in front of me, watching me intently as she pulled an orange lollipop from her robe pocket.

"Damian, hey," I said, the alertness in my voice betraying my effort to seem casual. Something told me this conversation would give me the closure and explanations I deserved—but it would come with a cost. Judging by the short pause before he spoke, I could already tell this was not a call to give his condolences. There was bad news at the end of this call. I could feel it pressing against my chest like a stone.

"Hey Noah... how's it going?" he said softly, barely audibly. Curiosity and shame gave his tone a particular quality.

"I've seen better days…" I chuckled. A dry, sarcastic chuckle, but a chuckle nonetheless.

"I can't even imagine. Listen, I just want to say how sorry—"

"Please don't," I interrupted. "It's okay. I know what you're going to say, and I appreciate it, but I would rather skip the pleasantries. Why are you calling?"

My tone had a trace of impatience, but I knew he wasn't taking it personally. He could hear my desperation and need for answers through my words. That's the thing when you've known people for years—there's no need for bullshit or small talk, and I was incredibly thankful for it.

"Okay, I'll cut straight to the chase. As you know, after the company officially filed for bankruptcy, Derek had to—"

"What?" I interrupted, confusion furrowing the space between my eyebrows as the wheels in my brain spun a million miles a minute.

There was a pause on the other end of the line; I could practically hear his eyebrows creasing too.

"Oh boy," I heard him whisper to himself. "He said he was going to tell you…"

"Tell me what?"

"Noah, the company shut down six months ago. Derek made bad deals that fell through and invested too much money. He had to scramble money from every which way just to keep the few clients we had left at bay. He had to get different loans from any bank that would agree to lend him money."

I didn't say anything for what felt like decades, but it must not have been more than a few seconds. I was processing everything as quickly as possible and, at this point, had even more questions than answers. I knew the company was in trouble from the forms I had seen on your desk, but I didn't think it had been shut down for months. I stuttered a few times before I could get my words out.

"If banks were turning him down, then that means the banks that did give him money had to get something big in return. What was the collateral?"

A pause.

"Damian, what was the collateral?" I repeated sternly, as if he hadn't heard me the first time.

"Your house," he mumbled.

My world shattered. The home we had built together—reduced to nothing more than a mere safety net. A security deposit. How did it get to this... I was having trouble processing this information, and in that moment, a strange thought crawled into my mind; how little did I really know you? You, the man I thought I shared everything with, had made decisions and kept secrets I had never glimpsed. I felt like I was discovering a stranger in the body of the person I loved.

"He was willing to give up our home? So what—if the house hadn't burned to the ground and the bank came to collect it, he would have had us sleeping on the street!?"

My voice cracked. Anger coursed through me, but no tears came. I wasn't sad; I felt cheated. Betrayed by a man I thought I knew. It was the feeling of being trapped in someone else's story without permission.

"How could he make that decision without me?"

"He didn't want to, trust me. It killed him to do so. At first, his collateral was just the car, but the more money he asked for, the higher the price. At first, he convinced himself things would work themselves out and he would pay everyone off... but the deals kept falling through, and the numbers kept going down... I'm so sorry."

"So now what?" My anger rose. "The car got totaled in the crash, my house is now a pile of ashes, and I have no money. Everything I had burned in the fire. How do they expect me to settle his debt? Slave myself for them for the next three lifetimes to pay them back for my dead husband's mistake?!"

The cracks in my voice were gone, now substituted by no emotion whatsoever. Indifference was clouding my judgment. I was so tired.

Another pause.

"That's just it, Noah. That's why I'm calling. Technically, he wasn't your husband. Not legally, at least. You never had an actual wedding, no marriage certificate pronouncing you husband and wife in the eyes of the law. That also means there are no documents stating that what is his is also yours. Legally, you were not bound to one another."

With soul-shattering clarity, I realized he was right. When we got engaged on that pier, and I said yes to you, it felt like we were already married. That was enough for us. In our eyes, we were husband and wife, so the idea of an actual wedding was a thought I tucked away in the back of my mind. Damian continued.

"The car was his since before you met him, and the house was under his name because the company approved him for better credit. That means that legally, when Derek died, his debt died with him. You don't owe anyone anything. I know it seems like little consolation, but financially, at least you get a clean break."

Clean break. Yeah, right.

I couldn't help but wonder, was this the Derek I loved, or just the man I thought I knew? Every choice, every hidden deal—it made me feel like I'd been living beside a ghost of you.

"Okay then. Thanks for letting me know," I said flatly.

"That's it? You don't have any questions?"

Of course I have questions—so many that my heart was numb, and my brain was about to explode.

"Nope. Basically, you're telling me I have no house, no car, no husband, and not even his debt to tie me to him anymore. All the strings have been cut. On paper, it's as if we never existed."

I just wanted this conversation to be over, and even though I knew my indifference was hurting him, I wanted this to be done.

Damian said something that was supposed to be supportive and comforting, but I barely registered what it was. He sounded far away; I had mentally tuned him out. I was still running this conversation through my mind when I caught his last words.

"Is there anything else I can do for you before I let you go?" Damian asked.

"Yes, I just have one last question."

"Please. Anything."

"How can you be such a fucking joke of an accountant, Damian? Wasn't it your job to make sure you kept track of his money and kept him out of trouble? Didn't you warn him about any of this?"

I wasn't angry anymore, I was genuinely curious. My voice was so flat, I worried he would think I was an answering machine.

He exhaled slowly and spoke softly, completely unresentful of my poisonous remarks.

"I did, Noah," he said patiently. "You know I did. But you said it yourself; I am his accountant, not his dad. I keep track of his money and advise him on what to do, but I can't force him to listen to me."

I noticed then that Damian spoke of you in the present tense, and I immediately realized what a bitch I'd been to him. It was selfish of me to assume I was the only one brokenhearted over your death. You had friends. You had family that were grieving you, too. How could I be so inconsiderate?

During this call, I understood that grieving was not individual; it was a collective feeling of mourning and loss that left us vulnerable to those who loved us most. I scratched my head and felt my hot cheeks as they blushed with embarrassment.

"Hey, I'm so sorry for snapping at you. I had no right to say anything. I'm just so tired and angry, but I want you to know none of this was your fault. I know that, and so does he. He dug himself into this hole, and I should be relieved that, at least financially, he didn't drag me down with him. Again, I am so sorry, and thank you for calling. Please let me know if there is anything I can do for you. You have always been a great friend to us, and we were—*are*—lucky to have you in our lives."

I could hear him holding back the tears, like a knot about to burst in his throat. His following words were heavy with shame and sorrow.

"The funeral is on Friday, right?"

"Yeah, at 2 p.m. I'll text you the address."

"Thank you. I will be there. Take care, Noah. Talk to you soon, okay?"

"I'm glad we talked. See you Friday. "

I genuinely meant it. I hung up the phone and felt Grandma's stare burning two holes through my eyes.

"Fucking idiot," I whispered in a small voice, tiredly, to the phone as I held it with both hands.

"Derek, Damian, or you?" she asked.

I shrugged my shoulders, unsure which one I was referring to. All of us? Maybe? We all made mistakes that with proper communication could have been avoided. She pulled another purple lollipop from her pocket and shoved it in my mouth. I accepted it gladly, grateful for the sugar's ability to perk me up, even if it was a small amount.

"You're not going to ask me what we talked about?" I asked curiously.

"No need. When he told me he wanted to talk to you on the phone, I turned my hearing aids all the way up to save you the trouble. These things are mighty strong; it was like he was right next to us!"

"You eavesdropped?" I said, baffled.

"I doubt you can call that eavesdropping. I was sitting right here in front of you!" she defended.

I stared at her. She was as sneaky as always.

"Well, what do you think? Is this good news or bad news?"

She thought for a moment. "I think that's something we can discuss after you've had some rest. It's been a tough week," she said as she tucked me back under the covers. She kissed my forehead and took the lollipop away. "I'll wake you up in a few hours with some tea and toast, okay? We can talk about it then."

"Okay. Thank you. I love you," I said groggily, all too happy to surrender my mind and body to unconscious darkness.

"Love you too, baby."

The last thing I remember as I fell into a deep sleep was the realization that I seemed to have lost everything even before I lost you. I was set up for failure.

But as I tasted the remnants of grape lollipop in my molars and smelled my grandma's lingering perfume, I felt confident—certain—that day by day, everything would be okay.

It had to be.

month one

WEEK ONE

FRIDAY CREPT UP on me before I even knew it. I had barely any breakfast and could not stomach more than a single piece of toast. I was ironing the black dress Grandma and I had bought for the funeral, and every stroke of the iron felt like a punch to the gut. Each hiss of steam made my stomach lurch, and the faint tang of hot metal mixed with the new-fabric smell clung to my nostrils until I felt lightheaded. Every pass over the warm fabric brought back a different memory of us, and it felt like I was pressing my heart into the void you left behind.

I arrived at the funeral home at noon and sat alone in the room with your coffin before the wake even started. It was a closed-casket wake—we were asked what we preferred, and we decided as a family that we would much rather remember you from a time when we were all happy and healthy, and, most importantly, together. The ground was covered in flowers; it made me feel like I was walking in a garden blooming exclusively for you. The smell of jasmine and gardenias perfumed every corner of the room, and I hoped with all my heart you could somehow smell them too. You looked so handsome in the picture they had next to the casket. Those kind, dark eyes I fell in love with years ago greeted me through the frame, and I felt a welcoming sense of love and gratitude.

God, I missed you so much.

People wouldn't start arriving until 2 p.m., but Grandma was waiting at the café attached to the funeral home. She left me alone for a few minutes so I could process this by myself, before everyone showed up and it became about them instead of you. Your parents called earlier; they said they would arrive at 12:30 p.m., so we had a few minutes to talk. I had not been able to face them since the accident, but I was glad they were coming. I was terrified I'd collapse the second I saw them—but also desperate for them to see me standing. I was hoping the sight of them would provide me with at least the possibility of closure—and that I would be able to do the same for them.

I took a deep breath.

In and out.

In and out.

I just had to get through today.

Thirty minutes later, I heard a soft knock at the door. I heard the hinges of the wooden door give in, and what I saw first was your mom's almost perfectly manicured hand. Her nails were painted a nude color with French tips, but I could see the tip of the nail on her thumb had been chewed raw. No wonder—one of the many attempts to cope with the anxiety and despair that comes with the loss of a son. My stomach clenched so hard I thought I might throw up. I was clutching the hem of my black dress for dear life, rubbing the fabric between my fingers to try to steady my pulse and shaking hands. The smell of new fabric was still hovering, sharp and dizzying, almost suffocating.

As soon as your mom walked in, we locked eyes for a split second before her gaze shifted to your picture, and she stifled a sob. She squeezed your dad's hand so hard that I saw both of their knuckles turn white, and then she forced her gaze back on mine. She took small, premeditated steps, almost as if remembering how to walk with one foot in front of the other, and as soon as she had materialized in the room, I saw your dad's looming, strong presence behind her. He was still over six feet, but somehow looked smaller than when I saw him last week. He was hunched over, his shoulders sagging, dragging his feet as if willing himself to step into the room that would make the death of his son a reality. We had all lived through a different lifetime between last week and today.

He closed the door gently behind him, and for a moment, we stared at each other before I broke into a run and threw myself into their open arms. I sobbed openly and shamelessly, and I felt my shoulders wetting with each tear I shed. The pain was unbearable, but in their arms, I felt stronger—and I felt they were stronger as well. We needed each other.

Your mom cradled my face in her hands and kissed my forehead, just like you told me she kissed you when you approached the idea of leaving your dad's company. It was a symbol of love and quiet loyalty, supporting us through the undeniable love of a mother's touch. Her hand dropped softly from my face to my own and she gave me a gentle smile, walking slowly to the casket to bid you farewell.

I was left facing your father, who gently rested my chin between his thumb and index finger and lifted my head up slightly. A signal to keep my head high and stay strong, as he followed his wife's footsteps to say goodbye to his only son.

I quietly left the room to give them privacy. The last image I saw before closing the door behind me was your mom resting her forehead against the casket and your dad's arm around her, his head on her shoulder as they spoke to you between heaving, gut-wrenching sobs.

I went to use the restroom, washing my face with cold water and gathering my thoughts for a moment; my face was swollen and tender to the touch. Once I was able to regain my composure, or what was left of it, I went to the café to find Grandma. To my surprise, she wasn't alone. She was laughing, talking to someone who had her back to me—but whom I would recognize anywhere. And as if I needed any proof, I walked closer to them and found Grandma eating a warm, chewy caramel brownie. Before they could even spot me, I placed a gentle hand on the woman's shoulder and said:

"Hey, Dawn. I'm so glad you could make it."

She turned around in surprise, her hands to her chest, and instead of saying anything, she stood up and enveloped me in a hug. I felt like I disappeared into her arms and was struggling to breathe, but God, it felt good to see her and have her here with me.

She let go of the hug and grabbed me by both shoulders.

"My Lord… You sure have had a rough goin', sugar. Here, have some brownies, it's your momma's favorite."

I went to stretch out my hand but before I could protest, she shoved the entire thing in my mouth. It was as decadent as I remembered. I swear it tasted like love.

"Tasty, right?" Grandma said as I chewed. "Dawn used to come over to bake them at home all the time, and I would actually have to limit the amount your mom could have in one sitting. Otherwise, she would eat the whole tray and end up with a stomachache."

They both laughed at the memory. I was still busy chewing.

"We sure had some good times, didn't we? Your granny and I were just catching up—we hadn't heard from each other in ages. My heart's so full right now seein' you two together. I just wish it were under better circumstances, is all," she said as she pinched my cheeks with love and tenderness. "But you stay strong, all right, baby girl? I know it feels like your whole world's just about ended right now, but remember—everything in this life, whether it's good or it ain't, will pass. You hear me?"

I finally swallowed what was left of the brownie, pieces of walnut still stuck to my molars.

"Yes ma'am," I nodded, placing my hands on top of hers and resting my forehead against hers. We stayed there for a few moments before she spoke again.

"Good girl." She turned to Grandma. "Miss Nadia, I know it ain't much, but I brought 'bout a hundred brownies to the wake. Figured folks might need a little somethin' sweet to help 'em through the evenin'. If it's all right with you, I'll start passin' these around. You think Derek's parents would mind?"

I felt moved by how considerate she was.

"I think they would genuinely appreciate it," Grandma assured her.

"Thank you so much for coming, Dawn," I said earnestly.

"Of course I'm here, baby girl. You and your family mean everything to me. I love you both so, so much. Your granny has my number in case you ever need someone to listen, 'kay? You know my door's always open!"

She excused herself politely as she walked around the wake with four trays of baked goods.

Seeing Dawn try to help in any way she could warmed my heart. I sat in her chair to be with Grandma a little longer before I had to go back and see everyone else.

"Gosh, it was so great to see Dawn after all this time. The second I saw her, a hundred different memories of your mom flashed through my eyes," Grandma reminisced.

I smiled at the thought as I picked a corner of the treat Dawn had left us on a napkin to share with our tea. She was right, the taste of chocolate and caramel melting in my mouth made me feel a little better. I sighed deeply and stared into my grandma's eyes, always filled with curiosity and compassion.

Twenty minutes later, she broke my reverie. "Ready to make some more rounds? I think there's some people looking for you."

"Ready as I can be," I answered plainly.

As Grandma and I were making our way around the funeral home, I saw Damian speaking with your parents. Understanding flashed across their eyes as they nodded and hugged one another. I assumed Damian was explaining to them everything he told me on the phone a couple of days ago, and as both your parents leaned on one another, I silently thanked him for answering all the questions that would have otherwise gone unanswered.

He excused himself when we locked eyes and came over to meet us. I was halfway through saying his name when he hugged me, an intensity that told me his guilt and remorse had left him broken.

"Damian, none of this was your fault," I whispered. "You could not have prevented anything that happened, even if you had come to me sooner. What happened was outside of our control."

I tried to absolve him of all guilt, like how your parents did for me, and I felt the tension in his shoulders dissolve as he heard my words—as if he had been carrying the guilt around with him all along and he was yearning for someone to release him.

He grabbed me gently by the shoulders and stared at me intently.

"Let me know if you need anything at any point, okay? I am here for you."

He nodded, then excused himself once more before the tears flooding his eyes could fall down his face.

You were so loved by everyone. Why couldn't you see that, Derek?

I watched as the wake began to wind down, my chest heavy, my mind numb. Every face I passed seemed to carry pieces of you, fragments I wanted desperately to hold onto. And yet, a hollow throb lodged in my ribs. I wanted you to see it—the love, the grief, the whole tangled mess of it—but you were gone.

Two hours later, the wake was finally over, and I felt numb with sadness. My limbs were heavy, my insides vacant, and every step toward the cemetery felt like wading through water. Your parents looked drained of energy, but we still had to get through the funeral service. Burying you was going to be the hardest thing we'd ever done, but you deserved a place to finally rest in peace.

I couldn't stop thinking about how empty and broken I felt, how surreal it was to move through a crowd while my heart stayed rooted in grief. Every conversation sounded distant, every face a blur. I kept telling myself I had to stay present, but it was like I was crawling through fog, numb and untethered.

All the flowers from the wake were now adorning your casket. Tones of off-white and soft pink were placed all around you, and as the sun began to set, rays of golden orange and purple reflected off the flower arrangements—each petal a different shade of sunset. I swallowed hard, trying to anchor myself against the surge of grief that threatened to pull me under.

Several rows of chairs were placed beneath the cedar trees around the cemetery. The site was peaceful, with vibrant shades of green that celebrated the lives of those who called this place their home of eternal rest. I was making my way slowly toward a front-row seat, arm in arm with my grandma, when a man's voice cleared his throat behind me.

"Noah," the raspy voice said.

I turned around, surprised to see Officer Jones standing before me.

"Officer Jones! What are you doing here?" I stepped forward to hug him before he could react. He reciprocated the gesture with a grunt and two gentle pats on the back.

"I just wanted to see how you two ladies were holding up," he said, shaking my grandma's hand. "Officer Jones. I take it this is your sister?" He grinned, mischievous as always.

"I can also be more than that to you," my grandma replied, winking at him. Fierceless.

"Grandma!" I scolded. "Are you kidding me?"

They both chuckled, clearly enjoying themselves.

"Young kids, am I right? They get embarrassed over everything," Officer Jones said. I was mortified.

"I'm just teasing," Grandma said, brushing him off. "Old gal like me, all I've got left to enjoy is a good laugh. But in all seriousness, thank you for what you did for Noah. We'd be lost without you. If there's anything we can do to repay you, say the word."

"I'm just glad you're together. And Noah, I wanted to give you this. Forensics just released it, and I figured you'd want it back."

He stretched out his fist toward me and let something drop into my hand.

I froze.

A knot formed in my throat as I looked down and recognized it—I felt the rim of the wedding ring you bought me at the pier when you proposed. I traced the rough edge of the lettering with my thumb, desperate to feel your touch through the metal.

You keep me wild.

That small, circular piece of metal became a new breath. I closed my fist around it, urging the metal to hurt my hand—to feel something.

My heart sunk, tears welling in my eyes, and I struggled to find air.

"Thank you so much," I whispered, my voice barely audible.

This man had saved my life—twice. How could I ever repay him?

"You be good to yourself and take care of one another, deal? You have my number if anything comes up. It was a pleasure seeing you both."

He shook both our hands—firmly, but gently—and walked away with a solemn smile, leaving behind a silence filled with unspoken gratitude.

I removed my mother's necklace from around my neck and slid your ring onto the chain. A small piece of you I could carry, a tether to what had been, and a comfort I could hold close.

The ceremony was short but intimate. The officiant said the words of comfort everyone expected, and after the final *amen*, we all pretended his phrases gave us peace. But they didn't. Not really. We were hollowed by your absence, and every heartbeat felt like an echo of you.

The officiant invited your parents to speak. Your mom stood up and tried to say your name, but she choked, overcome by the weight of grief, and collapsed. Your dad was her rock—he helped her up with the aid of a few others, and they sat back down. He looked at me, pleading, and I understood the message—it was my turn now.

I took a deep breath and clutched the wrinkled piece of paper I'd been holding for the past ten minutes. It was soggy with tears, folded so many times the edges were on the verge of ripping—a distraction and comfort I clung to all morning.

I rose slowly, every step toward the casket heavier than the last. I was afraid that if I got too close, my body would fail me. My legs might give out. My heart might stop altogether, and I almost wished it had. Every inch closer felt like walking into a storm I wasn't sure I could survive.

But I finally made it.

I reached the officiant. He took two steps back, giving me space. I felt the weight of every eye on me, yet none of it mattered except the silent promise I had made to you.

I unfolded the paper one last time. The faded words at the top read:

To Derek. Do not open till I die.

It was your turn to hear my vows.

"Hello, everyone," I began, my voice cracking. "Thank you for coming. Mr. and Mrs. Burke and I are incredibly grateful for your support."

I cleared my throat and continued.

"Um... years ago, Derek and I wrote our final words for each other, in case something ever happened to one of us. We didn't want to leave this world without knowing exactly how we felt for one another. I recently retrieved Derek's letter to me, but I haven't brought myself to read it yet. I can't do it." I sighed and placed my fingertips over your name, wishing I could be tracing your freckles instead. "Even though I'm still here with you all, a part of me—probably the most important part of me—died in that crash, too. So today, I'd like to share my final words for Derek, because he deserves to hear them."

I was nervous. The sun beat down on the back of my neck, sweat dripping from my forehead. My voice trembled, my throat dry like a desert, my heart racing. I looked out at the sea of faces, searching for courage, and I froze.

I saw him.

My blood turned to ice, and then, just as quickly, my heart raced faster—for all the right reasons.

My dad.

I felt my breath hitch, my chest swell. He was here. Somehow, he had found the strength to show up. My grandma must've been behind it, I was sure. She glanced back at him and gave the faintest smile of approval.

He had come through.

He nodded at me from the back row, but it was enough. That was the quiet nudge of courage I needed to get through this part.

I steadied my hands and read.

"Dear Derek,

I hope and pray that you're reading these words with the full certainty that I loved you then, and I will love you always."

I cleared my throat as the word *always* wavered before me, blurred and trembling, while a flood of tears gathered beneath my eyelids, smearing the spilled ink of the letters.

"For some people, finding true love is a matter of failed attempts and disappointments—years and years of first dates and broken hearts. But for us, it was simple. Like falling asleep. Fast and weightless.

You were always perfect for me, Derek. I still can't believe life gave me you. I'm a little self-conscious right now, because you wrote me two whole pages and I'm afraid my half a page won't be enough—but the thing is, one tree makes 8,000 sheets of paper, and I would need the whole Amazon forest to tell you what you mean to me."

I searched for my grandma. She dabbed a tissue at the corners of her eyes and winked, a fresh tear tracing her cheek as she offered me a small, steady smile—one that anchored the space around me and softened the dizzy blur at the edges. I drew in one last deep breath and returned to the page.

"So here it is—short and to the point:

You gave my life meaning. You were the reason I got up in the morning, the reason the world felt bright. If a legacy is measured by the happiness you leave behind, then yours will echo through me forever.

Your kind eyes made me feel like the most beautiful girl in the world. And your heart—God, your heart—turned my life into the greatest adventure I could have ever dreamed of.

I have never felt safer than I did with you. You were my home, my constant, my everything. All the dreams we chased, all the futures we planned—they were worth every second, because I got to build them with you.

I've whispered it to you every night since the day we met, and I'll whisper it again now, even if it's for the last time, even if you can't hear me—

You were the best decision I ever made.

Thank you for loving me... And for letting me love you.

With all my love,

Forever and always,

Noah."

I couldn't see the letters on the page anymore. Tears blurred the words as blue streaks of ink bled down my trembling hand. I pressed my palm against your casket to steady myself, a yawning absence coursing through me as I wondered how it had ever come to this.

After I said my name, silence fell—so complete you could've heard a pin drop. It lingered for several seconds before I finally looked up, and everywhere I turned, red-rimmed eyes met mine. Then, quietly, the officiant stepped forward.

"That was so beautiful," he said, handing me a tissue.

"Thanks," I whispered, accepting it gracefully as I sat back down next to my grandma, who rested her hand on my thigh and her head on my shoulder.

After my speech, the officiant said a few more words, but I couldn't focus on any of them. My heartbeat had started pounding in my ears, louder than any voice could cut through. The moment to lower the casket came, and I felt my own heart being lowered with it.

I saw the pallbearers respectfully standing to the side, waiting for their signal. When they added the straps to lower the casket, your mom's screams—muffled by a handful of tissues—snapped me back to the present.

We were asked to toss a single rose each; your parents, Damian, my grandma, and me. One by one, we stepped forward and dropped our farewells onto the surface of the polished wood. The petals fell silently, as if carrying fragments of our hearts with them. We stood together in a small line—five people suspended in grief—as the casket was slowly, reverently lowered into the Earth.

The silence pressed down on me, the world reduced to the five of us. My mind spun with what-ifs and memories, every laugh and touch from the past mingling with the pang of loss. I wanted to cry, to scream, to fall to the ground—and yet, I just stood there, broken and silent.

I stood by the coffin until the last shovelful of dirt was packed. Most of the guests had already gone by then. Numbness had settled over me, but grief clung tightly, heavy and oppressive. I felt hollow, shattered, yet somehow tethered to life by sheer will.

The crowd thinned until it was just us. I hugged Damian tightly and thanked him again before he left. Then I turned to your parents.

"Remember, you will always be a part of the family," your mom whispered as I hugged her and your dad. Her words echoed inside me like a prayer.

This moment, as impossible as it was, gave us the smallest kind of closure. A line had been drawn in the sand—your life before, and our lives now. Whether we liked it or not, time would keep moving. The sun would still rise. And we would be asked to go on living, even if it felt like everything had stopped.

I stepped back, wiping my eyes. That's when I saw my dad approach from across the cemetery lawn. He stood quietly a few feet away, hands folded respectfully in front of him, as he gave your parents his heartfelt condolences.

As your parents walked slowly toward their car, hand in hand, your mom paused and glanced back over her shoulder. Her steps faltered as she turned toward my grandma, hesitation etched in every movement. She pressed a trembling hand to her heart, as though trying to hold the pieces together, and whispered, "How... how does someone ever get over losing a child?"

Her voice was fragile—quivering, almost afraid of hearing the answer—carrying the weight of a grief too vast to name.

Grandma reached out, placing a steady hand on her forearm, and squeezed gently. "You don't," she said softly, her eyes meeting hers. They stood there for a long moment, looking at each other as if sharing a secret only a mother could understand—the kind of solace that comes from knowing grief is a bond, not a burden. The silence between them was comforting, tender, and heavy with love.

My dad waited patiently, watching the exchange between my grandma and your mom with tears in his eyes. The last time I'd seen him, a little less than a year ago, we'd been strangers in a shared grief, unable to bridge the silence that had grown over years of distance. I had wanted his support, his presence, but he had retreated, trapped in his own sorrow after Mom passed. I had carried the weight of both our losses, often wishing we could talk, wishing he'd been there. Now, standing before me, he was real. Present.

I turned toward him cautiously.

"Hey, Dad," I said, unsure of what to expect. "I had no idea you were coming."

He wrapped his arms around me.

"Oh sweetie," he said, holding me close, his chest warm against mine, steadying me in a way I hadn't felt in years. "You think I'm so far gone that I wouldn't be here for you?" He pulled back slightly to look me in the eyes. "I'm so sorry, Noah. I know exactly how you feel. But both your grandma and I—we've been through this. I want you to know we're here now. You've got two people to help guide you, at least."

I smelled the crook of his neck, lingering on fresh linen and soap. His eyes were kind but alert, empathy all over them. He was calm—not fidgety or distracted like I usually found him. He'd changed.

He took something from his pocket—a coin with the number five on it.

I held it in my hand.

"What's this?" I asked.

"It's my five-month sobriety chip. For real this time. A few months ago, I noticed you weren't calling as much—and when you did, you just sounded so… disappointed. So I decided to get my act together—to show up for you like I should've done all these years. I didn't tell you before because I wanted it to be a surprise… I needed to make sure I could actually follow through this time. I didn't want to let you down again."

I stared down at the chip, blinking against a sudden wave of tears.

"Look, Noah, after losing your mom, I felt like time stopped for me. And that burden fell entirely on you, and I should've never let that happen," he said, his voice thick with regret. "Your grandma tried to snap me out of it throughout the years, but every time I saw her, she reminded me so much of your mom that I'd just go back to square one. I didn't know how to live without her… and I didn't know how to be a father to you in the meantime."

I swallowed hard, memories of missed birthdays, arguments that turned to silence, and the phone calls that went unanswered flooding back.

"But last week," he continued, voice cracking slightly, "she called me and told me what happened, and for a long time I didn't know what to say. So I figured I'd do what I haven't been doing… and I showed up. I hope that's okay?"

I could see the vulnerability in his eyes—the years of guilt, the isolation he'd carried, the grief that had nearly consumed him. And somehow, all of it was here now, laid bare before me.

Instead of saying anything, I kissed his cheek and hugged him again, letting him feel the pride and forgiveness I had for him in that moment.

"I'm so proud of you," I whispered, placing the token in his shirt pocket and laying my hand over his chest. "You just made my day a little better by being here, Dad. I've missed you. And I love you. I'm sorry I haven't called. Feeling the way I do now, I understand why you were so consumed by grief all these years. It's unbearable. And I forgive you… for everything. I can't imagine what it was like seeing me every day, reminding you of Mom. That must have been terrible."

He placed his hand on my cheek. "Noah, you're the only thing that kept me sane. Can't you see? You're all the best parts of her. I don't know what I would do without you."

The warmth of his hand grounded me, and for the first time since the accident, I felt a little alive. The crushing weight of guilt, grief, and isolation that had held us apart all these years seemed to loosen, if only slightly.

"I'm sorry to interrupt," my grandma said, somewhat impolitely. "I'm really happy you got your shit together after twenty-five years, but aren't you forgetting something?"

"Yes, Nadia. Yes, I am." He smiled as he rolled his eyes. "Here you go. Thanks for giving me the heads-up—I sure appreciate it."

He pulled a family-sized lollipop jar from behind the front row seats.

"Enjoy your diabetes," he joked.

They always had a passive-aggressive relationship. At first, I used to think they hated each other, but over the years I realized they were trauma-bonded and loved each other deeply. In their own twisted, passive-aggressive way, they were family too.

Her eyes lit up at the sight of the candy.

"Fuuuuck yeah," she whispered to herself, opening the lid and immediately unwrapping a cherry-flavored lollipop. She picked a grape one and stretched her hand out toward my dad.

"Here you go," she said. "Congrats on not being a lazy, sad drunk anymore. You deserve it. It sure is good to see you doing okay, though." She flashed him a devilish smile.

My dad took the candy. "Thanks, Nadia. I really appreciate it. And I'm really glad to see you too—honestly." I could tell he meant it.

"Hey. I haven't seen you both in a while. Do you guys have time for a cup of tea? On me?"

I smiled. "Sure. You guys go wait in the car and I'll be there in a couple of minutes, okay?"

"Sounds good, baby," she said as she tucked a strand of hair behind my ear. She looked at my dad, then gently linked her arm with his. He looked surprised, like he hadn't expected her to lean on him—but was moved by it all the same.

She saw our expression and blushed a little.

"What are you two looking at? This is very fucking uneven terrain. I could fall and shatter my hip! Then what are you gonna do?"

My dad and I chuckled, and they walked slowly toward the car, already bickering.

"So what's with all the cursing?" he asked her.

"Eh. You know… Early signs of dementia is what they say." She shrugged her shoulders. "I encourage you to stay young as long as possible, because sometimes I say inappropriate things that even catch me by surprise." She shook her head in fake disappointment.

I heard my dad's laugh echo across the quiet cemetery as he tilted his head toward her slightly. Despite everything, they still gravitated toward one another, searching for the missing piece of the one person they had both loved most.

I stood where the coffin sat a few minutes ago and knelt by your grave. The earth was freshly turned, and a thin breeze brushed my face. I kissed my palm and pressed it gently to the place your tombstone would one day be.

The emptiness around me was infinite. I pressed my forehead to my hands, imagining you there, imagining the warmth of your presence that the breeze could never carry. I ached with longing, and every inhale felt sharp and fractured. It was hard to reconcile the permanence of this moment with the memory of you alive, laughing, touching the world in ways only you could.

I closed my eyes and let the grief pour through me, feeling both broken and strangely whole.

"I love you, Derek. I love you so much. I'll come back in a few days, okay? I promise. You'll always be my forever and always," I whispered to the wind.

I drew a deep breath to clear my head, then rose carefully, brushing the dirt from my knees before heading to the car to meet my family—where they were already working on their second lollipops.

I felt the smallest flicker of hope stir within me. Life would never be the same without you, Derek. But maybe, with the people I loved by my side, I could one day discover that it might still be worth living.

month two

I THOUGHT ADJUSTING would be hard, complicated even, but my grandma and I fell into a routine that became comforting. But even with the comfort of structure, something in me still felt jagged. The silence between us was often peaceful—but sometimes, it was just quiet enough for the grief to creep back in.

Over the following two weeks, my emotions fluctuated like the weather—stormy one day, clear the next. But looking into my grandma's eyes always made me feel at peace. We found comfort in each other's company.

One morning, after deep cleaning the house, I stepped outside to water the plants. Grandma had loved gardening for most of her life, but now that she was older, I worried the physical work might be too much for her—the heat, the hose, the risk of getting tangled and falling. So every week, I tended the garden she had always cared for with such devotion.

I dug through a bag of fertilizer, moving pots and shovels, a cigarette tucked between my lips. I had the odd feeling Grandma had been watching me for days— the way she'd glance my way with her mouth set, like she was keeping inventory of my habits, but I tried not to let it bother me. I struck a lighter, feeling the warmth of the flame near my chin as I inhaled deeply, and in that moment, I thought about how much sense it all made.

I hadn't smoked in years. I used to be proud of that—proud of how badly I'd craved it and still never gave in. But what pushed me over the edge wasn't some small bump in the road; it was a full-blown explosion of heartache and trauma.

So no, lighting that cigarette didn't make me feel guilty or like a failure. I didn't feel like a hypocrite, or as though I was betraying the memory of you—or myself. Life had failed me, and this was my reward for not throwing in the towel.

One would assume that after a cigarette burned my house to the ground, I would feel evasive or resentful toward them. But I didn't. This cigarette was the one thing tying me to my previous life. The life where I had a husband, a house, and a plan for the future. Now, everything had changed—and maybe that's why I couldn't let it go, even when it hurt. It was the closest thing I had left to feeling like myself, before my world fell apart.

The first drag gave me permission—two minutes of pretending everything was unchanged. Then the smoke hit the back of my throat and a different image took over. The blackened door, the heat, and the deafening way the house had screamed. The sweetness of the cigarette curdled into something bitter. It tasted like ash and regret, and I knew this wasn't comfort. This was stitching a life back together with a match.

I hadn't spoken your name in days. At least not out loud. Sometimes I wondered if forgetting it might hurt less. But every night I felt your letter screaming at me from the nightstand; begging for me to read it. But how could I? How could I face your last words knowing it's the last I'd ever hear from you?

I wasn't halfway through my second drag when ice-cold water suddenly drenched me from head to toe. I gasped, shivering in the chill, but the anger rose fast and hot, reddening my cheeks.

I whipped my head to the left—and there she was. Grandma stood tall, eyebrows drawn together in a hard frown, the hose limp in her hands, water still dripping from the nozzle.

For just a split second, before the glare fully settled on her face, I swore I saw something flicker in her eyes—fear, sharp and fleeting, like she'd just caught me standing on the edge of a cliff.

"What the h—?" I sputtered.

Her eyebrows shot up like warning flares, and she dramatically waved her finger over the hose trigger again. Then I remembered; the words hell, damn, and Satan were no-gos in this house. But that sure as shit wasn't going to stop me from demanding an explanation.

I screamed louder this time.

"What the *fuck*, Grandma!? What was that for!?"

She dropped the hose without so much as a flinch and marched toward me with the kind of unwavering step that made me question everything I'd assumed about her age. I guess that cane of hers wasn't really for balance after all—more like a prop for theatrics.

Without hesitation, she snatched the soaked, soggy cigarette from my fingers and shoved it so close to my eyes I had to strain to keep them focused.

"This is a nasty-ass fucking habit, Noah! What are you trying to do? Die before me?" She held it away from her body, like it personally offended her. "Effective immediately, you are done smoking."

I stood there, frozen, teeth chattering, too cold for a decent comeback. So I groaned like an angry teenager and stomped off to my room.

I slammed the door for effect and stared blankly at the wall, trying to recapitulate what had just happened.

Grandma had officially lost it.

But as water dripped from my hair onto the carpet, the anger fizzled almost as quickly as it had flared. I could still see her face—stern, furious, and underneath it all, afraid. It was the same flicker of fear I'd seen at the train station weeks ago. Her hands had trembled when she took the cigarette, not from rage but from desperation. She was trying to protect me, even if her love came out raw and unrefined.

Maybe that was her way of loving me—loud, messy, and impossible to ignore.

Six weeks had passed since I lost you.

The shock was fading, but the sting remained; grief no longer screamed—it hummed beneath my ribs, steady as a pulse I couldn't ignore.

Tonight I sat outside this pub with the moonlight spilling across my face, and I felt something akin to peace. Breathing in the fresh air the wind blew in my direction—carrying the scent of dirt and pine—distracted me from the craving to light a cigarette.

Ironic, wasn't it?

Inside, three old men shared a pack of Lucky Strikes—the brand that burned my life to ash. The bar was so thick with haze it felt like wading through thunder-clouds. For a heartbeat I was tempted to join them, to disappear into that fog, but my lungs flared exactly the way they did *that night*, and instinct lurched me toward the door.

I paused, exhaling slowly. I used to find comfort in cigarettes. They once felt like old friends—but it was that false comfort that cost me everything. Now, they're just ghosts. Ghosts I refused to follow me home. Like a phoenix, ever since my life burned to the ground, I had been trying my best to rise from the ashes.

Out here, lungs soothed by cold air, I started to label my feelings. Grief used to scatter itself through my body like broken glass. A dull, stabbing pain in my ribcage, migraines behind my eyes, paralysis in my stomach, and anxiety shaking my hands while I chewed my bottom lip raw.

Now, beneath the soft hum of a jukebox's classic-rock riff, it felt heavier, denser, like all those shards had melted down and gathered in my heart, beating harder under the weight.

Breathe in.

Breathe out.

Instead of letting my heart explode through my chest and give in to panic, I took deep breaths, counting the seconds as I inhaled through my nose and exhaled through my mouth. Slowly. Deliberately.

The muscles in my shoulders unclenched. My jaw eased. My thoughts stopped stampeding long enough to notice the chill air brushing my skin.

I turned my wedding ring—*you keep me safe*—around my finger to keep a rhythm. For a moment, the metal felt warm, as if your hand still cupped mine, thumb brushing over my knuckles the way you used to when you thought I wasn't paying attention. My breath stuttered; my body almost leaning toward where you should be. I pressed harder on the band and turned my ring slowly.

Breath by measured breath, my pulse quieted, the night no longer roaring in my ears.

Breathe in,

Breathe out.

Breathe in,

Breathe out.

The breeze prickled at the cold sweat along the back of my neck, but I didn't mind. For the first time in weeks, a quiet pride stirred in me—for pushing through the panic, and somehow, finding this fragile pocket of stillness.

I could handle this. I was still here.

I lifted my eyes to the night sky, and within a few seconds, I found the Three Kings.

My lips parted. A lump swelled in my throat.

I was sure, without a shadow of a doubt, that you could see me—and were proud of me, too.

For a moment, I almost saw you there—head tilted toward the stars, a soft laugh slipping from your lips as if you've been here all along. The image flickered, then melted back into the night sky, leaving only Orion's belt twinkling overhead.

I smiled at the constellation.

Any comfort I once tucked into cigarettes evaporated, replaced by the comfort of knowing I could always find you in the stars.

Stars are time machines. What I saw tonight died millions of years ago, yet their light still reached me. Your body was gone, but your light remained—my past, my present, my future. Up there, you shined on my whole timeline. I felt you closer than ever, like if I spoke your name aloud, the sound might reach you.

I miss you, Derek.

I wanted the stars and I to become equals, so I promised the constellations, and you, that I'd try to shine back.

The faint spark in my eyes told me there was still hope, that I was still worth shining for, and I gave a silent oath not to disappoint them.

Tonight, I was grateful—

grateful for you,

grateful that we met,

grateful for what we had,

and accepting of what will be.

I took one last deep breath and decided to go home.

Opening the pub door, I flinched at the stale smoke. The smell that once brought me comfort now coiled in my stomach like rot.

I circled the building under the open sky, following you instead, Derek—my fourth king, the brightest star of all—guiding me safely home. For a fleeting second, I swear I felt the brush of your shoulder against mine, the faint scent of your cologne as you walked beside me.

Time is unforgiving, but not unkind. Tonight, under a quilt of late-winter constellations, I let the universe tuck me in and vowed to rise with the dawn.

Since I had officially moved in with Grandma—at least for now—my life had found something close to a rhythm. The plan was to stay until I could find my footing, until work felt possible and I could survive a night alone without the silence crushing me. For now, Grandma and I leaned on each other, both quietly aware we needed someone to keep the shadows at bay.

That morning, I woke up to the smell of blueberry pancakes and sizzling bacon. My stomach grumbled—which was a miracle. I brushed my teeth and ran downstairs, almost giddy at the thought of an appetite for the first time in months.

Grandma greeted me with a smile and a suspicious spark in her eye, but I couldn't bring myself to question her. She ruffled my hair the way she used to when I was little and gave me a quick kiss on my cheek as she wished me a good morning—a second-nature, loving gesture that made the kitchen feel safer. The pancakes were warm and fluffy, the bacon perfectly crisp, and for the first time in weeks, I felt energy stirring in my body instead of dread.

After breakfast, she started on the dishes while I tidied up, but when I heated the pan to pour off the bacon grease, the smell rose thick and hot, unfamiliar somehow, and my stomach lurched. Before I could even set the pan down, I doubled over the trash can, heaving.

"Sorry," I mumbled, still shaken as I wiped streaks of vomit off the corner of my mouth. My hands were clammy, and my head spun faintly. "I'll be right back," I said, excusing myself to go brush my teeth and gargle a full bottle of mouthwash.

By the time I returned, she'd finished cleaning and had two steaming cups of chamomile waiting on the counter.

"Sorry, Grandma, I guess that smell made me nauseous."

"Mhm. I'm sure it was just the smell," she said, lips twitching in a mischievous grin.

I narrowed my eyes. "What does that mean?"

"Nothing. I probably shouldn't tell you."

"Tell me what?" I growled. Impatience bubbled in my stomach like the bacon grease on the pan. The image brought the smell back, and the nausea with it, so I quickly got rid of that thought and focused on staring intently at her.

"You won't get mad?" she asked, her spoon circling the cup in quiet, practiced motions, the sugar dissolving as naturally as if her wrist had been born to the movement.

"I'm already mad," I chirped through a clenched smile.

"Then I won't tell you."

"Grandma!"

She leaned forward like she was about to share state secrets. "You're pregnant."

I choked on my tea.

"By the time I'd stopped gasping and dabbing the sweat from my forehead, she was sitting there, calm and curious, watching me with the kind of patience that told me she could wait forever—without a care in the world."

"There's no way," I said, panic prickling under my skin as I dug my fingernails to my palm hard enough to leave four small crescent moons carved across my hand. "Why would you even—"

"Because I'm old and wise."

"Because you're crazy."

"Okay then," she said cheerfully, folding her hands in her lap while I melted into silent, wide-eyed chaos.

There was no way. Absolutely no fucking way. This was anatomically and biologically impossible. I stared back at her, heaving as I felt cold beads of sweat dripping down my armpit. *Why was she so calm!?* The silence was deafening, blood roaring in my ears as our eyes locked. I wasn't about to back down—I wasn't going to let her win. Not today. Not after what she said.

The staring contest lasted about forty-five seconds before I groaned loudly, grabbed the car keys, and stormed out the door.

Seven minutes later, I was parked outside the drugstore. I took a deep breath as I shut off the engine, and at that moment, I decided that my grandma's dementia had escalated to preposterous proportions and she had gone nuts, so I strolled inside the store, got myself a six-pack of beer and some lollipops for my grandma to appease her deteriorating brain. I was about to pay at the register when something pink flashed out of the corner of my eye. It was like God himself shined the holy light on this thing. I tried to ignore it, but I was too curious. One quick, innocent glance just to convince myself that this was all a big misunderstanding. Nobody stocks pregnancy tests at checkout lanes anyways. But as soon as I strained my neck and my eyes landed on the stick, I sighed in surrender and nodded my head, because that would be my luck. Sure enough, it was a pregnancy test.

I groaned again. Louder. The young girl with spiky hair at the register tried to avoid eye contact but couldn't help but notice as I stomped my way to the pregnancy test and slammed it on top of the six-pack. Now she gave me a full-blown, half-horrified, half-judgmental look.

"Oh, for fuck's sake, relax, it's for my grandma," I said as I slapped $20 on the counter and told her to keep the change. I angrily marched toward the door and didn't look back, but I was able to catch a glimpse of her from the circular mirror on the top of the entrance doors. She had turned pale as her face contorted—confused, disgusted, judgmental as hell, and completely mortified.

Maybe that will teach her to mind her own business.

The drive back home was grueling. I turned on the radio to a heavy metal station that I didn't care for just to quiet my thoughts. By the time I got home, I was determined not to give Grandma the satisfaction, so I crept upstairs and slammed my bedroom door behind me… only to find her perched calmly at the edge of my bed, swinging her feet and holding a gigantic crystal from her neck.

This woman was a psycho.

"I assume you bought a test to prove me wrong," she said. "But that's just silly. Am I ever wrong?"

I glared. "You're unhinged," I muttered as I rolled my eyes, heading for the bathroom.

As I was struggling to undo my pants from the sweat on my fingertips and trembling hands, I cursed under my breath. I was holding an entire future in my fist. My mind spun at the possibility of raising a child alone, without you. *How could I?* How could you not be here for this? My chest ached, my ribs collapsing inward.

*I can't do this. I can't do this. I can't do this. Not without you. Maybe if you,
no. I fucking can't. Could I?*

Once I was finally able to undo my pants and sit on the toilet, I couldn't
concentrate on peeing. I was never a shy pee-er, but it was as if my bladder was
intentionally contracting itself to avoid answers at all costs. I could hear my grandma
outside rummaging through the bag like a delusional raccoon.

"Oooooh! Lollipops and beer!" she said with the excitement of a child.

"Don't touch the beer! That's not yours!" I threatened from the bathroom.

"It will be in three minutes…" she mumbled to herself.

I rolled my eyes again, almost wrenching my neck, and turned on the faucet—
anything to give myself a little privacy and drown out the urge to bang my head
against the sink. The steady sound of running water helped, just enough to slow
my racing thoughts.

I capped the stick and scrubbed my hands, as if scrubbing them raw would
bring you back. Bits of the towel clung to the scabs on my scarred skin, still healing
from the fire. I wiped the sweat from my face, gripped the sink for support, and felt
my pulse hammer in my ears.

And now we waited. The longest three minutes of my life started now.

I started pacing around my room. My grandma was patiently sitting on the bed,
eating the candy I bought her, which I was glad I did so she could entertain herself
instead of offering unwarranted advice.

After what felt like a whole eternity, the timer on my phone went off. It was
time. Before I looked at the results, my grandma grabbed me gently by the arm
and positioned me to face her. I didn't know why, but quite frankly, I didn't care.
I could barely breathe.

She nodded encouragingly, her now blue-tinted teeth showing behind her smile.
She could be intense, but I could never do this without her. She reached up and
squeezed my hand—firm, exactly like a promise. I leaned into it because I needed
something to hold onto.

I exhaled slowly, and before I looked down, I looked at my grandma's eyes.

"I love you," I said shakily. "But you've officially lost your mind. I'm not preg—"

The room spun twice, and everything went black.

Two lines.

Oh shit.

"Yup! Just like your mom did!" was the last thing I heard as I fell unconscious and heard my grandma's distant echo of celebration.

The room continued to spin as I regained consciousness fifteen minutes later. My grandma was on her—my—second beer and eating a red lollipop that stained her lips purple. She handed me water and another lollipop with surprising tenderness. I collapsed beside her and put my head in her lap like I used to as a child, tears slipping down my face. She patted my back the way she always had—slow, steady circles that said everything words couldn't.

"How did you know?" I asked her.

"I have been suspecting it for three days but wasn't sure until you threw up when you smelled the bacon grease."

"What does that have to do with anything?"

"When your mom was pregnant with you, bacon grease made her puke," she said softly. "Guess the apple doesn't fall far from the tree."

"You induced vomit to prove a point?" I was stunned.

"Um, no. I had a theory and tested it with an experiment. Me being right was just a happy coincidence." She shrugged the blame off her shoulders.

"I have no idea how to raise a kid; I can barely take care of myself," I said, containing the fear in my stomach.

"You don't have to do it alone," she said. "I'll be here. We'll figure it out together." She squeezed my shoulder hard enough to make me wince—a fierce, maternal squeeze that felt like a vow.

Her words landed like a warm quilt over my panic. Still, my heart cracked. *Derek.* This was supposed to be ours. You would never see our baby's face, never rock them to sleep, never hear their first word or teach them to ride a bike. You would never feel their laugh vibrate in their tiny chest. The grief surged fresh, fierce and raw, and for a moment I let it break me open. But I clung to Grandma's promise, even if it felt impossible to believe yet.

We stayed like that for an hour, until my hips went numb.

"Want to make a toast to celebrate?" Grandma asked at last, chipper as ever.

"I thought I couldn't drink while pregnant."

"You can't, which is why I bought you a six-pack of non-alcoholic beer. You'll get fat anyway, so why avoid the carbs?"

I chose to ignore the second part of that comment.

"I haven't seen any beer in the fridge."

"I hid it in the vegetable drawer, which you like to pretend doesn't exist."

For a moment, I was stunned into silence—then, against all odds, I laughed.

"I hope I am half as cool as you when I get older," I said as we went downstairs.

I opened the vegetable drawer, and sure enough, next to the broccoli was what I would soon refer to as pregnant beer. I brought two cans to the table.

"Noah, these past few months have been the most action-packed weeks I have had in a long time. You brought joy back into my life and gave me a purpose, and now, you have been given one, too. And I am blessed to be a part of it. I fucking love you both. To you and your baby boy! Cheers!" she said as she raised her beer in the air.

"Baby boy? Did your mumbo jumbo crystal tell you that when I was unconscious?" I said sarcastically.

"Crystals never lie!"

I laughed as I cheered to the chaos in my life and thanked God for giving me an angel on Earth. I thought of you, Derek, and how I wished you were here with me with every fiber of my being, but once again, you sent me a gift to remind me that you would never leave me alone, and I thanked you for that from the bottom of my heart. My grandma's words echoed in my brain and my heart clenched. I clung to them as if they might be true—as if the universe, in its own strange way, was letting me touch a fragment of you again. And for the first time in a long while, I believed that maybe, someday, things might be okay.

This baby would know you like I did—kind, strong, and full of love. I'd raise him with your memory stitched into every moment, so he grows up knowing how much his father loved us. You would always be with us—in our laughter, in our sorrows, and every heartbeat—watching from the stars.

month three

FOR THE FIRST few days after I found out I was pregnant, I went through every emotion in the span of a heartbeat. I realized what I thought was acceptance when we cheered with the fake beer was only masking the profound state of shock. Now, I felt like I was going to explode. The following morning, I woke up as if the night before was nothing but a dream. But then I saw your letter sitting beside me, the empty beer can next to my dresser, and it all came rushing back. My hands trembled as I clutched the sheet of paper.

Then came the fearful sobs at the thought of creating and being responsible for a whole new human when I couldn't even care for myself. My chest heaved, and my knees threatened to buckle under the weight of it. After that came the denial and acceptance masked as the resignation phase, which led us to now. Currently at the complaining-in-a-bit-of-a-psychotic-and-somewhat-dramatic stage.

This pregnancy came at an incredibly inopportune time. For starters, how the fuck does this even happen to someone? This baby was already doomed to an unfair fate, and he wasn't even born yet. He was going to grow up without a father. No male figure—no dad to teach him how to shave or tie a tie. All the plans we had made for a family had been reduced to an incomplete idea, a missing concept of a broken thought.

He will sit beside an empty chair on Father's Day—the ghost of a memory that wasn't even his own—surrounded by real-life dads, questioning what that would feel like.

And on top of that, he was granted to the world's most inexperienced mom. My stomach twisted, and I rocked back on my heels. How could so many odds be stacked against such a tiny heart?

This kid didn't stand a chance.

And by the way things were looking, neither did I.

Fucking shit.

I gripped my stomach and looked down at my hands, feeling the tiny life inside me twitch at my anxiety. This baby might as well get used to his mom in a state of crisis.

"How on Earth did you end up here?" I whispered to him, my voice breaking slightly, the words hanging in the air like smoke. My fingers traced my belly absentmindedly, a small attempt to soothe both of us.

It had become a tradition for me to sleep in Grandma's room the night before the appointments with the obstetrician. I would always get nervous about the test results, and sleeping beside her gave me a little peace. Sure, she snored when she slept—more than you would think possible for someone her size—but the company was nice. She always slept on the right side of the bed because Grandpa would always sleep on the left. Ever since he passed, she's stayed put. When I questioned her, she said that Grandpa's body had formed an indentation on his side of the bed, and she did not want to mess it up. She said that waking up in the middle of the night and seeing his imprint gave her the illusion that he was making coffee or drinking water and would be back to bed soon.

I'm surprised she let me sleep here at all, but I assumed she realized that it would take more than 130 pounds once or twice a month to erase a mattress' 50-year-old, solidified memory. You'd think I spat in her face by the way she reacted when I once suggested buying an orthopedic upgrade. Sometimes, you just need to pick your battles.

At the same time, Grandpa's body was significantly bigger and sturdier than mine, so sleeping in his silhouette felt like I was wrapped in his embrace. It smelled like him, too—a hint of cigar, oak, and soil after morning rain. Even if the mattress didn't actually hold his smell, the memory associated with him brought the scent into his shape. The whole experience comforted me, and I liked to fall asleep thinking of him, hoping my memories would prompt him to visit my dreams.

Now, I have grown accustomed to the routine. The night before appointments, I would get in bed, avoid any comments about mattresses that are older than I am, let her kiss us both—my forehead, then my belly—and be lulled to sleep by her bulldozer-like snoring. I was having a great night's rest until a whisper stirred me awake. It took me a couple of seconds to realize I wasn't dreaming.

"Noah… Noah!" she said. I groaned, unaware of the time but hoping for just five more minutes.

"Noah!" she hissed.

"What?" I mumbled impatiently.

"I think I had a wet dream," she whispered, a little embarrassed.

Even half asleep, my eyebrows creased, and I got nauseous. Even for her, that was a wildly inappropriate comment.

"Eww," I said, completely appalled. "Aren't you a little old to have those?"

"I actually think this is about the time that you start having them," she said matter-of-factly.

My forehead crinkled. Something wasn't right.

"What are you even talking about—" I hadn't completed my sentence when my eyes shot open, and all the tiredness and laziness I felt suddenly evaporated. I was fully awake, completely aware, and terrified to move.

"What do you think having a wet dream means?" I asked, though I already knew the answer.

"It's when you piss yourself in your sleep. You know? You have the dream where you get up to use the bathroom? It just felt so real!"

I paused.

I didn't move.

And yet I felt it.

My lower back and my thighs felt cold and sticky.

Another small pause.

A deep breath.

And then I threw my body toward the edge of the bed and puked on the floor. While I retched, she added, "Oopsie indeed."

"We are getting you adult diapers," I said, my voice muffled by the pillow but with an air of finality that didn't waver.

"Sounds about right." She nodded. It was not resignation that I heard in her voice, but acceptance. She knew she was getting old and that we had to adapt to the new realities we were facing. I felt proud of her for being so mature and accepting of time, but deep down, I also felt a profound sadness because it would be a slippery slope from here on out, and I wanted her to stay like this forever. Nonetheless, we would tackle this together, just like we did everything else. This new reality, so it seemed, would include a lot of pee, both newborn and senior. Why did my life suddenly involve so many bodily fluids?

We mopped the floor, stripped the bed, stuffed the sheets into the washer, and showered until the water ran cool.

When the timer on the toaster went off and butter melted into the slices, the house smelled of chamomile and warm bread. Lately, all I craved was avocado toast; and Grandma's breakfast had always been the same; both ends of a French baguette with butter, guava jelly, and avocado.

At the table we discussed the plans for the day—doctor, then mall for baby clothes, and an urgent stop at the grocery store for her nighty whoopsies—that's what she chose to call them. Of everything she could've said, that's what she went with. I rolled my eyes at the joke, but it punched a hole through the morning's tension.

Mid-morning sunlight winked off the windshield as we drove to the clinic; the car smelled faintly of sanitizer and Grandma's cinnamon perfume.

We arrived at the appointment fifteen minutes early and were told to wait in the lobby. I was nervous and fidgety. Like she always did, my grandma noticed and placed her hand on my knee in silent support, offering me a comforting smile assuring me we would all be okay. Today was the appointment where we found out the baby's sex, and while I already knew it was a boy because my grandma said so—and apparently, she knows everything—I was still holding on to some skepticism for the sake of logic and rebellion.

The doctor called us in. I laid down on the bed and lifted up my shirt, exposing my belly. I had a small but visible bump by now; the hip dimples I was once so keen on now replaced by a small human the size of a lime. Its heartbeat filled the room with a steady melody of love and miracles.

I watched her rub the blue gel near my abdomen, and took a sharp breath as the cold substance touched my naked stomach.

The lime jolted a little bit, too.

"Sorry, I should have warned you!"

No shit. I smiled politely, secretly wishing I could squeeze that freezing gel into her face. See if she found it funny then. My hormones had been haywire as of late, and I found myself quite passive-aggressive—but really leaning more toward the aggressive side of the spectrum.

The doctor asked me how I felt, and I assured her I felt okay. I was a little more tired than usual, but she said that was to be expected.

"Any morning sickness?" she asked.

I gave Grandma a knowing, cynical look and answered with an icy cadence in my voice. "Not by choice."

"What do you mean?" the doctor asked.

"She threw up this morning," my grandma said mockingly as she unwrapped her third lollipop of the day. It occurred to me that taking her to the dentist and checking for cavities may be a good idea.

"Oh! Has that been happening often?" the doctor asked curiously.

"She better hope not," I whispered to myself.

"No ma'am! First time in about seventy years!" my grandma said.

The doctor lowered her eyebrows in confusion.

"I really don't think it will be a daily occurrence. I feel okay. It has only happened twice, and it's not too bad," I assured her, amused by my grandma's purple-stained guilty smirk as I shot daggers at her with my eyes. The doctor kept examining and poking my belly.

"So…" She smiled coyly. "Would you like to know the sex of the baby?" she said as her eyes lit up.

"Let me guess, it's a boy?" I asked, unimpressed.

Her face crumbled. She looked hurt—almost as if we had stolen her thunder, her big revelatory moment.

I pointed at my grandma. "She told me the day we found out I was pregnant," I explained.

The doctor looked at my grandma incredulously and then back at me. "That is scientifically impossible."

"Don't get her sta—" I managed to say before getting interrupted.

"You people and your science," my grandma scoffed. "I'm like a hundred years old; you learn a thing or two when you reach so many laps around the sun."

The doctor looked at her, me, and then back at my grandma. Her glare was as sour as the lime in my belly. She didn't look too pleased. The appointment was over shortly after.

Waiting in the elevator, my chest swelled with a strange mix of disbelief and awe. I realized, just for a second, that this tiny human I carried already felt like part

210

of me. I reached over and squeezed Grandma's hand, grateful for the solid anchor she always was.

Surprise, surprise. I was having a boy.

A few days later I was sweeping the floor. My body was sore, and I felt fifty pounds heavier, but I had only gained maybe three or four pounds. My belly wasn't showing yet, so it was hard for me to actually *feel* pregnant. The only indication that anything was out of the ordinary was the constant, bone-deep exhaustion—as if this baby was siphoning every ounce of energy from me and leaving only fatigue behind.

I was glistening with sweat, wearing sweatpants and a black tank top, and my hair was up in a misshapen knot above my head. The years of trying to look good were over. Now it was just my grandma and me in a house alone—we could afford to be comfortable.

My grandma was playing dominoes in the living room, but I could feel her glancing my way every few seconds. It was a little irritating.

"What?" I asked, tired of being examined under a microscope.

"Nothing. Don't you wanna throw on a bra, though?"

"Why would I? It's just us here."

"I mean—I'm wearing a bra. I just thought you might like to wear one too."

Now that I looked at her—really looked at her—she wasn't just wearing a bra. She was wearing real clothes—not the typical bathrobe she shuffled around in. And not only that, she had combed her hair. It looked good today. Usually she only fluffed it with a comb in passing.

"All right, spit it out. What did you do?" I asked, narrowing my eyes.

"Who says I did anything?" she said defensively.

Before I could answer, the doorbell rang.

We looked at each other.

"You might wanna get that," was all she said before turning back to her dominoes.

I sighed loudly and opened the door with unnecessary aggression.

And suddenly, I was standing in front of your parents, neat, composed, and well put together.

"Oh my god. Mr. and Mrs. Burke. Hi!" I said, crossing my arms over my chest. "This is such a nice surprise!"

Their smiles were polite, but their eyebrows furrowed.

"Your lovely grandmother invited us for tea. Didn't she mention it?" Your mom asked kindly.

I was gonna kill that lady.

"Oh! No, yeah! Totally, she definitely mentioned it—" I stammered, "it's just... time got away from me, and I didn't realize it was time for me to get ready. But please! Do come in!" I stepped aside and lunged for the hoodie that *someone* had—strategically and miraculously—laid across the couch. I met my grandma's eyes as she entered with a tray of freshly brewed coffee and tea.

You're so dead, I said telepathically.

Ooooo look at me, I'm so scared, she mocked me with her eyes.

"Mr. and Mrs. Burke, it is such a pleasure to have you here! Please, help yourselves to some tea or coffee. Noah will help me bring out the rest of the snacks— we'll be right back!"

Your parents nodded gratefully, making themselves comfortable on the couch.

Back in the kitchen, we lowered our voices to a whisper.

"Are you *crazy*, Grandma!? Why didn't you tell me you invited them!?"

"Because you would have panicked and stressed about it and probably tried to talk me out of it! But when you bring out the snacks, you definitely might want to mention the fact that their *late son* is having a son of his own!"

"Shhh!" I pleaded. "A heads-up would've been nice! I'm filthy and—if that wasn't enough—I am not wearing a bra!"

"Well, whose fault is that? I suggested wearing one ten minutes ago! Your in-laws are in the other room and you're just letting them hang like that—have some decency, kid!"

We both rolled our eyes and growled at each other as we turned away to grab the snacks. By the time we reached the living room, we had pasted two polite, hostess-grade smiles on our faces.

The small talk was a little awkward. It felt like they were also wearing some kind of mask, trying to convince themselves they were doing better—even though their hearts were just as shattered. But hey, at least they were trying.

"How have you been doing?" I asked.

They both sighed and concealed a small glance at each other.

"Oh you know. We've been trying. One day at a time. We have been attending support group meetings for parents who have lost a child and that helps. It helps us realize that we are not alone. We also set up a small foundation in Derek's name." The sound of your name still made my heart skip a beat and formed a knot in my stomach. "It's called Hearts of Hope, and it gathers funds for people who have been battling with depression and mental health issues in general. It doesn't really help us, but it is nice to know it may be helping others, you know?"

I honestly didn't. They were trying much harder than me, I've just been consumed with grief over losing you and anxiety over our son.

I thought about the foundation, *Hearts of Hope*, and I caught myself smiling at those two words, thinking back to when we went to the fair—when we had our whole lives ahead of us and wanted to conquer it one candy apple at a time.

My grandma cleared her throat, snapping me back into the living room.

"Huh?" I said, caught off guard.

"I was asking how you've been doing," your mom said.

I looked at her openly, earnestly. I couldn't bring myself to lie and say I was fine—I was exhausted from faking smiles, pretending this storm would pass, feeling held together by nothing more than tape and glue.

So instead, I let your parents read me like an open book. I shrugged, offering the ghost of a tired smile, and I knew they understood.

They nodded in quiet reciprocity.

I reached for my cup of tea and felt my grandma's stare at the back of my neck. My hand started shaking so violently I had to set the teacup back down.

This woman was relentless.

Your parents frowned, concern flashing in their eyes.

"Everything okay, sweetie?" your mom asked gently.

My heart was pounding. *How do I tell them?*

"Yeah, I'm okay. I just haven't been sleeping much. I've had a lot on my mind lately." I spoke faster than usual, stumbling on a few words.

I was sweating profusely now. My shoulders were visibly moving with every shallow breath I took. I was having an anxiety attack.

"What's wrong, Noah?" your dad asked. He was always blunt and to the point; I couldn't imagine him finding any kind of vague detour remotely entertaining.

I looked at Mr. Burke, and in his eyes I saw yours—your curious, searching stare—and a gasp caught in my throat.

Then I looked at your mom, her eyebrows raised in quiet expectancy, jaw tense, her lips forming a small pout.

"Noah, what's going on?" Your mom placed her hand over my knee, concerned.

I kept breathing, fast and short breaths were making me a little dizzy, and by now my hoodie was sticking to my lower back.

Finally, I looked at my grandma, trying to ground myself. The mastermind behind this whole operation.

Go ahead, she told me with her eyes.

I sighed, defeated.

Apparently, I couldn't keep this secret any longer.

I placed my hand over your wedding ring, the one hanging from my necklace, and silently wished you could be the one to tell them. I didn't know how they'd react, but with you here, I knew it would all be okay in the end.

I took a deep breath, my mouth parched, as if the two words lodged in my throat would decide the rest of my life.

"I'm pregnant."

Both of your parents were blinking furiously, struggling to process the words—and I understood the feeling completely.

"What?" they said in unison.

"I'm pregnant," I said again, lifting my gaze off the floor and meeting theirs, my words came out rushed and fast, afraid that if I got interrupted I would never speak again. "I found out a couple of weeks ago, and I'm freaking out. I'm definitely not ready to be a mom, much less without Derek to guide me." I was crying quietly now, still hyperventilating but feeling a weight off my chest by having finally said the words out loud.

I plowed on. "You're having a grandson. And I know you just lost your son, so I don't want you to feel forced to be involved in this baby's life. If the pain is too much, I get it. Trust me. But... if you want to be involved in any way... We need you." I rubbed my temple, aimlessly pushing the oncoming headache away.

My grandma sat stiffly next to me, and I could tell—even she was a little tense.

Five seconds passed.

They stretched on forever.

Then your mom brought her hands to her chest and screamed—more like shrieked—and smiled through her tears as she leaned backward on the couch, overcome with emotion.

I wasn't sure what I was expecting, but her reaction gave me a tiny glimmer of hope and comfort.

Your dad was still silent, staring at me. And then—

Waterfalls.

Tears streamed down his face. His nose turned bright red, and his lip trembled as it lifted into a grin that stretched from ear to ear.

Then your mom threw herself—literally threw herself—at me and my grandma with open arms, laughing through her tears.

"Oh, Derek, Derek—my baby, Derek! I knew it! I just knew it!"

She dropped to her knees and placed both hands on mine.

Relief washed over me, they were… *happy.*

I was a little hesitant, but after seeing their reactions, I allowed myself a moment to imagine our life as a family and with everyone we love right behind us, and suddenly I felt a little spark of joy as well, quieting my fear and anxiety.

By now, my grandma and I were laughing too, celebrating the legacy you had sent us from heaven.

"Oh, I can't believe it!" she cried, squeezing my hands and resting them gently on my stomach, as if she needed to physically connect to the life now growing inside me.

Your dad was still crying.

Shrieks of joy echoed all over the house.

"Come here, Mr. Burke! Join us!"

And to my surprise, he did.

He stood and came to sit by my side. With his giant arms, he wrapped around his wife, my grandma, and me, pulling us all into a single, warm, overwhelming hug.

"We're having a grandson!" Mr. Burke shouted, the words cracking under their own weight. I felt the thunder of his heart against my shoulder—rapid, steady, unmistakably alive—and, for the first time in weeks, my lungs loosened, knowing your parents were getting a second chance. Joy burst around us like applause, but beneath the cheering I caught a tremor, a breath that never quite became a sentence.

"Oh, my baby boy," he whispered—half prayer, half apology—"my sweet, sweet boy."

I hugged him a little tighter, not just for me, but for you too.

We laughed and cried and celebrated for the rest of the night.

My grandma brought out a twelve-pack of non-alcoholic beer.

Where had she been hiding that massive stash? That doesn't even fit in the vegetable drawer. I wondered to myself.

Each of us had a beer in hand, and together we toasted to you, Derek—

And the life we had created.

"Thank you, Noah," your dad whispered, wiping his nose.

"For what?"

"For giving us a piece of our boy back."

Tears pricked my eyes as I looked at him, your memory weaving an invisible bridge between us.

"To Derek," your dad raised his beer, choking a sob in his throat, a smile breaking through the grief.

"To Derek," we all echoed.

We each drank a few more beers and started talking about the future.

"What will his name be?" your mom asked, brushing a strand of hair off my face.

"I don't know yet," I chuckled.

"Oh, okay," your mom said quietly, asking a million rapid-fire questions. "And what about summers and holidays? Can we come visit?"

"Of course," I said. "No question about it."

Your mom raised her arms in celebration and let out a small shriek, like a kid opening a Christmas present.

"Look, guys... we're going to need all the help we can get. I want you both to be as involved in his life as you want. I need him to know where he comes from, and having you in his life will help keep Derek's memory alive. We're a family, and we'll raise him together. I know flying from Florida isn't always cheap, but maybe we can arrange visits a few times a year. We'll figure something out."

Your parents looked at each other, and to my surprise, they had a silent conversation of their own—turns out that superpower doesn't just apply to Grandma and me.

"There's no need," your dad said. "There's a retirement community about an hour from here. In a few months, we'll make arrangements to move back, and we'll be at your disposal. And I don't want you worrying about money, either. We'll cover any medical bills, daycare, clothes, tuition, college—whatever's needed. We've had a very difficult year, but this baby... this baby changes everything. It's giving us a chance to be happy again. Like it's giving us a... a—"

"Purpose?" my grandma offered, smiling gently.

"Yes," they both said, almost in unison.

"He's a gift, Noah," your mom said softly. "Derek sent us a gift. A chance to be a family again. And we will make him proud."

She placed her warm hand on my belly.

We had a few more beers after that and toasted some more. We laughed, cried, and reminisced about you, Derek. The past was painful, but the future held this new life—a second chance, and while we imagined a future where you were still here with us, we were comforted by one undeniable truth:

Our baby boy would grow up wrapped in love. Yours. Ours. Theirs. All of it. A legacy he might never know, but would feel in every heartbeat.

The front door clicked shut behind your parents, leaving the house in a hushed silence that felt almost sacred. The kind of quiet that wasn't empty, but full of possibility. I sank into the couch, my heart still fluttering from the whirlwind of their tears and joy. I could feel you in every word they had said, in every glance they had shared.

Grandma perched beside me, resting a warm hand on my shoulder.

"Thank you," I whispered, resting my head on her hand, "for forcing me to talk to them."

She gave me a small, knowing smile. "Sometimes you just need a shove, Pumpkin. You were ready—you just didn't know it.

I nodded, letting the weight of the evening settle in. "I don't know what I would do without you."

She patted my hand. "Honestly, me neither. You're a bit of a mess, but I'm sure you would've figured it out eventually." She teased. "You're stronger than you think. Always have been."

We shared a quiet laugh, said our goodnights, and I followed her up the stairs, setting a glass of water by her bedside. I watched her fragile frame as she steadied herself on the dresser, carefully slipping off her slippers. The years had taken their toll—loose skin hung from her elbows and neck, and she had lost so much weight. A pang shot through my heart, a sudden surge of protectiveness, and I vowed to always be there for her.

"I love you, sweet dreams," I mumbled as I closed her door gently.

Upstairs, the house felt hushed, the echoes of the night lingering in the walls. My bedroom was dim, the soft glow of the nightlight casting gentle shadows.

On my nightstand, your letter waited patiently. My fingers trembled as I reached for it and remembered the panic I had felt at the bank, the tears that had blurred the words I hadn't been able to read. But tonight was different.

Tonight, I had felt the love that I had been too consumed in grief to allow myself to feel.

Tonight, right now, I was ready.

I slid the envelope open, unfolded the letter and began to read.

Dear Noah,

I suck at writing. Words have always been more your thing, but I'll give it my best shot. After all, I'd do anything for you.

I've been racking my brain for forty-five minutes now, trying to figure out how to say goodbye to you—how I want you to remember me and what I hope will be my final words. But to do that, I'd have to imagine a life without you, and I don't think I can.

Maybe I'm being selfish. Maybe I'm a coward. But I don't want to live without you. I don't want to read your letter. I don't know how to immortalize my words, Noah, but I will say this: I want to die first. Ideally, just a day or two before you. But I hope you're the one reading this, because reading yours would send me into a spiral of eternal fucking torture.

I still remember the exact angle at which the sun hit your face that afternoon we met outside the coffee shop. I remember how easily your fingers moved as you shaped different chords, and I can still feel the butterflies in my stomach as I tried to work up the nerve to talk to you. I was terrified of saying the wrong thing because you were perfect. I couldn't mess it up. You were my only chance at love. My only chance at living.

Noah, you are my everything. You came into my life and gave it purpose. You are light and joy, and I need you to know that. I admire you—how you carry yourself, your confidence, the way you see the best in people and smile at strangers, how easily you love and how openly you show it.

This letter... It's poorly written. A pathetic attempt to express my love for you. But if I die, there are only two things I need you to understand:

First—You were, are, and will forever be my home. And I don't mean just a place where we lived. I mean my Home, with a capital H. You are my core, my heart, my happiness. You capitalize my whole life. You are my entire world, and I need this to be understood: they say home is where the heart is, but my heart will always be with you. My Home will always be You.

Second—Thank you for the lessons. Even if you didn't realize it, I learned from you how to be a better man. You taught me to see the world with childlike wonder, to ask questions, to be curious without shame. You showed me how to live freely, without guilt or judgment. You helped me let go of what others expected and embrace who I truly was. In doing that, you set me free. And lucky for me, that path led me straight to you.

You were my compass when I was lost and my North Star when I needed guidance. You became the best part of me. I am grateful, Noah. You showed me how to live.

I don't know how old you'll be when you read this. But I want to leave you with some words of encouragement—the same ones you once gave me:

Take your own advice, Noah. Find your purpose. Seek your happiness. Follow your path.

You are unique, and I have no doubt that wherever you end up, you will shine bright. But whenever you feel alone, look down at your wedding ring and close your eyes. Think of me. Picture me there with you, holding your hand.

You made me the happiest I could ever be. I am proud to call you mine. I will never leave you. I'll always be with you, even if you can't see me.

Don't be scared, Noah. I'll be waiting for you.

I love you forever and always. Thank you for letting me love you.

—Derek

I sat there for what felt like hours, absorbing every word, every memory, every heartbeat you had captured on the page. Tears streamed down my face, hot and steady, but they were not the same tears I had shed in despair. These were tears of love, of connection, of something unbroken.

When I finally folded the letter and placed it gently back on the nightstand, I felt lighter. Tomorrow, the world would return to all its messiness, but tonight, I could breathe. Tonight, I let myself feel both the sorrow of what I'd lost and the promise of what was to come.

I held my belly as I thought of you and whispered to our baby, "I will tell you all about him. You'll know him, and you'll carry him with you, just like me."

I took a deep breath and slid under the covers, finally letting myself rest, carrying your words, my family's love, and a small, glowing spark of hope for the future into the night.

As I reached the end of my first trimester, my grandma and I had fallen into a comfortable routine. Tonight was Scrabble night, and we had already picked seven tiles each, but right before we started playing, I got an incomprehensible craving for s'mores. I went outside to look at the little backyard fire pit we had. It was one of those you can buy at Home Depot. You can't cook a full-blown family barbecue on it, but it does the job of roasting marshmallows. I was still indecisive; I didn't feel like driving to the store, but the baby needed the s'mores as much as I did.

I hadn't even said a word yet, but I swear that woman could read minds. As I stepped inside the house and closed the sliding door, a bag of marshmallows smacked me in the face. Good thing she didn't throw the skewers next.

"That's an amazing idea, I love those little suckers. Scrabble can wait! Let me get some lighter fluid, and I will be right there," she said chipperly.

I nodded dutifully and spun on my heel. My grandma was so cool.

We ate our third s'more of the night as we sang along to the tunes on the radio. Enticed by the fire pit's beauty and the mystery of its colors, I asked my grandma when she had last used it. It didn't seem completely abandoned; there were still remnants of ashes and unburnt coal at the bottom of the pit.

She thought for a moment. "The day after I hit my head against the sliding door," she said without a trace of doubt.

"You were craving s'mores?" After a night at the hospital, I figured she deserved a treat.

She chuckled. "Oh no, no. I had to burn a letter."

"Burn it? Why not just throw it away if you wanted to get rid of it?"

"Because it was symbolic." She paused for a few seconds. "Ever wonder why I rarely get angry?"

The thought hadn't necessarily crossed my mind; I hadn't really seen her get angry often—cigarette episode aside. More often than not, I saw her going crazy, but not angry or resentful. I stared at her but encouraged her to continue.

"When I'm angry—and I don't mean just pissed off over something silly—I mean really angry, the kind that throbs in your head and weighs down your chest—I write it all down. I pour my heart out onto the page and address it to the person or thing I'm angry at. Once I'm convinced I've said everything I need to say, I seal the envelope and burn it. Watching my anger physically burn to a crisp helps me let it go. I've been doing it for years. Therapy was too expensive, and I preferred burning the letters instead of airing my business to strangers."

I looked at her intently, curious and interested in her coping mechanisms. Although many of her quirks were ridiculous (like the lollipop obsession), this one made sense. It felt right. I could almost feel the weight lift off her shoulders as she explained it, and I wondered if I could do the same. Could I write to you, Derek? Or to our son? To life itself for being so cruel? The thought both terrified me and lit a small spark of relief I hadn't expected.

"Who were you angry at the day you hit your head?" I asked.

She sighed, remembering the scene like a flashback in a movie. "Not who, but what. I was mad at Age. I was angry at the fact that time kept ticking, and my body was lagging behind. I'm so weak, Noah. I have to watch where I walk and what I eat. I have to wear fucking adult diapers," she said, wiping chocolate from the corner of her mouth, all childlike and vulnerable. The sight tugged at my heart.

"Aging has been one of the toughest things I've had to go through. I went from being fearless and independent to counting pills each morning and checking labels like my life depends on it. It probably does. So I wrote a letter to old age and told it to suck it. I can still hold my own, and my spirit never wavered, so I decided that I would continue to be this way until I can't anymore."

I held her gaze. I watched as she stood up and went inside the house. The night was chilly, but the heat radiating from the fire grazed my cheeks with comfort and warmth. The flames cracked and hissed, and I couldn't help but think of them as both destroyers and protectors. They devoured everything in their path, yet they also lit the darkness and kept me warm. Grief and hope, dancing side by side in sparks of orange and blue.

I heard my grandma's footsteps crunching on the dry leaves as she made her way back to me. She kissed my forehead and placed a pen, paper, and envelope on her now empty seat. I got the hint—this was my turn.

"Who would I even write to?" I asked.

"Who are you mad at?" she replied as she walked away, her voice a little muffled from the giant marshmallow she had just put in her mouth.

I grabbed the pen and placed it between my fingers. I hesitated for a moment, feeling the weight of her lesson settle in. Your name rose to my lips, then the baby's, then my own. Maybe I was mad at all of us. Maybe I was mad at the universe. The pen felt heavier the longer I held it, as though it already carried the words I was too afraid to write. I could let go—or I could hold it tighter than ever. But what did I have to lose anyway?

Dear Time,

I fucking hate you.

My anger isn't only directed at you. I'm angry at Derek. I'm angry at myself. But most of all, I blame you.

Years ago, when I was young, quiet, and naïve, I thought you were endless. God, I felt invincible. I believed I had control over my hours, my choices, my life. I was wild and reckless, and it felt fine—because I had all the time in the world. I was young, and you were infinite.

Tick tock. Tick tock.

But as I got older, your presence felt heavier. I felt you breathing down my neck. I started hearing you whispering in the back of my mind—do it right the first time, don't waste me. I started to believe you were slipping away.

Then I met him.

And suddenly—you stopped.

Time didn't exist when I was with him. You didn't matter. His time and mine combined into something new, something timeless. We ignored you. We lived above you.

And you hated that.

You got jealous. You ran ahead of us. And you didn't even have the decency to take us both.

Instead, you were cruel.

And in your cruelty, you took my purpose.

In your selfishness, you took my joy.

And with your absence, you stole my soulmate.

I ran out of You, and in doing so—I ran out of Him.

Why couldn't you just let us be?

Why couldn't you run your course and let us run ours?

With emptiness,
N.

I sealed the envelope and addressed it: "To Time." I dropped the letter on the fire and immediately watched as the flames rose in the corners of the paper, darkening it as the charred bits of parchment curled into dust. Within a minute, all that was left of my grief was a small pile of ashes.

My grandma had called this ritual symbolic. Cathartic.

That was an understatement.

It was an irony if I had ever seen one. I watched my grief and my anger burn down to a crisp the same way that my home did—engulfed by the fire that crackled around it, fearless and merciless as it destroyed everything I ever knew. The pop of the wood, the smell of smoke—it was too easy to imagine that night all over again, the heat pressing against my face, the terror clinging to my skin.

I stared into the blue flame as it slowly burnt out. Then I paused. *Burn out* didn't feel right. Fires don't just burn out—they die. I noticed one last little spark of life left on the corner of a dry leaf, fighting with all its might to reignite the fire, but the fight didn't last too long. A few seconds later, as if by magic, the spark disappeared into a tiny cloud of smoke. And that was that.

I put the lighter fluid between my forearm and chest and picked up the chocolate, marshmallows, and skewers from the chair. I popped one last marshmallow in my mouth, just like my grandma had, and walked into the house without looking back. I felt lighter, as if the weight of the anger I had been carrying had dissipated into the cold, misty night.

As always, she was right.

I wasn't angry at Time anymore.

But that didn't mean I forgave it.

month four

TODAY OFFICIALLY MARKS the start of my second trimester. It has been a wild ride. Grandma is constantly making sure I'm taking care of myself, eating well and getting the right amount of sleep. I have told our baby boy about you every day; I want to make sure he knows who you were and how happy you made me. Since Grandma and I talked about writing letters, I have been journaling a lot. At first, it felt silly, but it became as powerful as she said. I wish I could write you a letter, send it to heaven, and wait for the mailman to deliver your response. It would be simple, just a few lines about memories and reminiscing.

I wouldn't mention how I shattered your autographed Eagles CD and spent two nights forging Glenn Frey's signature, or that I gouged your car door with a runaway shopping cart and blamed it on an old man. Some secrets are best kept until the next lifetime.

But do you know what I would say?

I'd start with how much I missed you. Some days it hit me like a wave, knocking me off balance before I could catch my breath. Other days it's softer, like a draft slipping under the door, reminding me you're gone before I've even opened my eyes. But that pain, the sense of loss, was always there.

I would tell you that I missed our conversations and adventures. The way that I laughed *at* you and *with* you. I'd ask if you remembered how I would lie next to you and get lost counting the freckles on your nose? How I fell asleep in the crook of your shoulder? How I would impatiently wait for the sun to go down every night so we could do it all over again the next day? Every night with you was perfect.

I'd ask you about New Orleans. About the night you dragged me down Bourbon Street, your warm hand in mine, powdered sugar clinging to your smile after we split that beignet. I could still see the glow of the streetlights on your face, illuminating the night sky like fireflies, and heard Jazz music tumbling out of every doorway. That was the night we discovered Five Minute Poetry.

I could see it in your eyes. The curiosity to know what the poet would write about us.

I wish I remembered his words. The poem itself had slipped away, but the poet remained crystal clear in my mind. The young man balanced a typewriter on his scrawny legs and perched himself on a three-legged stool. I remembered wondering what those eyes had seen. He was so thin, the bones of his spine protruding through his flannel, but the fire in his eyes told me he was exactly where he wanted to be. He had found his home writing poems for strangers, providing the words of wisdom we longed for and aimlessly searched for most of our lives.

He was fascinating. I know you felt it too because I caught you looking at his hands. He was wearing fingerless gloves, but the frays and undone thread on the edges told us he had cut them himself to expose his impeccable nails—not a single smudge of dirt. The dichotomy of the thinness and frailness of his body against his pristine hands was odd. He valued his art and wanted to respect it. He was proud of what he did and how his fingers grazed each key, but he needed to keep the machine as pure as it deserved—free of sins and impurities.

That night, I knew—really knew—that I was hopelessly in love with you. Every freckle on your nose. Every off-key note you sang. Every way you could make me laugh even when I didn't want to.

I would give anything to read that poem again. It was so simple and beautiful. Just like you. Just like us. But I know I never will. That small piece of us had vanished in the wind.

The thought made my chest ache, and the letter in my nightstand felt even more fragile. At least I had this. At least I still had your words—words that fire would never take away.

I remembered this story one day during our daily afternoon tea. I kept telling my grandma about the poem repeatedly because I remembered the title—"The Word" was its name—but I could not recall where I put it. It did not matter anyway, because if it were in the house, the poem would have turned to ashes. That sounds incredibly romantic and poetic, but it only emphasizes its melancholy and nostalgia for what will never be again.

"We should take nude painting lessons," my grandma said in response, casually, as if that was a normal conversation to bring up mid-tea.

I froze, buttered toast an inch from my lips. "What the fuck," I whispered with an air of resignation, shaking my head as I placed the toast gently back on the plate and looked at my grandma.

"You want to paint naked people?" I said calmly. I was getting used to the irrational ideas that populated my grandma's brain, but this was something else.

"I think it could be fun. Explore human astronomy and whatnot."

"You mean anatomy?"

"You are getting hung up on the details too much. You sound like a schoolteacher." She chewed her buttercream cookie and rolled her eyes.

I nodded quietly, trying to figure out how we got here.

"Okay. Let me wash my hands, and we can return to this insane conversation."

I went to the bathroom to wash my hands, the butter on my fingers making them shiny and slippery. I was only gone for about two minutes, but by the time I came back, I was still trying to figure out how to hopefully not paint a live penis. I needed to tread this subject carefully.

"So, about that idea of painting nude people…"

She creased her eyebrows and looked at me slowly.

"You're into that? Painting asses? Well, I never thought about it, but now that you mention it, I think it could be a fun activity for us. We can learn about human astronomy. Where did you hear about that?"

The clink of her teacup against the saucer rang louder than it should have, like a bell marking the loss I couldn't name out loud. I was frozen and stood quietly for a few seconds. She looked confused, a little lost even, almost as if stranded in a forest—an unfamiliar space—but she was trying to mask her fleeting moment of amnesia. For a second, her brief certainty made me wonder if I'd imagined the whole thing. But deep down, I knew I was not only right but that this was a defining moment. From now on, nothing would ever be the same.

I walked slowly, smiling reassuringly at her. I scratched her back softly as I gently removed the plates and placed the pot of tea on the stove, trying to distract the heartache in my chest.

"Oh. Never mind that. I thought you had mentioned it a couple of days ago, but I must have misunderstood," I said, hoping to be done with this conversation so I could stop being reminded of the consequences to come, how I was losing her.

"You better watch it! Or you'll be forgetting things like me before you know it!" she joked, unaware of the gut-wrenching irony drenched in her words.

I pretended to laugh to hide the urge to cry. These episodes became more frequent, and my fear and concern grew stronger. It was like watching a crack spread across glass—you knew it would shatter eventually, but you're powerless to stop it. I realized then that what I thought would be painful to her would be worse for me. She would forget in fragments, pieces falling away until the hole was too big to notice. But I would remember everything. Every slip, every blank stare, every lost thread of a sentence. I would carry the weight of what she no longer could, as I unwillingly witnessed every distant gaze when she chased a thought that was always out of reach.

The worst moments were when she looked lost on the surface. But there was always that flicker—her hand searching for the shape of a memory and finding only a question. When that doubt clouded her eyes, I answered it with soft facts; a name, a date, a story. I would remind her who she was. I would be patient. I would be steady.

Her world used to be made of wonder and glass, so I decided to hold her fragile, paper-thin planet together with scotch tape and glue, carefully assembled to keep the illusion of safety and peace within—filling it with crystals to reflect her memories off of the light that shined inside her. She shone as bright as the sun, and I would do everything in my power to keep that fire ablaze, because that was what she deserved. She deserved an entire galaxy of memories available within reach.

Ever since Grandma's episodes became more frequent, I kept us on a tight routine. Breakfast, lunch, and dinner, always at the same time. Predictable meals she loved. It made her feel safe.

But today, I had broken the routine. Last night, after pacing the kitchen floor for what felt like hours, I finally dialed Dad's number. My thumb hovered over the buttons, my stomach tightening, already bracing for a slurred hello or an excuse I'd heard too many times before. Your parents already knew about the baby, and it was only fair that he knew as well. He showed up as a new man at your funeral, and I wanted to believe that change was permanent, but I'd been burned before. Each ring of the phone felt like a test. When he answered, his voice was alert, awake—steady. No haze, no fog. Relief poured through me so quickly I almost dropped the receiver. We exchanged hellos. Mine was careful, his was hopeful. My words came out shakier than I wanted, but I invited him over, and to my surprise, he immediately said yes. No excuses this time, just an open and earnest willingness to come and a note of gratitude that assured me I had made the right call.

So the next day, when the doorbell rang, I didn't flinch. I already knew who it was.

"Hey Grandma, sorry to spring this up on you, but I invited Dad over to break the news. Is that okay?"

She raised her eyebrows comically over her glasses, a million thoughts crossing her mind. "Of course, Pumpkin. I'm proud of you for taking the lead. How do you think he'll take it?"

Deep down I knew that the most prominent thought she had was whether or not this news would send him over the edge. I had the same fear, but I was done keeping him in the dark for the sake of protecting him. He is not made of glass, and if his determination to get clean has proven anything to me these past few months, it was that he was stronger than I gave him credit for.

"Your guess is as good as mine."

"Hmmm. Well, this shall be fun. I'll make us some tea!"

I walked toward the door and let my hand rest on the knob for a few beats before I opened it. The cool brass against my palm flashed me back to that night—the burn, the sting, the smell of smoke. My hand trembled before I forced myself to curl my fingers tight as goosebumps crawled up my arms.

When I was finally ready, I twisted the knob and swung the door open.

My dad was standing on the porch with a Coke Zero in the crook of his elbow.

He looked exactly like he had at the funeral—hopeful eyes, awkward smile, like he wasn't sure if he was allowed to feel welcome. The sight of him sent a weird jolt through my chest. For a split second, I wanted to slam the door again, to protect us both from disappointment. But I didn't. Seeing him anxious for reassurance broke my heart a little, but I knew this was necessary. Rehab programs had this whole mantra about penance and for their members to feel some sort of guilt or regret for previous behavior. Some sent apology letters to the people they hurt, but I knew my dad. His penance was to show up, even knowing he might not always be welcome. That's the thing about us though—even when he didn't always show up for me, I would never turn my back on him. That's just the way we worked. We depended on one another, and right now, he deserved every bit of support coming my way.

"Dad! Hi!" I welcomed him with open arms. He felt heavier under my arms, sturdier. I could tell he was eating better and taking care of himself. He smelled fresh and clean, his skin looked radiant, and his eyes showed kindness and an open heart. We held each other a little longer than usual—long enough for me to realize how much I had missed this simple act. Neither of us wanted to let go.

"Hi, sweetheart. Am I too early? I know your grandma usually has her tea around four. I can wait in the car for a few minutes if you're not ready."

"What? Wait in the car for what, Dad? No, you can just come in."

He sighed in relief.

"Sounds good, here, let me help you with the door then." He reached over and held the door with his right hand.

"Nadia!" my dad called warmly as he stepped inside. "Thank you for having me!"

"Well, it's my pleasure. How's sober life treating you?" she asked as my dad leaned towards her in a one armed hug.

"I just got my seventh month chip! Wanna see it?"

He was like a proud boy showing off a brand new toy. The sight of it warmed my heart.

"I'm proud of you, kid." She winked as she squeezed his arm gently, letting her hand rest there for a few seconds. I was glad to see this moment; he needed validation and to know that we were rooting for him.

"So!" I cut in quickly, trying to be as discreet and subtle as possible. "Dad, go ahead and have a seat—we'll bring out some snacks. We'll be right back."

"Actually," he interrupted, eyeing the bowls, "is that coconut ice cream?"

"Sure is! Would you like a bowl?" I said.

"Hmm, would you mind scooping some up in a cup? I brought soda, and an ice cream float sounds pretty good right about now!"

We both scrunched our faces.

"You want soda with coconut ice cream?"

He shrugged sheepishly. "Ever since I quit drinking, I've been craving some weird combos."

"Umm… Sure thing, coming right up!" My grandma answered, trying to be a good host, but as we walked to the freezer I heard her mumble under her breath. "Your daddy has some nasty-ass taste, but hey, to each its own."

"He looks good, right? You think he'll handle it well enough?"

"Pumpkin, I've known your nasty-ass father for almost twenty-five years. Ever since your mom passed away, he's been a broken shell of the man I used to know. But now? It's different. I've never seen him this way. He's ready. I promise. This won't push him over the edge, on the contrary, it will center him more than ever. He needs this."

She winked at me as she placed a spoon and a cup on my hands. Her touch was always warm and gentle, and every day I was so grateful to have her in my life.

I scooped three spoons of coconut ice-cream and walked back out to the living room, where Dad was patiently waiting with his soda in hand. I handed Dad the glass. He lit up.

"Ahh! I love coconut ice cream. I love chewing on the flakes. You know, it was your mom's favorite flavor too."

I studied him for a second.

He could talk about her now.

No spiraling. No breakdown. Just… a memory, spoken with love and steadiness.

Seven months sober. And here he was, showing up for me.

And somehow, that almost brought me to tears.

I looked at my grandma, who was staring at him intently, and I could tell she noticed it too. She shot me a quick glance.

He's finally ready, her eyes told me.

And for once, I wholeheartedly agreed.

I wasn't anxious like when I had to tell my in-laws about the pregnancy. I had now had time to adjust, and seeing my dad's strength and resolve to show up gave me the bravery I needed. He deserved to know—and to hear it from me—sooner rather than later, so he could be a part of his grandchild's life.

"Hey, Dad," I said carefully. "Did Mom ever talk about wanting more kids?"

His eyebrows rose, his eyes softening. "Oh yeah. She dreamed of a big family— more than I thought I could handle. You as the oldest, a little brother named Jonah, even twins. She used to laugh about it, said she wanted a full house of noise and chaos." His voice caught a little. "She would've been a wonderful mother to all of you."

Dad cleared his throat. "Hey, Nadia, would you mind bringing me a cup of water. Ice cream always makes me thirsty," he said, almost as if asking for permission.

She left the kitchen and returned with three glasses of water.

I hesitated, my heart pounding. "And grandkids? Did she ever…?"

His face brightened. "Of course. She said if you all had two each, she'd need bunk beds for eight. Pajama parties, movie marathons… She wanted to be the kind of grandma who made everything magical."

His eyes softened as he spoke. Mine filled. I thought of you, Derek, and how you would never get to see our baby, but somehow, this conversation made me feel closer to you.

"And what about you? Would you ever like to have grandchildren?"

"Oh, sweetie. That would be so nice. I'm hoping that with time, a few years from now, when you're ready to meet someone again, you'll bless us with the grandchild your mom always wanted."

"Well," I said softly, "you won't have to wait forever."

"Oh." He paused, concerned. "Are you seeing someone already? Don't you think it's a little too soon? Call me old-fashioned, but I feel like you might need more than a couple of months, Noah."

My grandma rolled her eyes loudly.

I didn't remember my dad being this slow.

"No, Dad. That's not what I mean."

"I'm not saying wait twenty years to grieve like I did, but I feel like maybe two or three ye—"

"Dad! I mean… I'm pregnant. You're going to be a grandpa."

The words hung between us, fragile and terrifying and beautiful.

For a moment, he just stared. My chest tightened. Ten seconds stretched into forever. In those seconds I imagined him storming out, spiraling back, shutting me out completely. My throat ached with the urge to fill the silence. Then the cup he'd been holding slipped from his hand and shattered on the floor, splashing water on our ankles. He didn't react to it. He was still processing.

Then his face crumpled—part joy, part fear. "Sweetheart… oh, wow. My God… That's…" He covered his mouth, his eyes filling. "Are you okay? I mean—after what happened to your mom—I can't help but worry—"

"I know," I said quickly. "But I'm okay. The doctors say I'm healthy. And I'm not doing this alone. I've got you. I've got Grandma. And I've got Derek's love with me, always."

"Uhhhmm, but Derek, h-how did—?"

"You don't need us to explain that part to you, do you?" my grandma said dryly.

He blinked a few more times. He still hadn't moved from the chair. "I'm… I'm going to be a grandpa?"

"Yup." I smiled softly.

His shoulders shook, and he pulled me into a hug that almost lifted me off my feet. "Oh, sweetie. I can't believe it. This is incredible news. I'm so proud of you. Your mom would be, too."

Grandma sniffed loudly. "Well, finally. About damn time one of you said it."

We laughed through tears.

"Nadia, did you hear that? I'm going to have a grandson!"

My grandma had misty eyes. I could tell hearing my dad talk about Mom made her feel the absence a little deeper. But seeing him celebrate this news, for both of them, gave life to her memory.

My dad kissed my forehead and hugged my grandma. Then, to my surprise, he lifted her off her feet and spun her around a few times, rekindling a strange moment of love between them I hadn't seen in years. He set her down gently and they smiled at each other—honest and intentional smiles—and they were both crying.

"Now *this* calls for a celebration," my grandma said. "Tell me your thoughts on non-alcoholic beers."

My dad blinked back tears. "Huh. I never really thought of that. I do know some of the people in my group drink them socially. Do you guys think it's okay?"

We shrugged our shoulders.

"I mean, it's ideal for expectant mothers and recovering alcoholics. No pressure though. We can toast with tea if you prefer." Grandma chimed in nonchalantly.

My dad thought for a moment. I don't know why, but this felt like a defining moment. And then he spoke.

"Well, it's a little past four in the afternoon. If I remember correctly, you typically have some tea at this time. How about we toast with tea to avoid any slippery slopes? We can eventually work up to the fake booze." He winked at us.

"Three cups, coming right up!"

My chest swelled with pride to hear my dad's words. My grandma was right. Our baby was grounding him in a way I never thought possible. While grandma went to the kitchen, I ran to his open arms. We rocked side to side, and it brought me back to when I was a little kid and I'd place my feet on top of his, pretending to walk with a giant.

Swaying left, then right.

Thinking the possibilities were endless.

Then something changed in my dad.

Any trace of addiction or despair softened. He would always love my mom, and the grief of her passing would always pulse quietly beneath his ribs. But now, he had a little boy to love—for both of them.

He had a chance to begin again.

We all did. Even if your body was gone forever, your love was still here—in this child, in my dad's healing, in every choice I made to keep us moving forward.

This baby was coming into our lives like a bundle of hope—a reminder that the future could still be full of love.

That the people we lost were never really gone.

That their stories, their laughter, their legacy, would live on.

And we would all be a family—whether here on Earth or up in heaven.

Together.

month five

GRANDMA HAD COGNITIVE and occupational therapy today. Every Thursday morning, I drive her to the senior center down on Longfellow Avenue, where she does activities to help her memory retention. There's no way to improve her condition, but we can slow the inevitable. For three hours a week, she plays Sudoku and association games, then answers rapid-fire questions about fruit and world capitals. She isn't thrilled; she says her fellow patients are old and drooly, too religious for her taste, or "cuckoo for Cocoa Puffs."

Without a filter—or any subtlety—she claims to be the sharpest tool in the box, but I think she enjoys the sessions more than she admits. After each one, she tells me endearing stories disguised as complaints, proof that she's bonding with the others. She notices everything. A trembling hand steadying a domino tile, or the way Mrs. Green hums before she answers a question. Having only me for company was limiting her, so it's good to watch her open up and socialize with others, even if she does it grudgingly.

While she's there, I always drive to the pier down the road—to the quiet, half-forgotten, deserted beach. The restaurants that once stood there have been closed for years after moving to the tourist area across the city, so hardly anyone comes here anymore. I am usually only surrounded by the cries of seagulls and the soft hum of the ocean. The solitude is calming, it helps me think. Of who I am now, and who I want to be. Unsure where to start, I always fall back on the five basic Wh-questions—the little test doctors use for concussions or amnesia, hoping it can tell me something I don't know.

Where am I? Physically, on the beach. Mostly, at home with Grandma. Easy.

When am I? Currently, I was still tangled in the past. But I was trying to be more conscious and aware of the present and look forward to the future. *Getting there…*

What am I? A mess. That's a given.

How am I? (Yes, I know this technically isn't a *wh* word, just bear with me.) Honestly? Confused, scared, overwhelmed, and often in denial—but trying.

Who am I? I'm Noah. But the question wasn't asking for my name; it's asking who *Noah* is—what defined me?

I've spent years not knowing the answer to this question. I was lazy and complacent and accepted the labels given to me. At first, I was a girl, so I acted like one. Then, I was a teenager, which mainly consisted of rolling my eyes. After that, I became a woman, a musician, and a wife. So, I walked confidently, played a guitar, and cared for my husband. Now I'm about to be something new—a mother.

The bump in my belly grows a little each day, and my sweaters cling tighter around my midsection, but I don't mind. Our bond strengthens with every kick, every flutter, and each day that passed I felt more excited to meet my son. As I strolled down the sand, I pictured the mother I never had but always imagined, the kind that tucked me in every night, spinning stories and inventing games. I smiled at the fabricated memory—and at the thought that I could become what she would have been.

I kept one hand on my stomach and studied the footprints scattered across the beach, thinking of the thousands of people who have walked before me. Footprints are excellent storytellers; some break your heart, and others inspire you. There is something nostalgic and romantic about them—life's unpredictability etched in sand.

To my left, small, delicate prints. The arch so pronounced only heels and toes kissed the sand. A dancer, I decided—leaping through rehearsals, her feet blistered from chasing perfection. I hoped her next spin was flawless.

To my right, broader, confident steps. The heel sinks deeper, the stride longer. I saw a thirty-something year old runner who trains for health, not vanity. He hated his cubicle job but loved collecting passport stamps and wanted to learn all about other cultures. He was hungry for life, hungry for adventure. I hoped he found it.

Closer to the tide, four tiny prints, spaced mere inches apart. Two boys racing. One will grow up to choose a simple life—marry his sweetheart and raise his kids in a modest house. He'll unfortunately lose his wife after fifty years, but he'll stay faithful to her memory, hoping his life will still glow with quiet devotion and one day they'll meet again.

The other boy will be a successful millionaire, owning properties in New York and Los Angeles with his private car collection. But his search for money will distract him from love, and unfortunately, by the time he realizes this, it will be too late. He will be eighty years old and married to a twenty-three-year-old with a whole life ahead of her, just waiting for him to die and inherit all his fortune. He has accepted this inevitable truth. He read his newspaper on a park bench, hoping to get distracted from his sorrows, alone in his solitude, when a man sat beside him and said:

"Excuse me."

"Whatever you're selling, I'm not buying. Go away!" the millionaire snarked grumpily without looking at the man.

"I didn't come here to ask you for money; I came to offer some company," the old man said with a smile.

"I don't want your company!" snarled the old man.

"You always did when we were kids," his old friend replied.

Ever since that day, the two old friends met at every sunset at the bench and reminisced about their youth to the sound of clinking glasses that toasted to two lives well lived.

Footprints. So many stories that come and go. I thought about how fragile we are. One moment, we are here; the next, we get washed away like footprints in the sand.

Sometimes I still looked for yours, half-expecting to see them beside mine. I imagined the weight of your stride pressed into the sand, solid and certain, always next to me. But the tide took them long ago, and I'm left walking alone.

And yet, even as the ocean erases what was, life insists on beginning again.

Soon, I will have a small human inside of me. Kicking and moving and ready for battle. Ready to come out into a world that has already failed him. My unborn child had already suffered the worst loss a child can experience. How cruel of this world to strip the joy out of something so pure and innocent. I tell him about you all the time, Derek. I press my hand to my belly and whisper your name so he knows who you were, who you still are. I promise you both, that I will give myself entirely to protect his love and happiness. I feel undeserving of such purity, and every night, I pray that I am good enough for him.

In the blink of an eye, I had treaded three miles' worth of footprints of my own, and more than two hours had passed. It was time to pick up Grandma. My feet were sore and tired, and I wanted to see her.

I walked in quietly and watched through the window. They were doing clay figures, and I could tell she was miles ahead of the others. They were working on the basics—houses, snowmen, flowers… very simple shapes.

And then there was my grandma's. A considerably large, detailed, prominent, one-foot-tall male figure danced between her hands as she crafted the final details. He had hair, fingers, and even eyes. It was surprisingly detailed, considering her shaky hands and the fact that it was made from clay.

It wasn't until I focused my attention on his crotch that I realized he was naked. And sure enough, he had a penis—a *whole*, detailed penis; balls and all. I knew that thought was still swimming around somewhere in her head. I tried not to laugh.

Her condition started to make more sense. Her dementia was able to retain information, just not in a part of her brain that could be accessed voluntarily. The thoughts and ideas popped up of their own volition. And my grandma's persistent thoughts seemed to revolve around naked men.

Fucking awesome... I thought to myself, but my inner dialogue was interrupted by the scream the nurse tried to contain at the sight of the man. She was turning neon red after my grandma handed her the naked man and suggested the nurse needed it more than she did. But her embarrassment and babbles were muffled by the other patients' uncontrolled, loud, and contagious laughter. My grandma slapped the table and threw her head back, laughing along with them.

Within two seconds, I was laughing, too. Who would've known... my grandma was the class clown, and she was fucking incredible at it.

You would have loved this, Derek. You always said she had a crazy sense of humor—I just didn't realize how far it went.

Now we have a new art piece to display at home.

Loud and fucking proud.

month six

AS THE DAYS went by, so did her memory. Every day, I could see small changes that gave it away. She would take half a second longer to recall someone's name or ask me the same question twice in a minute. Sometimes, she would catch herself and try to play it off. "*I'm just making sure you're paying attention,*" or "*Oh yeah, that's right, I had asked that already... silly me!*" she'd say as she swept her hand dismissively. But I could see it in her eyes, the fear of slowly fading away creeping into her gaze and blurring her memories.

One cold evening, after doing the dishes, she caught me absently rubbing your wedding ring—the one I'd hung on the same chain that held Mom's pendant. *You keep me wild* was still engraved inside. My chest tightened with the weight of all the words I wanted to say but couldn't.

"You should go talk to him," Grandma said.

"Huh?" I turned my head around abruptly, snapping my thoughts back into reality.

"Derek. You should talk to him about what's on your mind. I can see something is worrying you."

Her words shattered me. For weeks, I had been bracing myself for this moment—the day when her slipping memory would collide headfirst with the unbearable truth of your absence. My pulse quickened, my hands cold and trembling. Would I have to break her heart all over again?

"Grandma..." I said softly. "Derek died a few months ago… That's why I am living here with you, remember?"

She stared blankly at me. I stared back. My body braced itself like a soldier before battle, terrified of her reaction. Would she be in denial? Angry? Confused? My heart sank as I blinked twice, ready for what was coming. Then her face changed. Her eyes narrowed. Her forehead crinkled. Her voice became louder. A little too loud.

"No shit, Sherlock! What the fucking shit, Noah? Do I look like a dumbass to you? Why are you talking to me like I'm an old, decrepit, absent-minded idiot?" she shouted, offended. She waved the broom for punctuation. "I know he's dead, Noah. I saw it on the news. I picked you up at the train station. You live here, for God's sake." She stressed some of the words in those sentences for effect.

I was shocked. Eyes wide as could be. And suddenly, relief coursed through my body.

"Oh, thank God, I thought you had forgotten," I said.

"No, I didn't fucking forget! I may be old, and my memory is going to shit, but I think I would feel compelled to remember such a life-changing event!"

"Right! Of course! I just thought—"

"Well, think harder next time." Exasperation tightened her face. An involuntary smile threatened my lips—she caught it.

"And that better not be a grin." She jabbed the broom lightly at my chest. "When I said talk to Derek, I meant figuratively—like I talk to your grandpa. Makes the absence less… lethal."

With that, she handed me the broom and headed upstairs for a nap, shaking her head slightly with each fragile step. The whole ordeal had exhausted her.

A few minutes had passed, and I was done sweeping the first floor, so I went upstairs to sweep our bedrooms. The floorboards creaked under my feet as I reached the end of the steps, but I froze when I heard my grandma scream.

"Who's there!?" she yelled. I could hear the raw panic in her voice.

"Grandma, it's me." I walked towards her door.

"Who is that!?" She was panicking now. When I opened her door and turned on the light, I saw her small frame drenched in sweat as she clasped her sheets with frail, bony fingers. I stood by the door so she could assimilate me in the light as I recovered from the shock myself.

"Noah?" she said through quick, shallow breaths. "What are you doing here?" She was calmer now, but her eyes still darted around me. I couldn't believe it. Forty minutes ago, she was perfectly fine.

"I live here, Grandma. With you," I said softly. She looked at me incredulously.

"Since when?"

"Since Derek died."

Her eyes filled. They flicked to the tiny bump under my T-shirt; a sharp breath left her smaller, fragile. I watched memories flicker across her face—the exact instant she re-remembered. Grief crashed into her all over again. I sat beside her and let her lean into the crook of my shoulder; silent tears soaked my sleeve.

It wasn't until then that I realized what was going on. Just as my heart had taken a hit when you left, her mind took an even worse one when Grandpa died; it went into defense mode. Their lives together remained intact in her mind, but like ripped pages in a book, she couldn't remember the present. Not always, at least. She seemed to worsen during any kind of emotional distress, so I vowed to make adjustments and live a quieter life around her, making sure she wasn't caught off guard so that the memories didn't escape. I needed her as much as she needed me; I was her home as much as she was mine.

I was terrified of losing her, but I realized she also feared losing herself. Watching someone you love forget is a particular kind of heartbreak. She stands before me, not only a broken soul but also one who is unaware of her brokenness. It's grief within grief—losing her in pieces while still holding her in my arms. I'm scared that one day she won't remember how much I love her, so I repeated it. Over and over again.

"I love you, Grandma."

"I love you too."

"I love you, Grandma."

"I love you too."

"I love you, Grandma."

"I love you too."

I fucking love you.

I waited until I felt the weight of her head on my shoulder, and I softly placed it back onto the pillow. I kissed her forehead before I tiptoed my way out of the room and gently closed the door to keep her dreams uninterrupted.

I immediately went downstairs, making sure I skipped over the loose floorboard, grabbed a pen and paper, and sat outside by the fire pit. I closed my eyes as I felt the warmth of the fire grazing my feet and the few drops of cold rain landing on my cheeks, disguising themselves as tears. The only thing that told them apart was their temperature. One was cold as ice, sliding down my neck, and the other hot and salty, dripping into the corner of my mouth, reminding me that life was bitter.

I opened my eyes and saw through my breath. I grabbed the pen. *Click, click.*

Dear Grandma,

I am so sorry.

Sorry for the questions you forget, for the moments I can't explain, for the times I lose patience when all you've shown me is endless love. I will gladly have the same conversation every thirty minutes with you because hearing your voice reminds me you're still here.

I feel powerless sometimes—against time, against the memories that slip away, against the fear that you might forget how much I love you. But I need you to know; you've given me everything I have ever needed, and I will spend the rest of our time together trying to make you feel as loved and cared for as you have always made me feel.

So please forgive me. Forgive me for doing my best and for not being enough. You raised fighters, but you'll always stand as the ultimate warrior. You are brave. You are magic. You are my home.

I love you.

I need you.

And I am, have been, and will always be proud of you and everything you are. You always took the most selfless and genuinely remarkable care of me. Now, let me try to do the same for you.

With all of my heart and soul, for everything I am is because of you,

—N.

When the ink finally blurred under my tears, I folded the page and tucked it carefully into my journal. I knew I had to start thinking ahead—not just about me or the baby, but about her. It broke my heart, but maybe love meant facing the possibility that one day, keeping her safe might mean finding help beyond what I could give her alone.

It was nearing the end of month six… I was about to enter my third trimester, and my fear and self-doubt were worse than ever. I went to my grandma's room with two cups of tea, balancing one mug between my chest and wrist to knock on the door softly. I sat next to her in her bed. She turned off the TV and looked at me, those kind eyes bigger and brighter than ever.

"What's on your mind, Pumpkin?" she asked curiously.

I took a sip of my orange peel tea. "I would like to know more about Mom. What was she like?"

She smiled. A lifetime of memories flashed through her eyes in a fraction of a second. "She was iconic. Fierce, brave, and ambitious like no one I had ever seen before. She was honest, too stubborn, and confident. The most beautiful girl I had ever met, inside and out. She was a marvelous young woman. Despite all the mistakes I have made in my lifetime, your mom was the one thing I did perfectly right."

Her eyes got watery, but not from sadness. They were tears of pride. My mom was her proudest creation.

I thought for a few seconds. "I'm afraid of not being good enough. I wish I could be more like her," I confessed shyly.

My grandma looked at me skeptically. "Afraid? Noah, the qualities I mentioned in your mom are the same qualities I see in you. You are one and the same."

"Yeah, right..." I scoffed, refusing to believe that someone I had placed on a pedestal could be anything like me. I was trying to compliment my mom, not insult her.

Grandma paused for three seconds and squeezed my hand as she told me to wait a minute. I watched her get up from the bed and immediately felt a sharp, stabbing pain in my heart. She moved so much slower than she did six months ago. Her arms and legs were thin and wrinkly; the pigmentation faded in prominent areas of her tiny body. I saw how careful and aware she was of her surroundings; one more fall or injury could very well lead to the rest of her days in a wheelchair—or worse...

The sight of her made my heart ache. The paradox of the situation seemed ironic to me. Here I was, growing and creating a whole new life, as I watched the person I loved most nearing the end of hers. It felt unfair. Like life was mocking me again.

I was paralyzed with sadness and heartache, so I did what she requested of me and waited for her as I sulked in my grief. She returned two minutes later, walking as slowly as she had when she left the room.

Grandma sat back next to me and placed a photo album between us. It was dark green, with a gold frame around it. Its age could be determined by the pages, yellowed and heavy with time. I immediately recognized my mom and saw her grow in age, along with the dates documented in this album. Halfway through it, I stumbled upon blank pages and thought of all the pictures that should have been here.

I imagined the photos my grandma would have taken of her. Some smiling, some taken without her knowledge; the unexpectedness was a breath of fresh air. She was gorgeous, one of those people who couldn't be caught in the wrong angle.

I noticed that Grandma would take yearly pictures, without fail, on her birthday. There were only twenty-five pictures documented. I tried not to linger on that thought longer than intended. This album should hold fifty birthdays and counting, not only twenty-five. But I pushed the negativity away; I wanted to rejoice in the Polaroids before me, insert myself in them, and experience life through her eyes.

I liked to imagine what her perfume would smell like. Would her fingers feel calloused from playing the guitar like mine? Or would they feel soft and tender with love and care? I imagined the sound of her laugh and the spark in her eyes as I wished I had her bravery and thirst for adventure.

One picture caught my attention. It showed my mother as a teenager, maybe fifteen or sixteen. She was wearing ripped jeans and a crop top, a few strands coming out of her messy bun. She was stepping on a silver crown, a bouquet of flowers in her left hand, and her right middle finger up in the air. She looked fierce; her left eyebrow and smile were crooked. I stared at it, entranced. She looked rebellious and challenging, like authority was a game, and she knew how to win. I noticed the writing on it: *Beauty Pageant '83*. It wasn't until I read it that I heard my grandma snicker.

"Your mother was wild," she reminisced. I looked up at her, too curious to interrupt.

"Back in the eighties, beauty pageants were all the rage. The prettiest girls in town would gather, spending fortunes on dresses, hoping it would make them winners. Your mom... she couldn't stand it. She thought it was all shallow nonsense, she never liked what these competitions turned girls into. She would go on about 'social construct this and body image that...' She was always too ahead of her time, too smart for the rest of them. But because she was so effortlessly beautiful, she entered anyway. And of course, she won. When the host asked her what the crown meant to her—oh boy, you should have seen the look on her face."

Grandma chuckled, shaking her head. "She lifted her chin, squared her shoulders, and said, 'This crown? It means nothing to me. It means you all would rather starve us and shame us than see us for who we are.'

She went on about how she'd overheard girls throwing up in the bathroom stalls, while others smoked outside just to kill their hunger. She pointed out the girls who had nearly fainted from crash diets and pills, all just to squeeze into a dress for one night. 'This isn't beauty,' she said. 'It's cruelty dressed in sequins.'

Then, to everyone's horror—except mine—she snapped that silver crown in half. Tossed it right onto the stage. And she told the judges, 'We deserve better than starving for your applause.'"

I gasped softly, my eyes wide.

"And then she led the girls out of that hall like a general leading her army. She marched off that stage, took the prize money, and bought every girl greasy fries and burgers. I can still see it—heels tossed onto the stage, corsets unraveling, girls piling into trucks laughing with the wildest smiles. Your mom became an icon that night. The whole town was buzzing about it for weeks. And would you believe it? The next year, not a single girl signed up. The pageant was canceled and never returned. That was your mom, Pumpkin. She took down an entire institution before she was even eighteen. She had guts."

I looked at my grandma with bright and hopeful eyes. I felt incredibly proud of the woman I got to call my mom, wishing more than ever that I could hug her. "She sounds like a legend," I said.

"She was… And so are you, Noah. Your mom would tell every soul who crossed her path how happy you made her. She kept talking about how she would raise you right and always be in your corner, encouraging you to be exactly who you chose to be. She would claim to know you, even though you had barely developed a heartbeat, and tell stories of how bold and authentic you'd be, how you would conquer the world with a bright smile and a kind heart." She placed her hand on my face and looked at me through loving eyes. "And she was right. Maybe she couldn't raise you, but she did guide you and still does. I have felt your mom ever since you were born. When she died at the same time you lived, a part of her stayed in you. You have always carried her, and ever since you moved in, I feel her more than ever."

I was speechless.

"When was the last time you asked your mom for help?" she asked.

I held her gaze. "I don't know that I ever have. I've always thought about her as some sort of angel, but I've never talked *to* her."

She smiled softly and nodded to herself. "If you admire your mom and wish to be more like her, you have nothing to worry about. She is with you. Whenever you feel scared or have doubts about what you are doing, close your eyes and talk to her. Ask her for help, and trust your instincts, because like I said—you two are one and the same."

And suddenly, with the sharpness of a finger snap, every feeling of doubt and fear dissipated from my body. I could do this. This baby was not alone, and neither was I. Generations of warriors were by my side, guiding me in the right direction.

I smiled and took a deep breath.

In and out.

In and out.

In and out.

I laid my head on my grandma's silhouette. I closed my eyes, grabbed my mom's pendant between my index finger and thumb, and kissed it. During that kiss, I felt my mom closer than ever as I placed my other hand on my stomach. At that exact moment, my grandma sighed. She could feel her too, I knew it.

The four of us would be okay.

And for a while, we were.

Until we weren't.

—month seven—

MY THIRD TRIMESTER had officially begun, and I was in a much better place now, both mentally and physically. I tried to play my guitar today, but it was impossible to rearrange it around my belly, so I gave up after a few attempts and drove Grandma to the coffee shop to treat her to some vanilla chai before therapy instead.

Grandma's memory had been worsening at a quicker pace, just like the doctors had predicted, and now she went to therapy three times a week instead of two. Every new appointment felt like a quiet surrender to something we couldn't stop, no matter how much I wanted to fight it.

After dropping her off at the center, I took a detour to the mall while I waited for her to be done with her appointment. I planned to buy essentials for the baby, but it became painfully obvious once I wandered aimlessly down the aisles that I had no idea what I was doing. Thankfully, the kind lady at the store took pity on my cluelessness and practically held my hand as she led me through each aisle and told me what to buy and, most importantly, how to use it.

Thank God for her. I could almost hear you, Derek, teasing me about how our kid would be the test subject of my trial-and-error experiments. This baby would probably be running barefoot in an oversized T-shirt with fewer diaper changes than necessary if it weren't for her.

These past few months had been difficult, but we had handled the changes as best we could—me balancing new life and looming loss, and Grandma fading slowly as I carried the weight of tomorrow. Until that Sunday morning when everything shifted.

On Sunday morning, I jolted awake with a weird feeling in my stomach. It was a kind of anxiety I hadn't felt before, but my eyes flew open effortlessly. Any trace of tiredness was washed away, replaced by a sharp, electric alertness that gripped my senses. This feeling ran deeper—through my bones, chilling my spine in a way that felt foreign and wrong. The house was unnaturally quiet, and there could only be one explanation.

Grandma.

I sprang out of bed, fear and caution flooding my chest in equal measure. My belly solidified with stress. The baby felt it, and so did I.

"Grandma?" I called, but there was no answer.

This was not uncommon—she could be outside tending the garden or in the shower—but I already knew this wasn't the case. I checked her room. Nothing. Her bed was made, the slippers that always sat beside it were gone. My heartbeat quickened, and I could feel cold sweat dripping down my neck, my knees trembling. Something was very wrong.

I ran downstairs and heard the faucet running. While this should have given me peace of mind that she was probably in the kitchen, it only worried me more—and with good reason. When I entered the kitchen, it took me less than a second to notice two things.

First, the faucet was running, but no one was doing the dishes. It had to have been running for a while because the water level had reached the top of the sink, and now it was overflowing, spilling over the edge and onto the floor.

And second, I immediately noticed the coppery smell that tainted my nose. I wanted to throw up, but there was no time. I had to get my priorities straight.

I willed my feet to move, and as I went around the kitchen island, I saw her. She was on the floor. Swimming in blood. Unconscious. *What the fuck.*

"GRANDMA!"

She must have hit her head against the edge of the kitchen counter when she fell because there was a gash on her forehead and blood all over the floor. I could not see how serious it was because the water from the sink was diluting the blood, and now I was standing on a huge scarlet puddle that only seemed to be getting larger by the second.

I frantically shut off the faucet and grabbed the kitchen rag. Kneeling beside her, I barely noticed the pain that radiated up my knees as I forcefully landed on them against the ceramic tile; I'd surely bruise by tomorrow, but I'd be lucky if I made it that far. I felt like dying right on the spot. I gently put the rag over the cut on her forehead.

My hands shook as I contained the blood with one hand and dialed 911 with the other. Bloody strokes were covering my screen as I tried to keep it from slipping off my sweaty palms. My grandma's life was on the line, and my valid, definitely not irrational feelings could not get in the way.

Each ring felt like an eternity. Why the fuck were they taking so long? Weren't emergency services supposed to be immediate? After three never-ending rings, they finally answered.

"911, what is the nature of your emergency?"

"I need an ambulance—my grandma fell." My voice was even, but the edges of panic cracked through every syllable. My chest heaved, my lungs burning.

"Address?"

"Um, eh—it's, uh… ugh!" The numbers jammed in my brain.

"Take a deep breath, ma'am. What is the property address?" Her voice grounded me back to the present.

"1947 39th Ave." I sighed in relief.

"Is the patient currently conscious?" she asked. I was always amazed, and frankly a little disgusted, by the coldness and apathy that all emergency operators exhibited. I always thought they should sound a little kinder and more empathetic. Being on the receiving line, I now understand why they are so blunt. They were simply being efficient and could not afford to indulge in panic. Their command of the situation kept me level-headed, and I was incredibly grateful for them.

"No," I half-sobbed.

"Any open wounds?"

"Um. Yes." I nodded even though she could not see me. "On her forehead. I'm pressing a rag against it." I was not even sure if the words came out; my eyes were blurry from the effort of trying to make sense of the sounds coming from my mouth.

"Is the front door unlocked?"

"I think so."

"Please hold; the ambulance will arrive in six minutes."

The phone slipped from my grip, landing in the puddle with a wet slap. Silence roared in my ears. I clutched her hand—it felt so fragile, like it might crumble under my desperate grip.

I felt so worthless. She had been taking care of me—of us—for several months, and in return, I had her bleeding on the kitchen floor. I felt guilty, scared, and alone. So, I did the only thing that brought me comfort. I couldn't deal with the sight of her like this—passed out in her own blood, so I closed my eyes, took a deep breath, and spoke to her.

"Hey, Grandma,"—my foot couldn't stay still from the adrenaline and anxiety coursing through my body—"please wake up. I cannot do this without you. I know it seems selfish of me to ask you this, but I really need you to wake up and push through for me one more time. I need you; we need you. I am not ready to do this without you. Not yet. So do me a huge favor, and please open your fucking eyes."

My voice cracked with every other word. I opened my eyes slowly, expecting hers to be staring right at me. Nothing happened. I felt defeated and hopeless. If she died, surely I would too. I couldn't survive another loss like this. As I stared blankly at her fragile and innocent face, suddenly, it came to me; there was one last resort, one last thing I could do. I looked up to the sky, imploring and hopeful. I shut my eyes once more and squeezed her hand, and with all my effort and all my might, as my breath pierced through my lungs, scorching my throat, I prayed to my mom.

Ma. Please help us, I pleaded.

A second later, the paramedics burst through the door.

"*Thank you*," I whispered to her, gratefulness washing over my body like a wave. Grandma was right; she had been with me all along, and I had just been too oblivious to see her.

I watched how the paramedics calmly took in the scene in front of them before springing into action. One led me away carefully and sat me down in a chair. He asked me if I was okay and assured me he would be right back. The other guy, the taller one, was already kneeling behind my grandma. He took her pulse and pried her eyes open to shine a flashlight in them. They placed my grandma carefully on the gurney and led her to the ambulance.

The shorter guy instructed me to stay seated, but my body refused to obey. My baby was fine. I needed to be with Grandma instead. As they led her outside, I stood up quickly. I felt weak, and with a swift rush of blood that went straight to my head, I got dizzy. I grabbed onto the wall to keep my balance, leaving a scarlet handprint against the white concrete, and I couldn't help but notice the four sets of reddish footprints on the floor leading to the door.

When the paramedic saw me, he gave me a stern look. He did not like to be disobeyed, but he had compassionate eyes, and I could tell he understood. He rushed toward me and held me by the elbow. He tried to take me to the second ambulance that was arriving, but I refused.

"I am leaving with her," I said, leaning toward the opposite side with an air of finality that left little room for argument. He hesitated. "Do what you need to do to me, but I am riding with her." I didn't wait for him to agree or disagree; instead, I led him to the ambulance where my grandma was, and he had no choice but to help me climb inside.

Once we were settled, I asked them how she was. She was still unconscious, and I was still petrified.

"It's hard to know the reason why she passed out. Right now, the important thing is to stop the bleeding and stabilize her. Her blood pressure is low, probably from the head wound. I will stitch this up right now, and once we get to the hospital, we'll be able to get more answers."

The shorter paramedic was taking my vitals. I could hear him speaking to me, but I could not figure out what he was saying. I felt numb on the drive to the hospital. Memories of these past few months were flashing through my brain like vignettes in an old, classic, sepia-filtered film. *How could this have happened?*

The blaring of the ambulance sirens sounded faint in my ears. I went from being in a state of total awareness, alert and ready to spring into action, to shock and suspended worry. I held her limp, fragile fingers in mine as the paramedic assured me her vitals were stable.

All I knew was I couldn't lose her. Not like this.

The shorter paramedic directed his words at me. "Your blood pressure is very high."

"Yeah... I wonder why." I replied.

An eternity later, we finally made it to the hospital. What happened next was too fast for me to recount the exact details in order, but this is what I remembered:

The ambulance had not even entirely stopped when both paramedics and I stood abruptly as a third paramedic flung open both ambulance doors. He was an older man, probably about sixty years old, but by his frame and gaze I could tell he'd seen a lot in his life.

As they raised the gurney to wheel my grandma out, I felt it. A light, almost impalpable squeeze in my hand—like a magical, divine assurance that she would be okay.

Two seconds later, there was a sharp pain in my stomach. I winced. It came and went in the blink of an eye, but the paramedic next to me didn't miss a single beat. It took me a few seconds to piece it together.

He was pale. He looked at me and immediately placed a firm grip on my shoulder. He glanced at my seat and ordered—authoritative yet pleading—to bring another wheelchair immediately. He held my gaze once again. My forehead wrinkled slightly in confusion, but something in my peripheral view caught my attention.

I didn't even have to look to know what had caused this reaction, but I turned my head anyway. There was a blood stain on my seat.

My whole body stiffened as I looked at him again. His deep, fiercely blue eyes were the last thing I remembered before my world turned black, and I fell into an ocean of darkness and uncertainty.

I am not sure how much time had passed between the ambulance episode and now, but as I slept on my side, exhausted and lulled by the rhythmic beeping of the machines, the baby decided to move. A kick in my midsection jolted me awake.

For a few seconds I let myself lie there and breathe. Then the room found me. The pungent sting of rubbing alcohol and stored medication; light blue and white everywhere; the red hazard trashcan in the corner like a punctuation mark. I pressed my hand to my belly. The baby kicked hard, and for a brief second, I focused there—on this tiny life moving inside me—before the morning crashed back in. The blood, the kitchen, my grandmother.

Grandma.

Where was she? Why wasn't she beside me if we came in the same ambulance? Something wasn't right.

Something wasn't fucking right.

I desperately pressed the alarm button on the remote next to my bed. I was persistent, and I didn't stop until I made sure somebody listened. A nurse came rushing into the room.

"Is everything okay?" she asked quickly, checking everything on my monitors to ensure my vitals remained stable.

"I need to speak to the doctor right away, please."

"He will be in shortly. Is there something that I can help you with in the meantime?" she asked, gently placing her hand on my shin. I could tell she wanted to be comforting and soothing, but this was not the time.

"I need to talk to him now," I said sternly and nodded slightly as I pulled my leg away from her reach. I couldn't afford to be nice right now. I could tell there was something she wasn't telling me. She simply nodded and walked decisively to find my doctor.

Three minutes later, I heard a sharp knock on the door.

Knock, knock-knock.

"Come in," I said quickly.

The first thing I noticed was how well-presented he looked. Even in his late sixties, he was shaven, his hair combed, his shirt tucked in tight, and he had shiny shoes that squeaked with each step. Then I noticed his eyes. They were kind and caring. He had a soft smile and slightly crinkled eyebrows that conveyed sympathy. The dichotomy of his whole presence confused me. He wasn't like other doctors I had encountered. He had a palpable sense of humanity and kindness that told me he would tell me exactly what I needed to hear, which was the truth.

"Hi there, my name is Dr. Jane; I'm happy to say that I'll be your doctor during your stay," he said chipperly as he stretched out his hand and shook mine gently. "How are you two feeling?"

I looked at his eyes for a moment. "What are you not telling me?" I said in a small, vulnerable voice.

He furrowed his brow and took off his glasses.

"Is it my baby or my grandma?" I asked, petrified of the answer. I could barely articulate my words.

"As long as you care for yourself and rest as much as possible, you and your baby will be just fine," he said reassuringly.

My heart sank once again. I nodded slowly in understanding.

"So it's my grandma?" I looked at him, tears already spilling from the corners of my eyes.

"I'm afraid so," he answered. He sat by my feet at the corner of my bed. The staff in this hospital had no issues violating any kind of personal space. I didn't mind it, though; right now, he was the only person who could give me any peace of mind, or at least accurate information. I welcomed his comfort and hoped he could tell I appreciated it.

"Your grandma took a hard hit to the head. She has a substantial concussion, and it has somehow accelerated her condition."

For once in my life, I said nothing. I just listened. The room narrowed down to his voice.

"Has she been exhibiting episodes of dementia lately? Forgetfulness, obliviousness, repeating conversations?"

I nodded. His lips were framed in a tight line as he nodded in acknowledgment.

"I want to be transparent with you, Noah. This won't get much better. Her mind is more fragile than her body. There will be days she's lucid—good days—but they won't indicate long-term improvement. I tell you this because I do not want you to get your hopes up. Good days won't mean progress anymore; they'll just mean a welcome hiatus from the inevitable." He named it plainly, and the bluntness kept panic at bay.

"The important thing is for you to be patient. Try not to take anything too personally; sometimes, she may struggle to recognize herself. Try to have routines at home; make it a little easier for her. Be very loving and understanding, which, according to the story I heard from the paramedics about you refusing to leave on a separate ambulance, I can tell you love your grandma more than anything."

I looked down, shyly. "Yeah, I was a little stubborn, I should probably apologize to them."

Dr. Jane chuckled. "It's okay, Noah, you should never apologize for loving someone too much."

He went through a list of more recommendations, but I was too busy fast-forwarding into the near future and trying to imagine a life without the one person who had been a constant in my life.

"Noah," the doctor said. I snapped back into the present. "I will leave it up to you what you want to disclose to your grandmother. You know her best, so do with this information what you think is best. There is no wrong answer here; it will be a learning process for you and her."

He pulled out two small devices attached to a lanyard.

"I will give her this safety alarm that goes around her neck. If anything happens—anything at all—to either of you, you can press this button, and an ambulance will be dispatched to your house immediately. I will give you one as well, in case you can't get to her in time for any reason."

I grabbed her device and placed it around my neck.

"Things are going to be a little different now, too. Your grandma will be more dependent on her wheelchair. If her bedroom is upstairs, I would rather you both sleep downstairs for the time being. We will schedule a home plan and follow-up visits, and I would also feel more comfortable if we had a nurse come over and help you while you get adjusted—at least four times a week, if that's okay with you."

Once again, I nodded. I had nothing else left in me. All I could do was muster up the energy to absentmindedly move my head.

"Do you have any questions for me?" he said lastly.

"Can I see her?"

"She's asleep right now. We are monitoring her vitals but she's stable. I can get a nurse in a few hours to wheel you to her room if you'd like. I just can't have either of you walking right now."

I nodded once more. I didn't know what to say.

Dr. Jane gave me a small smile and an even smaller nod.

"Okay, then, I will let you be for a couple of hours while you process all this new information. I'll come back later to check on you. I'll keep you all here in the hospital for two days just for observation, and then I'll send you three home. Does that sound like a plan?" he asked, a hint of hope in his voice.

I looked at the alarm around my neck and nodded as he got up from my bed.

"Thank you," I said, as exhaustion and fear drenched my voice. He squeezed my shoulder twice to show his support, and I placed my hand on his for a moment before he left the room.

A few hours later, Dr. Jane came back to check on my progress, and just like he promised, he called a nurse over to wheel me to my grandma. They drove me one floor down to the Intensive Care Unit. The ICU smelled like antiseptic and quiet fear. I watched the other patients from the bed; their faces half-hidden by tubes and families who spoke in urgent whispers, and I prayed for my grandma to be okay.

They wheeled me into her room, which barely fit both of us, and they placed my bed right next to hers. She looked small and bruised, with an oxygen cannula at her nose, and a stitched gash across her forehead. I felt the baby press into my hand like an answering heartbeat.

The nurse said she was medicated and comfortable enough to be left until she woke. I nodded my head and thanked her for her time and willingness to bring me here. She was extremely kind and helpful, which made ignoring her instructions more difficult.

I smiled gratefully as she shut the door and moved on to her next patient. Reaching for the surgical scissors on the metal tray between our beds, I let them slip from my hand and clatter to the floor. The sharp clang was enough to stir her awake. I watched as confusion flickered across her face, her gaze darting around the room while her fingers brushed against the tubes threaded into her veins. She winced at the raw stitches in her forehead. Within seconds, her eyes found mine.

"Hey, Pumpkin," she croaked.

Tears came hot and immediate. I couldn't hold them back.

"Well, that was scarier than a sad clown, am I right?" she tried to joke.

"Stop joking." I demanded. "Why would you joke about this? You almost died!" My voice cracked before I could stop it.

She blinked at me, startled. For once, the humor drained from her face. She looked small, vulnerable. "I know, Pumpkin. I'm sorry. I just... I didn't want you to see me like that. To worry more than you already do."

The silence stretched between us, heavy with truth. I grabbed her hand and rested my other on my stomach. The baby shifted under my palm, tiny kicks pressing against my worry, grounding me.

"We can't keep playing around like this," I said, my voice steady. "We have to take care of each other now—for real. No more pretending it's fine when it's not. When we're allowed to go home, we're turning the living room into your bedroom, and we're hiring a home aide to come by a couple days a week. That's non-negotiable."

Her eyes welled, and she nodded slowly. For the first time, I saw the fear she carried too.

Then her eyebrows knitted in confusion. "Wait... I know why I'm here, but why are you in bed? Are you okay? Is it the baby?"

My throat tightened. "We're both fine. The doctor said as long as the three of us rest and take care of each other, we'll be fine. But you have to tell me how you're feeling. Even if you forget things sometimes, I need to know. I have to be prepared for next time—this can't happen again."

"Next time? That bad, huh?" Her face fell. "Is my memory slipping away?" Tears pooled in her eyes, trembling on the edge of fear, and I knew she needed the truth. She deserved nothing less.

I held her hand tightly, feeling the frailty in her grip. "It's not looking good, Grandma. You hit your head pretty hard, and these episodes… they might happen more often from now on. But we'll face it together. I promise. You're not alone in this."

Her tears spilled freely. "I just don't want to forget you," she whispered, her voice small, almost breaking.

"You won't," I said, my own throat tight, my voice cracking. "But even if you do, I'll remind you who I am. Every time. It'll be fun—like meeting your favorite grandchild all over again," I teased through my own tears.

She nodded, a small smile breaking through.

"Just promise me you'll always remember how much I loved you," she said, clutching my hand as if letting go would erase us both.

"You don't have to worry about that. You'd never let me forget," I murmured, holding her hand to my lips as if sealing a promise.

Three days later, we finally went back home. Everything was different now—subtly, but undeniably.

In the following weeks, things worsened at a quicker pace. I found myself repeating the same conversations with her over and over, sometimes only minutes apart. Moving around the house became harder; my belly heavier than the rest of me, and almost all my attention was on my grandma, leaving little time for anything else. I could see her slipping away by the second, and some days, I barely recognized her.

The home aide arrived on Mondays, Tuesdays, Thursdays, and Saturdays at noon. She would run my grandma's vitals, change the sheets, help me shower her, and refill her prescriptions. More prescriptions were added each week, threatening to overfill the pill container as the small squares overflowed. She also cleaned the bathrooms and swept the house—tasks technically outside her job description, but we had grown close in the hospital, and even closer during these visits.

She was young, full of energy, and had a heart of gold. She offered her help gladly, and I showed my appreciation by making us two cups of tea at the end of each visit. We would sit with cookies, sharing updates, observing progress, and finding small moments of calm in the chaos.

Right now, she was my primary support system. Her unwavering spirit and positive attitude made her visits not just helpful but something I genuinely looked forward to. At the end of each visit, our routine became a small sanctuary—a chance for both of us to escape our daily struggles and anxieties, to enjoy each other's company, and to build a fragile but comforting rhythm of friendship and care.

"Dear pain,
Please spare me from this everlasting hurt I live in.
It's un-fucking-bearable.
—N."

With age, I came to understand that pain is complex, uncomfortable, scary, and found in unknown territory. The fear of the unknown only worsens the pain, but with knowledge and awareness comes acceptance and relief. As my grandma's condition became more apparent and I was told what to expect, my understanding of the situation grew, and suddenly, accepting it became easier.

Her condition was real—a tangible object that had to be introduced and accommodated into our lives—but we weren't scared anymore. It hurt to see my grandma become someone I used to know, but like Dr. Jane said, some good days still prevailed, and hearing her laugh as she told a dirty joke through purple teeth from the grape-flavored lollipops gave us hope. Each good day was like going back in time, and it made it easier to look forward to the future.

I often think of how she used to write her letters and then burn them, as though the fire would carry her words into the sky. For her, that was release, a way of letting go. But I couldn't bring myself to do the same.

Instead, I wrote to you, Derek. I folded each page with care and tucked it into the drawer of my nightstand, as if one day I might discover a way to mail them to heaven. They sat there like a quiet archive of love and longing, each letter a conversation paused, waiting to be picked up again when we're reunited.

It wasn't letting go. Not for me. It's holding on. It's my way of keeping you close—of making sure that when I whisper into the silence, there's proof that I never stopped talking to you, never stopped needing you, never stopped believing that somehow, in some way, you heard me still.

It's the only way I knew how to survive without you—by writing you back into my life, over and over again, until the day the silence finally answered.

"Dear Derek,
Sometimes I wonder how we would've navigated this part of life together. Would you have held my hand when my grandma forgot my name? Would you have made me laugh, just to pull me out of the heaviness of it all?

Taking care of her makes me think of how we might have cared for each other if we'd grown old side by side. I like to imagine us aging together, with the same tenderness I'm learning now—the kind of love that aches and heals in the same heartbeat. Each moment I spend with her, I feel you there, in every careful act that both hurts and comforts me.

We would have shared that rhythm, that quiet patience that only comes from decades of love. I can't give you that now, but I can offer it to her—with the same devotion and kindness I would've shown you. Maybe, in some way, caring for her is practice for the life we were meant to have together.

I'll love you, always. Until we meet again,

-N."

month eight

A WHOLE MONTH had passed since her fall—one crisis barely survived before another loomed ahead. Still, we were staying strong. And amid all the chaos, there was one bright truth holding us together; we were four weeks away from meeting our baby boy. It was the final countdown.

The morning had unfolded as usual. I would even dare say it was one of the best mornings we'd had in a while. I made us our typical breakfast—nothing too complicated; toasted bread with avocado and jelly and a cup of English-breakfast tea. We did memory exercises together, which by now were more of an activity to pass the time than a way to ward off memory loss. She picked Word Search again; it was her favorite game, and I'd gotten so good at it that, to her frustration, I was finding each word within seconds.

Shortly after, we strolled through the park, showered, ate a light lunch, and napped. These days we were exhausted most of the time, so naps had become a recurring necessity.

By nine o'clock, I had finished my nightly routine. I had put on my favorite pajamas, drenched my stomach in coconut oil to avoid stretch marks, and cleansed my face before bed. I turned off the bathroom light, rain hitting my window, as a fast-approaching thunderstorm made its way toward the town.

At ten past nine, I heard a shattering, ear-piercing thunder strike so furiously that it shook the windows. I instinctively got worried and walked—more so, waddled—downstairs to check on Grandma. It was late, so I expected her to be in bed. I hadn't even reached the first floor when I felt the sharp, cold breeze that told me the front door was wide open. Cold sweat dripped down my back.

No, no, no.

I was carelessly running now, using every surface I could for support. I had taken five steps out the door when I saw her. She was drenched in water, her hair completely flat against her head as she walked against the wind a few yards ahead of me. She looked so small and fragile that I worried the wind would sweep her away. I yelled her name. Nothing. I ran toward her as I desperately called her name over and over again.

The soft, wet grass gave way under my feet, but I couldn't take my eyes off her. I ran as carefully as I could while using my arms to counterbalance, but I should've paid more attention to my feet, because soon after I started running, I placed my foot on a patch of mud and immediately knew I had made a mistake.

The moment my toes touched the dirt, I slipped, fast. My belly hitched, as if bracing for impact. Luckily, I was able to react in time so I landed on one knee, both hands planted in front of my body, preventing what could've been another tragedy. I got up carefully, adrenaline coursing through my body, painfully aware of how close I was to losing everything once again. Raindrops hit the back of my neck as I tried to get up, my hair sticking to my forehead and making it hard to see. Panting, I scrambled upright and hustled to the sidewalk where footing was solid. Once on solid ground, I sped up again until I reached her.

I grabbed her sternly by the shoulders and abruptly turned her around to face me.

"What are you doing!? Are you insane!?" I yelled through the roar of wind and water.

"I have to meet him at the station," she said, determination burning in her watery eyes. She tried to pull free.

"Meet who?"

"Your grandfather! He's coming home from Vietnam today, and I promised I'd be there. Now move, Noah—I'm late!" She tried to push me aside, her fragile bones barely forcing me to sway in place.

Shock left me speechless. Vietnam? Grandpa had been gone for fifteen years. I couldn't speak, couldn't move. What just happened?

She turned around and started walking again but lost her footing. I grabbed the crook of her elbow to stabilize her and motioned her to sit with me by the curb.

"Come here for a second; sit with me for just a moment."

"No. I can't, I'm running late," she insisted.

"He's not coming, Grandma. Just sit here, please!" I begged, urging the anguish in my voice to make her snap back into reality.

"Let fucking go of me!" she sobbed.

"He's gone, Grandma! He's not coming to the train station. He's not coming back at all. Grandpa has been gone for years! Cancer, remember? I need you to snap out of it, please; just sit down next to me for a goddamn minute!" I pleaded, defeated and exhausted. My stomach was rock solid.

Her face twisted in confusion. She was so disoriented. It was heartbreaking. She finally gave in and sat down next to me, her eyes wide in search of answers and explanations.

"I–I–I don't understand; what do you mean?" she stuttered. I could see her kneecaps protruding from under her nightgown. She was withering away.

I sighed as I held her gaze, trying to figure out what to do next. How do I offer comfort to a broken child?

"It's okay," I said. "Everything's going to be okay."

She looked terrified, lost, and confused—like a small child in a crowd full of strangers. I wrapped my arm around her as she placed her head on my shoulder; I could barely register the weight of her head. I thumbed the red button on her medical alert pendant. We waited beneath the streetlight, my arm around her shoulders, rainwater and tears running together until distant sirens cut through the storm.

Flashing red-and-blue washed across the house one last time before we climbed into the ambulance—again.

They gave us towels to dry off as they asked my grandma routine questions.

"Ma'am, what's your address?" the paramedics asked.

"Uh, 39th Ave," she said groggily, taking longer than usual to answer.

"How many fingers do you see?" asked the paramedic, holding up three fingers in front of her face.

"Six." My grandma answered with absolute certainty, her voice steady, but she looked dizzy. She placed a hand on her cheek.

"Grandma. Are you okay?" I asked.

"My head hurts, and my face feels funny," she complained, wincing in discomfort.

Immediately, the paramedic tried to shine a light in her eyes, but she flinched and mumbled something, pushing his hand away. Suddenly, an incomprehensible string of sounds spilled from her mouth—words that made absolutely no sense.

I didn't know what this meant, but the paramedic sure did. He spoke into his radio, and the urgency in his voice sent an icy chill up and down my spine.

"This is Unit 62; we are eight minutes out. Please prepare for a possible stroke. The patient is seventy-six years old and displaying symptoms. We need to act fast."

Oh shit.

They wheeled my grandma into the emergency room with impressively choreographed urgency, and once again, the tests, treatments, and observations began.

Despite my begging and constant protests, two nurses grabbed me by the elbows and guided me to the waiting room. They were firm in their decision to keep us apart.

They brought me a pair of sweatpants and a shirt to change into. I was to sit, enclosed in four musky walls, and wait for further updates.

"She's in good hands," was the last thing the nurses said as they handed me a small pillow and a blanket before they disappeared through the doors.

It was going to be a long night, but there was nothing I could do.

How many more nights like this could I survive before I completely unraveled? One crisis after another, like the universe was testing the limits of my endurance. I pulled the blanket tighter around me and closed my eyes, wishing you were here, Derek—your steady voice, your stupid jokes, the way you always managed to make me feel safe. Without you, the weight of it all pressed down harder, and I wasn't sure how much longer I could carry it alone.

I fell asleep in the waiting room thinking of you. The chair was cold, and the air carried the heavy scent of tears and anxiety. Rubbing alcohol and sanitizer clung to the atmosphere like a dense fog, sharp and inescapable.

The little pillow they gave me barely fit half my head. It did a better job shielding my face from the chill of the vinyl chair than providing any real comfort.

At five in the morning, Dr. Jane walked in. Seeing him brought a flicker of comfort—but it vanished the moment I registered the somber look shadowing his face. Compassion weighed in his eyes, dimming the room around us.

"She's not coming back home, is she?" I asked.

We were long past pleasantries.

"I'm afraid not," he said, shaking his head slowly.

"Okay."

I pushed myself upright, stiff and slow, moving one limb at a time. Each vertebra cracked as I stretched into standing, as though my body itself resisted the truth. Once on my feet, I took a deep breath and met his gaze.

"What's going on?"

He looked at me with a kind of pain that made my stomach twist. We both knew his next words would change everything.

"What your grandmother suffered last night is what I personally call a turning point in the form of a stroke. After the concussion, her brain never really had the chance to heal, and that left her more vulnerable. She'd already been having those little episodes of dementia these past few months—forgetting things, short-term memory loss, an inability to retain information, her body beginning to weaken."

His pause was heavier than his words.

"But now, there won't be any 'little episodes' anymore. From here on out, expect… Emmy Award-nominated blockbusters' worth of dementia."

I furrowed my eyebrows. His metaphors lacked tact, but they were effective. I think, in his mind, delivering bad news with entertainment references somehow made the blow less painful. But it hurt nonetheless.

"Is she going to stay in the assisted living unit or one of these rooms?"

"I'd rather keep her in one of the rooms with 24/7 care, if that's okay with you."

"I mean, you're the doctor… but she'll get bored after a few weeks and want to get out of here," I half-joked, half-hoped, clinging to the tiniest shred of denial.

His eyes softened, sharp with pity. I could practically feel his heart breaking for me.

"That's the thing, Noah. Your grandmother's dementia has progressed to the final stage. And by the way things are looking, I don't think she has more than a few weeks left."

I sat back down. Hard.

My body collapsed into the chair, spine cracking again under the weight of the news.

This was it.

Dr. Jane sat beside me.

"Would you like me to stay with you for a few minutes?"

I nodded. Empty.

Vacant tears fell silently down my cheeks into a hollow chest void of anything but grief.

He gave me a small nod in return and stayed quietly by my side until a nurse called him away.

Dad arrived an hour later, his hair disheveled, his face pale and worried. He must have left the house the second I called. In one hand he carried a smoothie, and in the other, a small paper bag with a toothbrush and toothpaste from the convenience store downstairs.

He spotted me and exhaled, relief flickering in his tired eyes.

"Oh, Noah." He shut the door gently behind him. "Are you okay?"

I pressed my lips together, trying to hold it in, but the moment he stepped closer, I broke. My shoulders shook as I leaned into him, resting my head against his shoulder. For a minute, I just let myself be small again.

He placed his hand on the back of my head, his thumb tracing soothing circles against my hair. Then he cupped my face with both hands, holding it gently in front of him. Our eyes met. Concern was etched into every line of his face.

"You haven't eaten," he said quietly, setting the smoothie beside me. "And you'll feel better if you brush your teeth."

I couldn't speak, so I just nodded. The lump in my throat was too thick to swallow past. He didn't push; he stayed by my side, his hand steady on my knee as if anchoring me to the world.

We sat like that for a long time—just the two of us in the dim hospital light, hearing the monitors blink, breathing through the same grief, both trying to figure out how to keep going without her.

I was so glad he was here. I would never have been able to hold it together without his support. He stayed with me for a few hours until he had to go to work, but before he left, he wrapped his arms around me and held on for a long moment, his chin pressed to the top of my head. His voice was low when he finally spoke.

"I'll be back later, okay?" he said quietly. "We'll take turns during visiting hours. I'll help with everything."

He didn't need to promise. I already knew he would. That was just who he'd become—steady and dependable.

"I love you, Dad. Thank you for being here."

"I love you too, sweetie. To the moon and back."

Hearing those words reminded me how much I've always needed him, and how proud and grateful I was for him. Despite everything, he showed up.

I was not sure how many hours had passed since I heard the click of the door as Dad shut it behind him, but it must have been a few—because now it was getting dark again, and there was a tangible shift in temperature. The air felt colder. I couldn't tell if it was the temperature dropping or an omen swirling around me, whispering that time was running out—that it was almost time to say goodbye.

Tick-tock, tick-tock.

The cheap tea the nurse had kindly brought me sat cold beside the untouched jello. I couldn't remember the last time I'd eaten a proper meal—not since the thunderstorm. When life unraveled like this, time stopped being measured in hours. Instead, it fractured into moments. The thunderstorm. The ambulance ride. The endless night in the waiting room. Each one suspended, withering into fragments of space and memory.

I stood up, feeling the passing of time in every muscle. My body was stiff to the point of shattering into a pile of bones, and my stomach was so heavy it felt like I was carrying bricks instead of a human.

I walked slowly but steadily, knowing exactly where I was going.

Knock, knock, knock.

"Come in," Dr. Jane said.

I opened the door but stayed rooted in the frame.

"When can I see her?" I croaked.

"Not just yet. Soon, though," he said, offering a small, reassuring smile.

I nodded.

"When are you moving her to the room in palliative care?" I asked.

"Tomorrow morning, if everything goes according to plan."

"Which number?"

He glanced quickly at his notes. "B-612. That's Building B, sixth floor, room 12."

"Good. Then I'm moving in." My voice left no room for negotiation. "I'll be back first thing in the morning."

For a second, he just looked at me—no protest, no lecture about policy, only a quiet nod. Empathy softened the weight in his eyes, and in that moment, I knew he understood.

I shut the door before he could speak, sealing the decision.

Under normal circumstances, he would have argued—family members weren't supposed to just 'move in.' But this wasn't about policies anymore, it was about prioritizing comfort. He knew how little time we had left, and how much it mattered for her to see this baby. So, just this once, he let me win.

I walked slowly out of the hospital's double doors and ordered a taxi back home. By the time I got there, it was eight o'clock at night. I opened the front door and went straight to my room. I gathered all the photo albums I could find, then I packed a bag and threw in a few shirts, sweatpants, and most of the clean underwear I could find.

Coming home completely alone terrified me, but I quickly pushed that thought aside, knowing that going down that rabbit hole would paralyze me. I finished packing and immediately undressed.

I turned on the hot shower to a scalding temperature, and as I felt the drops of water touching every inch of my body, I leaned my palms against the shower wall and took a deep breath.

My head pounded, my body ached, and my brain was a swamp of exhaustion. I hadn't slept properly in weeks. But rest wasn't an option—not now.

I gave myself one hour to enjoy the only decent shower I would have in the foreseeable future, and then I shut the water off.

I stood still for a few moments, feeling the water dripping down my body as goosebumps covered my arms and legs, a chill running up and down my spine.

I needed to allow my body to feel something aside from pain. I needed a distraction.

The shift between scorching heat and bone-penetrating cold did the trick for a few minutes, but once the baby moved with discomfort, I wrapped a towel around us.

I dressed slowly and took two pain relief pills before getting into bed, urging my body to breathe in and out, hoping the rhythm of my heart would lull me to sleep.

It didn't.

After restless hours of tossing and turning and bad dreams, I got up from my bed at six in the morning and made some buttered toast. Two hours later, after cleaning the house and making it as presentable and decent as possible, I was in a cab back to the hospital. I didn't know when I would be back.

I was already settled in the room when they wheeled her in. She looked ten years older, with dark circles shadowing her hollow eyes, every bone protruding from her small frame. Her body looked as if it had caved in on itself, fragile and breakable. I couldn't understand how she had changed so much in just a few hours.

She looked like a crystal glass on the verge of breaking.

Because the stroke hit while we were already in the ambulance, the doctors told me she'd gotten treatment faster than most—fast enough to save her voice, though the rest of her body had been left trembling and frail.

It was incredibly hard to see her like this, but I had been warned—so the shock dissipated quickly.

"Hi there, stranger," I said, silently praying for one of her quick-witted, sarcastic remarks.

She spoke slowly, dragging out her slurred words, and the three words I would've given everything to hear were not the ones she said to me.

"Who are you?" she whispered.

Ice shards cut into my heart. The smile evaporated from my face. I looked into her eyes but couldn't find any trace of recognition.

I balled my fists and squeezed them as hard as possible to keep myself from crying.

"I'm Noah," I said softly, though the words felt foreign on my tongue, like I was introducing myself to a stranger.

She said nothing more. She stared blankly at me, taking in the room, seemingly forgetting our re-introduction.

The nurse looked at me sympathetically, assuring me that some days would be better than others.

She told me that at this point, all we could do was make her as comfortable as possible, and to be as patient and loving as I could.

"She may not remember who you are, but the heart never forgets love," the nurse said.

I clung to that sentence as if it were gospel.

The heart never forgets love.

I thought of you, Derek, and how I never forgot yours. I repeated that phrase every day like a mantra, whispering it to myself when the ache became unbearable.

I found hope in words and found myself reciting them to my grandma too, hoping they would help her as much as they helped me.

The nurse got her settled into bed, and as I held her delicate hand, I was shocked by how cold she felt.

I grabbed one of the fuzzy socks I had brought and covered her feet, rubbing them between my hands to warm them up, but nothing I did could chase away the cold that seemed to have already claimed her.

I looked into her eyes, and even though she couldn't recognize me on the surface, I kept searching, desperate to believe she was still in there somewhere—buried beneath the fog, waiting for her to break through.

The nurse proceeded to explain the physical, speech, and cognitive therapies scheduled to help her regain her overall strength. I paid attention to every word, determined to be as involved with her recovery as possible—if "recovery" was even the right word.

The following two weeks were emotionally draining. My grandma still hadn't recognized me; she was barely able to move her legs, and her speech was improving, but only slightly. I could see where this was going.

Dad came by a few times each week, sometimes after work, sometimes after his AA meetings. He'd bring coffee or fresh flowers and sit with her while I tried to nap in the chair by the window. It wasn't much, but it gave me time to rest—and in his quiet way, he was making things right. Every time I saw him reading to her or brushing her hair out of her face, I realized that healing didn't always announce itself. Sometimes it just showed up and stayed.

I had come to accept the fact that my grandma would die in this hospital bed, but I promised I would stay with her till the very end, whether she knew it or not.

The heart never forgets love.

Years prior, I had read a book by Isabel Allende titled *Paula*. The book was based on a true story, and it followed Paula, Isabel's daughter, who had tragically fallen into a coma at only twenty-eight years of age.

To cope with her grief, Isabel wrote a memoir—*Paula*—to give to her daughter so that, in the event she woke up from her coma, she would be able to read the story of her family's life.

Unfortunately, Paula never woke up, and she died about a year later in a hospital in Madrid. Isabel published her memoir in honor of her daughter, paying tribute to a life that would live forever.

This idea has stuck with me ever since, and to this day, I believe it is one of the strongest, purest, most selfless acts of love I have ever seen.

So I decided, in my own way, that's what I would do, too; I would tell my grandma stories for the remainder of our time together.

I told her the stories of her most extraordinary adventures.

I recounted her fairy tale love story with my grandfather and the story of my mom's rebel-hearted act in the beauty pageant—daily.

I showed her the photos from the albums I brought from home and hoped it would spark a hint of recognition.

I told her about all the Fourths of July we spent celebrating her birthday—the fireworks cracking overhead, the night air sticky with summer heat. How you'd bring her lollipops, and she'd pinch your cheeks with a mix of gratitude and love only she had.

Sometimes, I could swear I saw something in her gaze shift; a small smile would trace her lips as her old self crawled back into her consciousness—but it would disappear as quickly as it happened, and I could never tell if it was my own imagination.

Whether she recognized them or not, I knew she enjoyed the stories, because after each photo, she would continuously place her wrinkly, shaky finger on the corner of the page for me to flip it and show her more pictures.

We continued the stories until her eyelids grew heavy and she fell into a deep sleep, her gentle breathing giving me solace.

I would rest my head against her bed and hold her hand while she slept.

My belly had grown so big that I couldn't find any comfortable position, so I focused on being as close to her as possible.

This routine became habitual until one Tuesday morning. I was watching my grandma sleep, wondering if she was dreaming of people she once knew, when I was startled by a warm feeling flooding my legs.

I looked down and saw my thighs were soaked.

Fucking shit.

It was happening. This was it.

Derek. God, I needed you. I searched for you in the corners of the room, in the silence, in the air itself—longing for your hand in mine, your voice steadying me. I searched for you everywhere, wishing you were here to meet your son.

From this moment on, I would have someone depending on me for the rest of my life.

Panic clouded my thoughts, sweat slicked my palms, and the pain in my lower abdomen clenched like a fist around my core, threatening to bring me to my knees.

I tried to breathe—in and out—but the moment the next contraction ripped through me, I clutched the sheets and let out a piercing shriek.

That shriek jolted my grandma awake too—literally, and figuratively.

And I don't mean the grandma that had been taken over by dementia.

This was *my* grandma—the one who cursed like a sailor, had the fashion sense of a toddler, and consumed enough artificial sugar to rival a kindergarten classroom. She came back to me when I needed her most, just like she had promised.

"Noah!" she said, clear as day, as she saw the situation unfolding before her.

"Oh fuck," she muttered, piecing it together.

Despite the stabbing pain and overall desire to jump out of a window, I couldn't help but laugh at her words. I had been waiting weeks to hear that phrase.

"Welcome back!" I said, tears pooling in the corner of my eyes.

She grinned, as if brushing off months of confusion. "Thanks! Where was I?"

"Long fucking story," I managed to say.

"Well, it doesn't seem like we have a lot of fucking time for stories now, do we?" She slammed her hand on the call button like a general summoning reinforcements.

I kept choking on tears and laughter.

"Now, I'm sure there's a perfectly good reason as to why I'm in a hospital bed," she added, "but do you know if they've got any candy around here?"

Her priorities remained intact.

"Way ahead of you." I reached into my bag and tossed a handful of lollipops onto her bed.

She smiled as she peeled an orange-flavored one with her teeth and continued repeatedly pressing the button with her other hand.

"You're a fucking legend."

"Right back at ya," I said.

We laughed, shaking our heads in disbelief at the absurdity of it all.

The nurse, however, was nowhere in sight. My grandma tried to sit up, only to realize she couldn't.

"Why the fuck am I fucking paralyzed!?" she snapped, furious at the inconvenience.

"Stroke," I gasped between contractions.

"Oh for fuck's sake," she huffed, rolling her eyes. "Give me a break."

Then, with all the drama of a Broadway star, she yanked her IV pole and sent it crashing to the floor with a thunderous clang.

"What does a paralyzed old hag and a bursting woman have to do around here to get some fucking help!?" she screamed.

The crashing noise was finally enough to get the attention of three nurses, who rushed into the room and frantically apologized. Apparently, a guy was having a heart attack down the hall, and they were rather occupied.

Judging by their reaction, they were unprepared for what they walked into.

I saw the panic reflected in their eyes—this was the terminal unit, after all, not the maternity ward.

"Jamie, run up to the fourth floor and tell them to get ready immediately," one barked.

Jamie bolted like an Olympian track medalist, vanishing in the blink of an eye.

The other two nurses helped me to a wheelchair, but as they started to wheel me away, I anchored my foot on the ground and clutched my grandma's bed. I wouldn't leave her.

Pain made words impossible—but thankfully, she spoke for both of us, coming to my rescue once again.

"I don't know where you think you're taking my granddaughter and great-grandson, but if you thought for one motherfucking second you were leaving me here to rot while I miss the birth of that boy, then you must not be very gifted in the brain department. And God knows I don't want a stupid nurse. So one of you better get over here and wheel my paralyzed ass right alongside her, because she's not letting go of this bed otherwise. And frankly, I don't think you ladies are qualified to deliver a baby."

Her gaze was stone cold, daring them to disagree.

Both nurses looked at me, startled. Up until now, they had only seen the fragile, amnesic version of my grandma, not the firecracker version I had known all my life. I braced for backlash, but surprisingly, none came.

"She's having a good day today?" one of them asked curiously, nodding in my grandma's direction.

"The best day," I smiled sincerely.

"Fuck yeah!" was all they said before one of them left my side and moved beside my grandma, ready to tow her behind me as we made our way to the fourth floor in noisy shrieks of pain and celebration.

And in that chaos, I felt it—the fierce, unyielding love of my grandma shining through. She had come back for me, and for *him*—our little boy waiting to meet her just when I needed her most, and I couldn't help but feel grateful that this was the version of her I got to see in this moment. Fierce. Defiant. Unstoppable.

For the first time in months, pain and fear gave way to something entirely different; awe, joy, and a sharp, perfect clarity that I would never forget. No matter what came next, we were in this together—and somehow, that made everything bearable.

The delivery was painful, exhausting, terrifying, long, and perfect all at the same time—but I was in so much pain that a lot of those hours blurred together.

These, however, were the two most important things I remembered clearly:

First, my grandma was the loudest cheerleader in that room. Through orange-teeth blasphemy, she had the whole room laughing as they delivered a baby with her running commentary. She lifted our spirits with enough energy for both of us.

Second, I felt terror in my bones; I wasn't ready to do this. In a matter of months, my life had changed entirely, and none of it had been under my control. I wasn't given a choice—the choice was made for me.

I had always lived independently, free as the wind, and now I would have to live for someone else. This level of selflessness scared me, but I was willing to try my best—and be forgiving of my mistakes along the way.

I didn't know how much time my grandma had left, but sooner rather than later, I would have to do this alone. I could feel it in the small, fragile beat of her hand as it rested near mine; time was slipping through our fingers. And I would never be ready for that.

Little did I know, I wouldn't have any time left at all…

Our son was born at exactly eleven fifteen in the morning.

I was exhausted, sweaty, and incredibly weak. They handed him to my grandma for a few minutes while I rested, and I saw her as she welcomed him into the world—lucid, overjoyed, and, most importantly, at peace.

She looked at me, pride exuding from her eyes.

"What's his name?" she asked.

"Theo," I whispered. My voice cracked on the name. You and I had whispered it to each other weeks ago in the quiet of the night, dreaming about this moment with your letter close to my chest. It was always supposed to be Theo.

She smiled. "Gift of God?"

I nodded in response.

She looked back at Theo's eyes and traced a cross on his forehead with her thumb as she kissed the top of his head.

Looking at them, a memory flashed in my mind of my mom doing the exact same thing to me when I was born. I know it was virtually impossible for me to have any recollection of that moment, but I saw it clearly—her sharp features emulating the scene happening in front of me only twenty-five years apart. She was so beautiful.

Grandma smiled as she handed Theo to me.

"He is so beautiful, and I am so proud of you both, Pumpkin." Tears streaked her face. "I want you to know that whatever happens, I will always be with you— *every step of the way*."

I nodded, mirroring her smile and holding her hand, showing every bit of love and gratitude I felt toward her.

"I know Grandma. I love you so much. Thank you for absolutely everything; I couldn't have done this without you. We are so grateful for you. You saved our lives."

"Oh, Pumpkin, and you saved mine. You gave me the best moments of my life. Spending these last months with you has been my greatest honor."

She grazed my face with her gentle touch.

"You brought light back into my life, and I love you so, so much."

She smiled and squeezed my hand.

"I love you too," I squeezed back through tears.

I had always heard tales about motherhood and how it changes a woman.

Suddenly, your senses sharpen, and an unyielding sense of protectiveness and love takes over.

I always thought they were exaggerating.

But it turns out—they were right.

Trumping every feeling of self-doubt or fear was love—pure, genuine, selfless love for the life I held in my arms.

Holding Theo's tiny hands, I realized I was finally complete. My purpose was fulfilled.

As I marveled at his eyes, an intense ray of sunlight warmed both of our faces as someone placed a protective hand on my shoulder.

I turned to my left to meet your piercing eyes, Derek, and cried as you brushed our son's cheek with a loving touch.

"He has your eyes," I heard you whisper in my ear.

"I knew you'd be here," I whispered back, the words quivering on my lip, wishing I could reach for you and pull you closer.

"I will always be here. I love you, Noah. I love you both. Always and forever." You brushed a steady finger across my lips.

Always and forever, I promised in return, the words carrying the weight of everything I had ever felt, everything I would ever feel.

I saw you looking past me as you smiled at someone across the room. That's when I turned my head and saw my mom standing beside my grandma's bed, smiling at me.

I blinked—tears pooling under my eyelids, blurring my vision.

She looked as gorgeous as ever.

"Hey, Mom," I said softly.

"Hi sweetie. I'm so proud of you," she said with a smile bright enough to light up the room.

I felt immense gratitude for the two people standing by my side, but my heart sank when a third person manifested next to my mom.

Grandma's brown eyes locked into mine as I felt her hand go limp. I squeezed it gently, willing her to hold on, but it was already too late. A cold emptiness spread through me, mirroring the chill that had crept over her fingers, and I felt the weight of the world crush my chest.

Utter silence.

The only sound was the beat of my heart as it threatened to tear itself from my chest.

I couldn't breathe.

"No," I sobbed quietly. Fire scorched my throat as I swallowed a desperate urge to scream.

"Every step of the way," she said as she winked at me and held my mom's hand instead.

The rays of the sun were almost blinding.

The room felt impossibly still, every tiny sound magnified. Theo's breathing, the faint hum of the machines, the distant footsteps in the hallway.

"I love you all so much," I openly cried as I looked at each of their faces one last time. "We need you. Please don't leave us," I pleaded.

I shut my eyes, letting the tears fall freely. When I opened them, it was only Theo and me on the bed.

My grandma's peaceful body laid next to me, the ghost of a smile still traced on her lips. I rested my hand on hers, wishing I could keep her warmth just a little longer.

The doctor and nurses regarded us with a quiet, sympathetic gaze. They left the room to give Theo and me a few moments alone while we grieved.

Theo screamed in my arms as tears fell down my neck; both of us crying for the people who would never leave our side.

"It's going to be okay, Theo. It's okay to be sad for a little while," I reassured him as I kissed his head in the same spot my grandma had kissed him—the same place my mom had kissed me twenty-five years ago.

We looked into each other's eyes and promised to always have each other's backs.

I vowed to him that all four of us—Derek, Grandma, Mom, and I—would always be there to protect him.

Always and forever. Every step of the way.

month nine

"(Dear?) Dementia,

In the end, you let me have her one last time—on the most important day of my

life—and for that, I am thankful.

-N"

Two days later, Theo and I were cleared to go home.

It was bittersweet; on one hand, I had lost a pillar of my life. On the other, I was being handed a new reason to live.

Dr. Jane was as sweet as always. After expressing his condolences for the loss of my grandma, he congratulated me on such a beautiful baby boy. I thanked him for everything—the accommodations, the patience, even for turning the other cheek when I'd passive-aggressively declared I was moving into the hospital wing (for which I also apologized). He had been patient and kind, an angel in disguise.

When he offered his hand as a goodbye, I stared at it for a moment before brushing it aside and wrapping my arms around his torso. He chuckled at the sudden burst of affection and returned it with two gentle pats on my back. For a brief moment, I let myself rest against someone who had carried so much of my burden without complaint. The man was a paragon of virtue.

He called us a cab himself and helped us inside, setting Theo gently into his car seat before closing the door. He bid us farewell and asked the driver to make sure we got home safely. I waved at him through the cab's rear window until the street bent and he disappeared. I had made his life more complicated these past months, but I was grateful for the way our paths had crossed. I hoped, selfishly, that he felt the same.

The cab dropped us off right in front of the house, only a few feet from the doorstep. I thanked the driver as I handed him cash and walked slowly, with heavy, fearful steps, toward the door. I hadn't been here in weeks; the driveway felt like an old friend welcoming me to our new life.

I was carrying Theo with my left hand, and when we reached the front door, I stared at the doorknob, paralyzed, unable to move for too many reasons; afraid that if I touched it, it would combust into flames. Touching it felt like crossing a line between two worlds—the one where Grandma still waited inside and the one where she never would again. The truth of that possibility was so foreign and heart-wrenching, it rooted me to the spot.

It was Theo's tiny sneeze that snapped me out of the trance.

"Bless you," I said politely, and turned the knob.

The house was exactly as I had left it last month, but a stale muskiness hung in the atmosphere, dusting the surfaces with an air of abandonment. I set Theo down just inside the entrance and opened every door and window, letting the fresh air sweep through. It was my way of inviting new life into these walls.

Walking through the rooms, the air felt dense—hard to breathe—but I knew the oxygen was fine. The weight sat in my chest, my mind struggling to learn how to breathe in a house without her.

Theo and I went upstairs. The crib we'd bought him still sat in the corner of Grandma's bedroom, brand-new, waiting to wrap its blankets around him and welcome him home. I laid him down; he fell asleep almost immediately.

Grandma had insisted the crib stay in her room so I could rest at night. She used to joke that she wouldn't stick around much longer and the room would become the nursery anyway, since this was only a two-bedroom house. The thought of him sleeping in her room comforted me; I could imagine him protected here, with three angels—Grandma, Derek, and Mom—watching over him. I'd get around to changing the ancient flowered-tapestry wallpaper and making this a room fit for a young boy soon enough, but for now, it was perfect.

I closed the door softly so he wouldn't wake up, and then I went to my room for a quick shower and a change of clothes. The smell of hospice and disinfectant clung to my hair and skin. I knew I had to call Dad and your parents soon to give them the news and invite them over to meet our son, but right now, I just needed a moment. A moment to gather my thoughts and feel the memories that this house held close to my heart.

The shower wasn't long, but it was necessary. I found a pair of sweatpants and an old tank top in my closet, and as I was ready to leave the room, something caught my eye.

The familiar curves of my guitar leaned against the wall. A rush of anger, guilt, and sadness collided inside me. My fingertips tingled with adrenaline as the past year flooded my mind.

Seeing it again made me think of my mom's callused hands from playing that same guitar, the songs Derek and I sang in the forest, and the new strings my grandma bought me after the fire burned through the originals. I thought of the three people I would never see again, and of the losses Theo had already accumulated in such a short life, and I felt angry.

Bound by scars of past trauma and blinded by memories that would never exist, I grabbed the guitar that had once brought me so much joy and marched downstairs. Hot, heavy tears slid down its neck like rain.

I walked to the patio and felt the cold breeze graze my tear-stricken face. I needed to sever my ties with the past to have a clean slate for the future. With a deep breath and an anguished, broken heart, I grabbed the neck of the guitar with both hands, swung my arms, and with a scream that left my throat raw, I shattered the instrument against the floor with a crashing, dissonant sound that reverberated on the windows.

I felt a rush of peace that grounded me to the present. As I wiped my nose, a string of snot connected the corner of my lips to my shaking wrist. I felt all the exhaustion, anxiety, and misery I had been sulking over leaving my body, and I immediately felt lighter. I stood there, focused on my chest as it rose and fell, until my heart slowed to a normal pace.

Once I had nothing left in me and my hands had steadied themselves, I let the remaining piece of the guitar fall with a hollow clatter beside me. That's when something peeking out from inside the remnants caught my eye.

From the pile of shattered wood and strings, I pulled out two envelopes. One was yellowed from the passing of time; it had no name addressed. The other looked fairly new; my name stood out in the center of the page.

Driven by curiosity, I opened the latter first. A warm rush of relief and surprise filled my chest as I slid down the wall and let myself sink into the ground, dried leaves crunching beneath me.

It was a letter.

"Dear Noah,

If you are reading this letter, it means that, unfortunately for me, I am no longer in this world—which I assume has you feeling angry and guilty. Why else would you shatter your guitar like a maniac? Am I right?

First and foremost, I'm so sorry for your—(my?)—loss. But I need you to know, without a shadow of a doubt, that these past few months, you were the light of my days. I'd been ready to go for some time—that's something that happens when you grow old—but having you back in my life reminded me why I was still here. You gave me a reason to hang on a little longer.

You were my purpose, Pumpkin, and I never want you to feel you were anything less. I have all the faith in the universe you'll be okay. You're a strong, smart woman—just like your mom—and you can take the world by storm.

Secondly, I made you the sole beneficiary of everything I own. All my savings, this house, and anything else under my name are now legally yours. Hopefully, it starts to make up for the inconvenience of my untimely death.

Also, remember that blanket I knit you when you were a kid? You left it here years ago, and I forgot to give it back, so I knitted a miniature version of that blanket for the baby. You'll find both of them in the first drawer of my dresser. I hope he loves it! And please tell him, every day, how much his great-grandma loves him too.

Lastly, and most importantly, I love you, Noah. As I've told you before, I will always be with you—but in case you need a reminder, whenever you see a sunset and a stray ray of sunlight falls on your skin, I want you to know that's me. I want you to picture me holding your hand, because I will always be there, every step of the way.

I love you always,
—Grandma

"P.S. You may be wondering how I knew to put this letter in your guitar. The answer is obvious, baby girl: I'm old and wise but, most importantly, a fucking genius.

Second P.S. I hid twenty secret stashes of lollipops around the house. I challenge you to find them all before they melt this summer. Love you!"

A warm, golden streak of sunlight fell onto the page as if on cue, illuminating every inch of it. I pressed the letter to my chest.

Thank you, I whispered to the sun.

After a few moments, I set the letter down and opened the second envelope. As soon as I unfolded the paper, the typewriter font told me exactly what this was.

The poem I had carried in my heart for the past year now rested in my hands. I was taken back to the sound of jazz drifting through the freezing streets of New Orleans, a night when dreams and adventure wrapped themselves around us.

I saw you, Derek, standing beside me as we spoke to the poet in fingerless gloves, watching him capture our story in five fleeting minutes.

5 Minute Poetry – "The Word"

Before we became people,
we were woven inch by inch
into a tapestry of ink
that wrote a thousand stories.

When borders tried to separate us,
art drew us back together.

We are specks in a galaxy
of moments and coincidences.

We live in time
with an expiration date on our hearts—
but the journey began before we had a name
and will continue after our last breath.

All that remains is the echo of the word,
retelling who we were, what we did, forevermore.

And that's when I finally understood the twists and turns of fate. I understood that who I thought would be the protagonist of my story for the rest of my life was a lesson I should have learned years ago—a lesson of love, strength, courage, and simplicity.

You were my beginning, and although you were not my end, I was yours. But even though you were no longer physically with me, you sent me the most important gift of my life—a gift that contained your DNA, an eternal reminder of all the good that you were and the magic we created when we were young and laughed under the rain.

I looked at the sky once again and saw it with different eyes. The grayish shade reflected on the palette of colors brought me peace, while the cold, sharp breeze caressing my cheeks reminded me I was alive—and that I had to be strong, waking up every day in an eternal quest to find tomorrow's sunrise.

Seeing the clouds reflected in the lake helped me understand that life was cyclical, that we were a unit, and that the people we love never truly left us. Those who died became guardian angels and accompanied us in every step we took. We never were, and never would be, alone.

I understood then that the future and the past are hidden in the present, and that pain taught the most promising lessons. I was grateful to the universe for allowing my soulmate, parents, grandmother, and son to be a part of my life.

My story began with a simple question—three words that changed the course of my life and created a world of wonders and madness, where I built my home and found my peace. We were very young when it all began, but everything we felt and everything we were came from a place of love—the purest, most genuine, and imperfect love that brought two strangers together outside of a coffee shop.

And thus began the rest of my life.

THE END

acknowledgements

Writing *Every Step of the Way* wasn't easy. I don't have a professional background in writing, so putting together this novel was, quite literally, a learn-as-you-go process. It took hours of research, months of writer's block, and more than a few moments where I questioned whether I had the life experience or imagination to fill these pages with anything meaningful.

I began this novel on my twenty-second birthday, December 28th, 2020. I ended up stepping away from it for nearly a year because everything I wrote felt off. I didn't feel a connection to the story. I hadn't lived enough yet to understand the emotions I was trying to portray. I just didn't get it—not in the way Noah needed me to.

But time has a way of filling in the blanks.

In the two years that followed, my world shifted. I came to know grief and loss personally. I experienced fear. I carried heartbreak and self-doubt so heavy it felt impossible to bear alone. My old coping mechanisms didn't work, they were short-term fixes for long-term wounds. It was like putting a Band-Aid on a broken bone.

So, I turned back to writing.

This time, I wasn't just creating characters—I was pouring my heart into them. The story became my lifeline. In writing Noah, I came to understand her. And in understanding her, I found parts of myself. Writing this novel helped me sit with emotions I had spent years avoiding. I've always struggled with vulnerability, but this story taught me how to feel—and how to heal.

And for that, first and foremost, I want to thank Noah. Not because she's my alter ego—far from it—but because she did something I never could: she faced me. Writing her story uncovered a version of myself that had been hiding in the shadows for far too long.

To Andie at Sun & Spines Editorial—thank you for being a phenomenal editor. Your kindness, patience, and guidance made this process far less overwhelming. You protected my voice while helping shape this manuscript into the strongest version of itself, and you never once made me feel silly or out of place for asking a million publishing questions. I'm endlessly grateful for you.

To Eva Polakovicova—thank you for giving this book a face. I needed someone who would not only see its potential, but also care deeply about the story behind the cover. Your creativity and heart are embedded into every detail, and I couldn't be prouder of what we created together.

To Ashley Santoro—you were the final piece of the puzzle; without you, readers would quite literally be unable to read this story. Your willingness to collaborate on the interior layout and your ability to match my vision so perfectly is something I'll value forever. You understood that every minuscule detail mattered to me, and the way you cared just as deeply confirmed I chose exactly the right designer for this book.

To my parents—God, I love you so much. I love you both more than words can say. Everything I am is because of you. If I lived a hundred lifetimes, I'd choose you as my parents every single time. Thank you for giving me a life filled with joy, safety, and love. You created an environment where even failure felt safe, helping me see it as an opportunity for growth and experience—one of the greatest gifts a parent can give. Every success I have had is thanks to you. I hope one day I make you as proud as I am to be your daughter. I love you both.

To my uncle, Tío Adrian—for cultivating my love for the lost art of handwritten letters. Being your pen pal over the past two years rekindled a kind of magic in me: a curiosity, a sense of wonder, and the quiet longing that comes with waiting for someone's thoughts—and the hope that someone will read my own. Thank you for all the letters. I've kept every single one.

To my grandmothers—this novel is yours. The bond between Noah and Grandma Nadia was inspired entirely by the love I share with you both. I see you in myself every time I look in the mirror—in my stubborn fire, in every eye roll, and in every dream I dare to chase. You were pioneers in your own fields, and I carry your courage, strength, and spirit with me always.

To the man I love—six years isn't nearly enough. I hope I get to grow old by your side. Most authors thank their partners for being their first reader, but since we can't seem to agree on whether you actually read the whole book… I'll settle for knowing this: life granted me my own fairytale, and my very own prince charming. You're perfect for me. I want to build my life with you. I love you forever and always, especially because you always believe that I can do anything. I will choose you every single day, in every single timeline. Matcha date soon?

And finally, to you—the reader.

If this book broke your heart, I'm sorry. Writing the final chapter broke mine, too. But every tear I shed healed something small in me, and I hope—somehow—it does the same for you. Thank you for picking up my first novel. Whether it brought you hope, faith, courage, or even just a small smile, I'm grateful beyond measure. I've said it before and I'll say it again—you're the reason authors get to do what they love. You are the heart of the literary world.

Thank you for letting me share a piece of mine with you.